HUSH

HUSH
JUDE SIERRA

CONSENT
an imprint of interlude press

ISBN 13: 978-1-941530-27-6 (trade)
ISBN 13: 978-1-941530-30-6 (ebook)
Published by Consent, an imprint of Interlude Press
http://interludepress.com

Book design by Lex Huffman
Cover Design by Buckeyegrrl Designs
Cover Illustration by Victoria S.
10 9 8 7 6 5 4 3 2 1

Cimms—if I'd never read the first of your beautiful stories, I wouldn't have known I had this in me.

CHAPTER ONE

CAMERON VARGAS'S INTRODUCTION TO COLLEGE, from its first days into weeks, turns out to be a blur. Later he'll think back to that time and wonder at how he managed to create the canvas of such a pivotal time in his life as a sort of watercolor, pastels that blurred into one another with few distinct shapes or forms.

There was a canvas: complete, yes, and from a distance a scene portrayed. But the finer points were lost, a fact he wouldn't realize until later. Until *after*.

Cam would like, in part, to say the difference is simple, that there was a distinct before and after. That his life before was simply *before Wren*. In chaos, in months of searching to find the ground, he'd say this: that Wren had come into his life like a freak storm, unexpected and swamping, leaving him capsized and floundering.

It's a great joke really, on himself, to realize that he has valued boundaries so much in his life—knowing and placing and naming—only to look back and comprehend that a life of such care and precision served only to blur one moment into another, and to so easily erase himself.

IT'S THE SECOND HOUR OF HIS DAY on the third day of his second semester when he sees Wren Allister for the first time. The class is absolutely packed, only a few chairs of the two hundred-person capacity lecture hall left unfilled. *There's nothing here to look forward to.* Stats are not his thing; he's here to fill a requirement quickly and move past something he'll hate. He's never been one for close crowds. He'd say he dislikes large crowds, but that's untested. And silly, really, considering that he's moved here, to Chicago, from a town smaller than any of the suburbs surrounding Carlina University.

A heat rises from so many young, bored bodies, a humidity shared by many lungs. The constant rustle and squeak of restless bodies confined to sit quietly for a two-hour period surrounds him. He'd tried to snag an aisle seat, but come just a little too late and is now sitting somewhere in the middle of a long bank of seats that curves around the podium and projector in the amphitheater classroom. The fold-out desk is roughly the size of his notebook, which is really irritating; as is trying to fit his entire six feet into this space without infringing on someone else's. At the end of a row, he'd at least be able to stretch his legs into the aisle.

Cam has only been awake for two hours, and it seems as though the rest of the day will go on forever, as if stats alone have the power to stretch time like taffy.

The professor is late—by four minutes, according to the clock on the wall—and Cam feels too hemmed in to do more than look around. The girl on his left leans toward him, which makes him feel self-conscious about getting on his phone. He can only see the few rows in front of him on his side of the room, just the backs of heads really; but he can see more to his right: faces and expressions and clothes. Looking at them makes for an interesting few minutes. He observes that patterned shirts seem to be the norm for guys his age. Nothing stands out to him.

That is, until he sees *him.*

He's seated two rows below Cam, close to the middle aisle. His dark hair contrasts with his pale, glowing skin. He's wearing a brown knit sweater; its collar droops to the side, exposing part of his shoulder and collarbone. There is also a hole in one sleeve. Cam can't tell if this is by design or from wear.

Cam has no idea why this boy has drawn his eye. He's looking away, and Cam can only see his face in quarter profile. One of his legs is crossed over the other and he jiggles a foot impatiently; the half-undone laces of his Chucks twitch. He's looking at his phone, scrolling over something with his thumb.

Suddenly, the boy seems to stiffen; he sits up a bit and looks up and around. Then he turns abruptly and looks Cam right in the eyes just as their professor bangs in through the double door, shuffling papers and apologizing.

The look is fleeting; just a moment and it is gone, as the focus of the room shifts toward the front. It's nothing.

Only it's not.

Two hours later Cam is still sitting in class, watching the other students stream out the doors and feeling his body vibrate from something so intense he doesn't even have the words to comprehend it.

THAT'S UNUSUAL. IT'S NOT THAT Wren's never connected with someone, just that he can't remember ever doing so when he wasn't open to it, or searching and testing the waters. Closed, sleepy and bored, he'd felt the moment that boy had seen him: a new warmth had rolled through him, and when he'd turned around, the boy's eyes on Wren had felt like wildfire.

On his long walk home, Wren takes a breath and looks up at the great big sky, watery blue and gray with scattered stratocumulus clouds. Nora would laugh, knowing he now names the clouds. Over a year of living with her and he can name weather patterns in his sleep.

He flips his keys at the door of the apartment building and tries to focus on the warm metal in his hands, the slight dig of a key's ridge on his thumb, the faint metallic smell that lingers. He can't manage to ground himself with details—instead he feels exposed, as if that boy touched something deeply personal with just one look.

Wren will see him again, and he'll have to be more careful with himself, stay watchful until he understands what that boy wants or needs. It's a large enough class that he can easily avoid direct contact until he has a better grip on the situation. In the meantime, Wren tries to ignore how it felt to look into the eyes of a boy so handsome it makes him ache.

"HELLO? WREN? YOU IN THERE somewhere?" Nora taps his forehead with her fork.

"Oh god, gross!" Wren wipes at his skin with a napkin. "Nora Chelsie Engle, what the hell?"

"I've been talking to you for five minutes and you're just staring into space. What's going on?"

Wren shifts a little. "Nothing."

"You're bouncing your leg like crazy, Wren," she points out, and he tries to still it. "I know your tells."

"It's..." He looks at her carefully. Nora does know him, and he knows she's safe. But— "I'm working it out," he says after a moment. "I promise I'll talk to you if I need to."

She looks down at her plate of cacciatore. "All right."

Wren bumps her foot with his under the table in a gentle acknowledgment of thanks and affection. "So, tell me about your day again, and this time I promise to listen."

CAM GETS HOME FROM SCHOOL early on Wednesdays—before his roommate Nate does, before dinner, with just enough time to go for a run and shower. Mostly, Cam is an evening runner; he enjoys the lingering ebb of day as night bleeds into the sky, the night air in summer and the crisp dark that presses in on him in the winter. In warmer months, the transition of late summer sky into night makes him feel expansive, connected, as if his body is melting into his surroundings. When December leeches the heat from everything, when night comes for the day sooner, the sky feels farther away. Winter is when he feels the smallest, the great big sky impossible above him, he himself shrinking against such a vast backdrop.

Cam may live here, but this isn't home. It's taken him months to figure out how to adjust to changes in schedule, how to fit all the things he likes into his day when his days are so different. He can't say that he has adjusted without resentment. He runs when he can, now. It's easier to run in the daytime or morning here, when it is quieter. He is still learning how to live surrounded by so many people and buildings.

A new semester and different classes have forced him to adjust again. Maybe he's growing a bit too, because while repeatedly having to figure out how to manage his time has been a pain in the ass, now at least he grasps the scope of the change to come before it happens. He explores a little more these days, takes trips into the city and soaks in the buildings, tall enough to take his breath away, and the bodies, so many bodies filling every space around him.

And he runs. He runs because his body asks for it, because running gives him what nothing else in his life has offered: an indescribable feeling he chases as fast and as far as his legs will take him.

* * *

Friday Wren comes prepared, but it's still not enough: his whole body alerts him when the boy swings through the classroom door. Inside—where he usually keeps his gifts held tight—he wants to unfurl, wants to know how the boy would look with all of Wren's focus on his pleasure. This urge strains against his insides, seeking the soaring rush that comes from making someone submit to what he can give.

The boy sits opposite him in the class, but Wren can tell he's hardly paying attention. Instead his eyes are seeking, scanning the crowd until they meet with Wren's.

Wren sucks in a breath, stills his bouncing leg. A seeking feeling pierces him. The boy must know; there's no way they could connect so easily otherwise. Wren returns the look with cautious intent, gives the energy a tiny boost and can tell the moment the boy absorbs it; Wren senses the reciprocal heat of longing. He smiles smugly. It's been a long time since he's played this game, a long time since he's found someone who understands the rules and wants to play.

He lowers his eyes coquettishly, picks up his pen and runs his fingers over it. More open now, he can feel this boy's desire even without eye contact. Anticipation is much better than confusion, delicious and heady and so, so welcome.

Wren lightly kicks shut the door to his apartment, shopping bag swinging from his arm.

"Hello!" he calls for Nora. He flings the bag on the table and calls out again. "Are you home?"

"Yes, yes, stop yelling," she says, coming from her room, pulling her sweater close around her body. Her long hair is in a loose and messy knot; her naturally blonde hair is darker now as the sun-kissed highlights of summer fade. "What is your deal?"

"I'm in a good mood," he says lightly. "I bought some new clothes and I thought we'd make something awful but delicious for dinner and maybe go out tonight."

"Wren." She gives him a smiling, indulgent look.

"Stop," Wren says with a laugh. "Do not read me right now, I'm just in a good mood." He's in a fantastic mood, which is a lovely change of pace. He's been bored and itching for something interesting for months.

"You found someone to play with, didn't you?" Now she looks a little condescending, or judgmental; it's hard to tell. Nora has no problem preventing him from reading her; it's not his primary gift, and he's not worked exceptionally hard at developing it. Mostly, the skill has come into its own as he's grown older. Reading peoples' feelings and moods has always seemed potentially intrusive; at least he can consciously choose to compel someone or not, and his sense of respect for others' boundaries and wills has always kept him from violating them.

"Don't read me," he repeats. It's a little annoying that she can see things he doesn't mean to emote. Her intuition works differently than his—she can see in his aura a lot of what he's feeling because she's not as good at controlling gifts as he is. Nora struggles a lot more, too, with closing off her perception of people she's intimately connected to. Early in their friendship, and then later, when they became roommates, he'd sat her down for a few conversations about it.

"I know you are struggling to control it," Wren had said, as he slid a cup of coffee across the table to her. "But can we figure out a way for you to respect my privacy, or *anything* that won't feel so much like I don't have any?"

"Should I just not say anything to you?" Nora had suggested.

Fiddling with the lid of his coffee, Wren had thought about it. He shrugged one shoulder. "I guess that will work, for now."

Later, when they became closer and began talking about living together, it was more apparent that even when she didn't broadcast his feelings to other people in small jokes or observations, she still read them and based her behavior and advice on them. There was little she could do about it.

"Listen," he'd said, "I need to you try *not* to change your behavior based on what you see. And I am going to ask you to please consider finding a mentor, because this can't go on."

"Wren," she'd replied, "I don't think I can. It's just how I work. You *know* this, it's how I function."

"It doesn't have to be that way. I know it's challenging finding people to help, and I know it *feels* like you can't change these things. But I really feel like you need to at least try. It's not just the reading. You know things even before I do, and then you change the way you say things and act patronizing. It's annoying, and I feel like I can never have anything for myself."

"I'm sorry." He knew she was sincere.

"And often," he continued, on a roll, "you assume you know what the reason behind what I'm feeling is, and you *don't*."

Nora swallowed and looked away, twisting a lock of hair in her fingers over and over, the way she often did when she was thinking. "Okay. That's valid. I guess I didn't realize that I alter my behavior that drastically based on what I'm reading."

"Listen," Wren said, laying his hands flat on the flea market table. Its cracked linoleum top was a hideous shade of pea green Nora had inexplicably fallen in love with. "If you see something that you are concerned about and you feel like it needs to be immediately addressed, ask me if I want to talk and let me know what you see. If not, you have to wait for me to come to you, like any normal person would."

"Wren, that's not entirely fair," Nora said. "Even if I weren't gifted, I'd be able to see you're in a bad mood based on your posture or face, and friends do shit like ask how your day was. Or, like, hey are you okay?"

Wren wrinkled his nose; she was right, but the whole thing annoyed him. "Yeah, that's probably true. But it doesn't have to be for us because *we're* different. I think the rules have to be different."

Nora huffed out a breath and ran her fingers through her hair. Bits of it stuck out when she mussed it; messy streaks of teal blue and pink showed through her naturally blonde hair.

"Wren—"

He could tell she was trying to hold back her temper. "Listen," he interrupted, "this is not a negotiable thing. If we're going to live together, you're going to have to respect this, for me. There are some things I want to keep to myself and *can't* around you, and that sucks because you are my best friend and I want to live here with you. But living with someone is different than being friends. You'll be able to see me night and day. Please try to respect this."

"Ugh." She thunked her head on the table.

"Look, if you're going to be like that, I don't—"

"Shut up!" she said. "I won't be. It's just hard. I'm gonna have to do a lot of thinking and practicing. Can we respect a learning curve, at least?"

"Of course." Wren covered her hand with his. "We'll make some rules and then a plan for how to implement them. And I'll help you find a mentor, if you'll consent to training."

"Fine. God, you and your rules," she had laughed.

"Shut up," he'd said, nudging her foot with his under the table.

"Sweetie," Nora says with a smile, bringing him back to the present conversation. "It's impossible not to read you. Your aura is huge. And bright—god it's gorgeous: reddish purples and streaks and bursts of this really dynamic gold—"

"Nora," he warns.

"Okay, okay, I get it," she says, holding up her hands in a placating gesture. "We'll ignore the incredibly gigantic, sensual, happy aura in the room and do something fun."

Wren rolls his eyes and lets her hip bump him. He feels too good to be annoyed right now. He's surprised that his aura isn't palpably sending waves through everyone within a hundred-foot radius. It's been so long since he's felt something like this connection to that boy; hot, sharp and immediate, and *god* is he looking forward to the game.

* * *

"DAMN, CAM, YOU WERE GONE for a while," Nate says when Cam stumbles into their room on half-dead legs. "How far did you run?"

"Really, *really* far," Cam wheezes. Nate glances at him for another second before going back to the tangled mass of laundry strewn over his bed. He folds with a haphazard carelessness that makes Cam cringe.

"Feeling the need for speed?" Nate says. Cam can hear the smile in his voice even though his back is turned.

"No. Maybe." Cam strips off his soaked shirt. "Something." His stomach growls faintly through the cramping clench of muscles that—like the rest of his body—feel tremendously overworked. He'd skipped his dinner and run far longer than usual, trying to pound the buzzing, shaking electricity under his skin out through his feet and into the pavement. His statistics classes had been... weird. Unsettling. His attention has been scattered—which wouldn't be unusual in itself, considering how much he anticipated hating this class. But it's the draw, the way his focus is constantly pulled toward that boy. It's as if, for the two hours they are in that room , gravity shifts; Cam's body wakes up, his senses sharpen and his thoughts move helplessly, helplessly.

"CAM," NATE SAYS THE NEXT DAY, setting his tray down on the table, "this is Mic, he's in my comp class."

"Hey." Cam looks up and half waves before looking back down.

"Hi." Mic begins to organize his tray of food. "So, Nate tells me you aren't from Chicago."

"Not even a little," Cam has to joke.

"You like it here though?"

"Love it," Cam says.

Nate grunts; Cam thinks it's an affirmative sound, but doesn't ask. Nate is devouring his lunch as though it's going out of style.

Cam continues, "Different. It's a bit of an adjustment..." *Maybe too big*. He squirms his shoulders against that niggling itch that's been plaguing him since yesterday.

"Have you been out much? The Teke's are having a party tonight; the first party of the semester is always *wild*," Mic says.

"Oh, I don't know," Cam says, then picks up his fork. Puts it down. Clears his throat. "I'm not much of a partier."

"Somehow Cam has managed to come to us the best-behaved boy in all of the Midwest," Nate says. From anyone else that would sound cutting, but from Nate it's clearly affectionate. "He's not totally hopeless though," he winks at Cam. "Last semester Julianne and I got him hammered right before Christmas break. It was amazing, he was actually singing carols. God, I wish I had film."

"Oh my god, shut up," Cam says, covering his face and laughing. "I had forgotten about that!"

"Yeah. I'm pretty sure you were sporting a three-day hangover, and we put you on a plane back home with it," Nate says.

"Uhh no," Cam says. "That was just a natural reaction to going home."

"That bad, huh?" Mic butts in.

Cam shakes himself a little mentally and closes off a bit. Nate's cool; he knows Cam well enough not to press and he's okay with waiting for Cam to confide in him. "Maybe it was just the hangover after all," he says, picking his fork back up.

Another kid from their hall, a transfer student whose name Cam doesn't know, walks past. He's slim and dark haired and reminiscent of that boy in Cam's stats class who keeps looking at him, who is somehow brightly burning in Cam's periphery even when they're not in class. Every time Cam thinks he sees him he tightens in a way that's unsettling but also feels... good.

THEY GO TO THE PARTY, Cam dutifully tagging along when Nate begs for a wingman, though Cam points out that he has no idea what a wingman is really supposed to do.

But it's all crushed bodies and spilled beer, fetid alcohol and smoke smell so heavy it feels like a wet blanket on his skin as soon as they manage to wedge through the door. Partygoers spill onto the lawn. They wrestle on the balcony above the front door until Cam wants to tell everyone to settle down before they end up with broken necks.

Thoughts like these must be exactly what Nate means when he tells Cam he needs to loosen up and act his age. No one here wants to be mothered, and, really, he has no desire *to* mother anyone. He's only been back in Chicago for two weeks, and they've only just rounded out their first week of the semester and everything is too much. Nebraska is still in his bones, disconnecting him. A boy in an impossibly hard class is haunting him, drunk people shouting variations of the same Saturday night party script are surrounding him and he has a visceral desire to run, and run, and run away until the dust settles behind him.

It only takes one more stats class for Wren to understand his role in this exchange; if ever there was a cat and mouse scenario, this is it. Everything radiating from this boy reads longing, hot desire unchecked. He is waiting to be led, wanting to be discovered. Wren feels new, newer than he has felt since... well, since Robert.

Wren shakes his head. Robert's name is at the top of the list of things he doesn't think about; thinking about him violates one of Wren's primary rules: *Don't give anyone the power to hurt you.*

This, the somehow-instant tether that formed between him and the boy and tugs and tugs at Wren every second they're in that amphitheater, *means* something. Whoever this boy is, he's pulling at Wren hard. If it weren't for the rawness of the boy's longing, Wren might think he wants to lead. No matter; it's not as if he'll ever put himself in such a vulnerable position again. Wren leads, and they follow.

* * *

Every day, Wren comes late to class and leaves early. Some days, he unlocks a little, lets himself feel that hot, sweet course of desire and enjoys how it winds through him. On days when he feels especially sexy and focused, or full of want, he'll find the boy in the room and pull from him the need to seek Wren out, pull their gazes together. Leading this gorgeous creature is incredibly thrilling; it tests Wren's willpower, but Wren drags it out because he's learned that anticipation can be even better than fulfillment. Wren has discerned that the boy has light brown hair and is tall but obviously fit. His eyes are a lovely almond shape—maybe brown, but Wren can't really tell—and his skin is a wonderful café con leche. Wren can't wait to get his hands on him.

"HOW ARE YOU TODAY?" NORA asks over dinner.

He rolls his eyes. She's always painfully obvious when she's reading him, though careful to follow the rules he laid out. He supposes it's the most he can expect, especially because, with her around, he's learned to sense when he's emoting most strongly. She can't help but see that. Her first mentor had been a total washout, and they've been struggling to find a second; a good, trust-based rapport is vital for this sort of teaching, and is hard to come by based on want ads. And Carlina's course offerings for the gifted aren't focused enough for the individual training Nora needs since they're intended as electives and not a part of a designated development program or degree track like some universities offer.

"I am fucking fantastic," he declares, then winks.

"Okay, Wren, I cannot take it anymore, you have *got* to tell me what's going on."

Rolling his eyes and biting back a smile, Wren pretends to sigh. "If you insist."

"God, you're adorable when you're happy," she says.

"Shut up," he smiles. "Okay. Try, *really,* not to be judgmental."

"Well that's a winning start."

Wren shrugs and fiddles with the plug in his ear, twisting it. Feeling whimsical that morning, he'd worn plugs he rarely breaks out, the ones shaped like elephants, for good luck. He's been contemplating going up a size.

"So..." He takes a breath. "There's a boy."

"Ahhh," she squeals happily, clapping her hands, "why didn't you tell me sooner? Oh god, what's his name? When do I get to meet him? When did you meet him? How—"

"Whoa, whoa, hold on, Nora, it's not like that." He gives her a look. "You know it's not going to be like that."

"Wren—" she says, too sweetly, too concerned. "I know it was hard—"

"I swear to god," he jumps in, "if you go there, I am leaving this room. It's a rule."

"Fuck," she says under her breath, "I hate your rules. Can you just stop with that?"

"Dislike duly noted," he responds, his voice rich with sarcasm. "I'll put that motion before the board."

Nora stares at him for so long he becomes a little uncomfortable. Finally she takes a breath, shaking her head minutely. "So tell me about this boy."

Wren closes his eyes. "I think his name is Cam—Professor Gibbs was talking to him after class yesterday and that's what I think I heard. He's... beautiful." Wren shrugs slightly and smiles. "There's just something there. And I can't wait for it to happen."

CHAPTER TWO

WREN KNOWS THAT CAM IS seeking him; during every class, Wren senses Cam's desire, the building force of attraction. Wren feels him pulling as soon as he nears the classroom. The feeling is heady, an exhilarating flush that envelops him the moment they connect. Sometimes it's overwhelming.

He'll not deny that one of his favorite aspects of his gifts is that he *can* gift. As much as he enjoys being pursued, and as much as he enjoys drawing it out, he loves giving those feelings back even more. His power to compel, he knows, is to be used with caution and respect. Many have used this ability in awful ways. Wren was raised to respect it—and also to enjoy it, to use it to compel pleasure, comfort or relaxation in others.

For every tug of longing and desire he feels from this boy Cam, he's careful to pull something from him as well: a rise of sensuality, a surge of confidence. Wren wants Cam, wants to take him apart and touch him, have him until they're both half blind. Wren wants to discover every secret space of Cam's body, and *god* does Wren want to make it incredible for him. And he can. Compelling Cam to small bursts of pleasure from across the room leaves Wren on a high that lasts for hours.

* * *

"YOU'RE GONNA GIVE YOURSELF SHIN splints or something at this rate, man," Nate says one day.

"What do you know about it?" Cam says, laughing and wiping his face with the hem of his shirt. "Have you run even once in your life?"

"Nope," Nate says, making the "P" sound pop. "I prefer my low impact but incredibly healthy swim/lift/flex routine."

"Flexing as a workout, huh?" Cam scrubs his hands through sweat-soaked hair. He's *gross*.

"Well, not precisely," Nate says, mischief all over his face. "It's what the flexing *gets* me, if you know what I mean." He waggles his eyebrows and Cam snorts with helpless laughter.

"You are ridiculous."

"And lucky. Or a player. Irresistible."

"All right, Casanova, I'm gonna shower. Feel free to flex," Cam says, then pauses when Nate bursts into laughter, realizing a second too late what he's implied. "I take that back; do not flex right now."

"I'm not the one who needs it, anyway," Nate says.

"What does that mean?" Cam asks.

"It means that I bet if you flexed a little more, you might not be killing yourself running."

"Uh..." Cam folds his towel over his arm, not really sure where he's supposed to go with this conversation. Is Nate implying that he needs to... take care of things more often? How would he know how much Cam does? If he did, he'd probably know that lately, things really have kind of... ramped up. Cam's not precisely sure why, other than the fact that that itch—that something that's been driving him to run more, to push himself, to work it out—has been getting worse lately.

"Get laid, dude," Nate leans forward to spell it out. Cam feels his face heat up and looks away. While they've talked about how Cam's never had a girlfriend before, he's never admitted to Nate that he's a virgin. He's not ashamed of it, but neither is it something he's ever wanted to talk to someone about.

"I have to shower," is all Cam says, toeing on his shower shoes.

"Flex it, dude," Nate shouts after him, laughing as Cam shuts the door with a little more force than is necessary.

* * *

"WHEN ARE YOU GOING TO talk to him?" Nora asks one night, curled next to Wren on the couch while they watch a rerun of *Law and Order: SVU*. She's painting her nails a lovely peach color. Wren shrugs.

"I'll probably wait until the end of the semester," he muses. "I won't have to worry about seeing him every day, then."

"What is this going to be, another one-time thing?" Nora caps the bottle and sets it on the table carefully, propping her feet up so that the nail polish won't smudge.

"You said you weren't going to judge."

"I'm not," she says. "I'm just trying to understand why you'd spend months teasing each other for one night."

"I don't know."

Nora sighs and squirms, and he can feel her irritation washing over him.

"Stop that," he says sharply.

"I can't help it. I'm feeling what I'm feeling," she snaps.

"Well, feel it less strongly, please," he says. He knows he's being irrational and also knows—though he's loath to acknowledge it—that her irritation stems from concern. What she wants for him are things he doesn't need—a companion, love, something steady and affirming. Wren closes his eyes and breathes and tries to find a way, again, to explain why those things just aren't on the list.

"I'm sorry," she says quietly, and lays her hand on his arm. "I didn't mean to judge. I just worry."

"I know." He leans his head against the couch and looks at the ceiling. His eyes feel tired and fuzzy; it's late and they've been marathoning this show for a while now. Wren has work to do and, while he knows that watching "just one" episode of *SVU* somehow sucks them into watching a whole run of shows, he hasn't wanted to leave the couch and the warmth of Nora's familiar body next to him. "It's not that I plan on it being a one-time thing, you know."

"Oh?"

"I mean, it could be. We'll see. I just want to be sure I have an out if things don't go the way I want."

Nora laughs a little. "Which rule is that?"

"Number two." He smiles wryly.

"How many rules are on this list now, anyway? Wren's 'how not to get burned' list, I mean."

He pokes her. "That's not what it's called, and it's none of your business."

Nora picks up the remote and begins to flip mindlessly through channels. It's late, and if one of them doesn't find a way to break free, they'll be stuck 'til midnight. Finding nothing, she puts down the remote.

"I think I'm gonna go to bed, honey," she says.

"All right." He catches her hand as she stands and gives it a squeeze. It's a small apology, but she understands him.

"I love you, Wren." She puts her hand lightly on his head.

"You too."

"Enjoy your chase," she adds quietly in parting.

"Oh," he says a moment later, to no one in the quiet room. "I am."

* * *

WREN DEFINITELY DRESSES DIFFERENTLY ON stats class days now that he's had three months of reading Cam's reactions to his appearance. He dresses to look smaller. Exposes little bits of skin. His collarbone seems to be a particular enticement, which really works for Wren because it's ridiculously sensitive.

He pairs Cam's affinities with his own for soft fabrics against his arms and neck and structured pants or even tops, depending on his mood. Most of the things with which he surrounds himself make him feel good, maximize his sensual pleasure: the light and fabrics in his room and wardrobe; the incredible, lush give of his bed. Wren textures his life with small luxuries, and rarely, but intensely, indulges in bigger, more raw ones. Whoever this Cam is, Wren knows he'll be incredible.

* * *

THE CLOSER THEY COME TO the end of April and the semester, the harder it is to hold off. Wren squirms in class; the tether between them is so taut and electric, it's only through the incredible self control he's rigorously practiced that he manages first to stay put and then to slip out of the room before Cam can find him.

"YOU ARE DRIVING US *CRAZY*," Nora says one night.

"God," Brokk adds, "please just fuck him and give us a break."

"Fuck you," Wren says, laughing. "What do you know about it?"

"Listen, I don't have to have your abilities," Brokk replies, using a fork to gesture between Wren and Nora, "to know you're so horny you make *me* want to go out and get laid."

"So go get laid, then," Wren says placidly.

"I will if you will," Brokk retorts.

Wren rolls his eyes, but Nora's laughter is bright and contagious. Several patrons around the restaurant turn toward the sound.

"Just—" Wren twists the sweating glass of water on the table before him, "lay off. It's hard enough." He breaks off when Brokk laughs. "God, what are you, thirteen?"

"Young at heart." Brokk winks at Nora.

"*Anyway*," Wren continues. "I was saying it's difficult enough, holding out. But we're almost there."

"Praise be." Nora wiggles her fingers skyward dramatically.

"Just be careful," Brokk says lightly, ignoring the displeased look Wren sends his way.

"Seriously?"

"Come on, Wren, you know he can't help it," Nora butts in. "He's naturally protective; all people have proclivities, and when we care about each other, they come out, even in those who aren't gifted. It's not a terrible thing, having a friend looking out for you."

"I know," he sighs. "I can feel you guys, you know. We're all way too turned on by my game," he jokes. "Here, let me do what I was made to do." He looks Nora in the eyes and quietly draws a calming peace from her. Then he looks at Brokk. It's a little harder with him; he's naturally guarded. Luckily, Brokk is both good-natured and comfortable with Wren. Wren's friends trust him; and while he's often irritable about Nora using her gift, he's always gotten joy and comfort from using his to make the people he loves feel good.

"That's lovely," Nora smiles at him softly. She pushes a sweet calm at him, too. It's not the same as being compelled; but there's something nice about feeling other people when they're like this.

They leave the restaurant, and Wren looks up at the sky. Nora threads her arm through his and shivers. It's not really cold, but there's a lingering chill in the air, an April night on the cusp of summer, leaving spring slowly behind. Above him, the sky is inky black. It had been a lovely crisp blue all day, hazy with cirrus clouds and full of gentle breezes. He knows that in some places, the sky is carpeted with stars on nights like this; but not here. The lights from the city and suburbs pollute the sky. It's no matter to Wren. Knowing that things like star-filled skies exist, beautiful and timeless things, grounds him. It is as it should be, and he is where he should be in this world. Every rule he's made has brought him here to good food, good friends and a great life. The buildings around him crowd like friends and family. He loves this, because so many small pleasures and great distractions mean he never needs to feel lonely.

* * *

DESPITE HIS STRICT RULES AND his need to have everything in its place, to plan ahead, Wren knows that spontaneity has its own pleasure and that getting caught up in something provocative and impetuous can be a liberating experience, made hotter by its unexpectedness. Sometimes even he feels constrained by the structures he uses to protect himself from the world.

Wren hadn't planned for this, but as soon as the elevator doors open to the basement level of the library, Wren knows Cam is there. He checks his call number. To find that section of books, he should follow the blue line, one of the colored trails taped to the floor to guide students. The blue line forks to the left, but Wren can sense that's the wrong way if he wants to find Cam. He takes a shaking breath, tries to control the excitement that shivers up from his core and turns right instead of left.

IN THE DEAD QUIET OF THE LIBRARY, Cam is too aware of the silence; the grinding hum of the movable stacks being opened startles him. The sound of faraway footsteps draws his gaze up from his bewildering class notes, and a cough from the other side of the reference stacks, where other study tables are tucked away, distracts him easily.

He's chosen this table in the basement because it's quiet. He can't study in his room, not stats. He can't focus on notes from that class because all he sees is *him,* the boy who has been ceaselessly drawing his attention all semester. Now, everything he's jotted down seems disjointed. In class, his hands take notes on auto-pilot; his ears are half tuned to the professor while his eyes stubbornly stray to whichever corner of the room that boy is in.

Math has never been his thing, and attempting to learn in such a distracting environment isn't working. Not only is he unable to pay attention, but what they're learning is also far beyond what he thought it would be. He's pretty sure that he'd be lost even without the added distraction.

Cam never struggled in school. Stubbornly, he wants to avoid having to admit defeat and go to the help lab. Dry-eyed and frustrated, he puts his head down on the table and takes a deep breath. With the final exam looming, he's beginning to feel a crest of panic. Cam doesn't get poor grades. He's steady, he works hard and he has faith in his intelligence. Well, that and a scholarship that demands his high performance.

Maybe it's the anxiety stealing in, or maybe some inherent grace and lightness of tread keeps Cam from hearing footsteps approach; Cam is startled by the sound of a voice.

"Rough day?"

Cam's head pops up, and he barely manages to keep his mouth from dropping open: it's *him.* There's a long silence, crackling with energy, during which Cam stares stupidly. The boy is wearing an asymmetrical black cotton sweater that unzips diagonally from his neck to his shoulder and bright blue tunnel plugs in his pierced ears. Cam can see the exposed left side of his collarbone. His mouth is suddenly too dry, and his heart rate picks up until the hard, battering beat feels as if it's shaking his ribs.

"Cat got your tongue?" the boy asks, one corner of his mouth lifting in a smirk. Cam's eyes follow the movement of his lips.

"N–no," he stammers a beat too late. "I mean—"

"Yeah," the boy says, eyes brightening. This close, Cam's curiosity is finally assuaged: the boy's eyes are a startling green and mischievous, as if he knows something Cam doesn't. His hair is a true jet black—not dyed, but rich, genuine and thick.

"I'm Cam," Cam offers inanely, barely suppressing a wince.

"Wren." The boy doesn't offer a hand, just shifts his weight onto one leg so his hip juts out a bit. He's wearing wide-buckled boots that come up almost to his knees. His pants are insanely tight. That's a strange thing to notice... Cam snaps his eyes up and the boy's—Wren's—smile only widens. He leans forward and eyes Cam's notebook. He smells like rain. Cam has to close his eyes against a disorienting wave of dizziness; it's a little frightening but also inexplicably *good*.

"Stats, hmm?" Wren shifts the strap of his satchel, stretching his shirt to reveal a little more skin.

"Yeah," Cam forces himself to breathe normally. What is wrong with him? "Not my thing."

"You should get a tutor," Wren says. "You'll get it down in no time."

"Final Wednesday." Cam shrugs and tries not to feel stupid. Obviously Wren knows this, since they share the class. "Not a lot of time."

There's another long silence in which they just stare at each other; it's not awkward, but something else, and Cam's unable to look away. A flush starts to rise through his body.

"I should go," Wren says. His eyes never leave Cam's. They're the color of May grass, and when they settle on Cam's that something hot, that something new, flares and falls deep in his stomach.

"Studying?" Cam manages faintly.

"Not exactly." Wren gestures toward the stacks. "Research."

"Oh," Cam says. His fingers buzz, and his skin, his muscles, his lips.

"I'll see you later," Wren says lightly, and bites his lip around a flirtatious smile. Cam has seen that sort of smile countless times as he watched others engage in that dance. He's never had such a look directed at him—not like this. It's disorienting, how much it makes him want more.

Cam turns to watch Wren go. He probably looks a fool, but he cannot take his eyes from Wren as he disappears into the stacks.

Cam closes his eyes and tries to breathe, and all he can see is the slim width of Wren's shoulders under that shirt, the fit of his jeans and those boots miraculously making his legs look miles long.

He lets a moment pass and inhales as slowly as he can. His fingers shake. Something is *insisting* inside him, pulling and pulling, wanting him to follow. When deep breathing doesn't work, and when trying to name the feeling and put it away doesn't work, when acknowledging that he hasn't any idea what the hell is happening doesn't seem to make a difference, Cam does what he can't seem to help doing and follows.

WREN DOESN'T HAVE TO WAIT LONG; maybe a touch longer than he expects, when he broadcasted so clearly. He sets his bag on the floor, leans against the wall between rows of books and props one foot against the wall. He doesn't untether, not for a second, not when Cam is in his blood like this. Impatiently, he pulls a little, touches the desire inside Cam's body and compels him to come closer.

Getting to look at Cam, to examine his face close up and for a longer period, was lovely. His triangular chin and slightly slanted eyes, a deep chocolate brown Wren's not seen before, are stunning and sensual. Something steady burns inside those eyes.

Wren tugs harder, and finally, satisfyingly, Cam is there. His eyes are wide and he looks unsure, but it doesn't really matter, not when Wren's eyes meet his, not when Cam's hands, wide and hot, come up to frame Wren's face. Wren's eyes want to flutter shut; he tilts his head back and feels them grow heavier as his body's imperative rises. He covers Cam's hands with his own and exhales brokenly.

"I don't—" Cam says, pressing and molding his body until it is curled around Wren's. It thrills him, the sharp bright desire flaring in Cam. Wren breathes him in, waiting. Cam is all boy and heat, and his lips are so, so close. Wren flattens his shoulders against the wall and shifts his knee so Cam can crowd closer, opens his mind and uses his gift to project his desire, hot and strong into Cam, and swallows the sharp inhalation of Cam's breath just before his mouth crashes against Wren's.

CHAPTER THREE

WREN'S MOUTH IS INVITATION. IT'S an inevitability Cam wasn't expecting but *feels*. Some part of him, deep in his core, recognizes that he has no idea how to do this. But his body moves instinctually, and no part of him second-guesses Wren's lips. Wren's tongue slips past his; his mouth pushes against Cam's and then draws back, as if he's expecting something, and Cam is defenseless. He has no idea what he's doing, he's never done this, but kissing Wren is intuitive. The slide of his tongue along Wren's, pulling his mouth back and nibbling at those lips before dipping back in, just happens. A primal need unlocks, their mouths are open and blazing and Cam is suddenly *ravenous;* a shocking chasm of desire is cracking open inside his body. The pleasure he feels at the touch of Wren's lips against his cascades through him until he aches. Pushing Wren roughly against the wall, he strains for more.

Wren's arms are around his shoulders and he's making delicious sounds of pleasure and encouragement against Cam's mouth. Cam pulls away, sucking in shaking breaths. He startles at the touch of those lips against his neck, kisses that feel like fire. He tips his head back, and one hand comes up to thread through Wren's messy hair and keep him close. Wren nips and sucks and holds Cam close as he trembles. He feels as if he's about to shake out of his skin.

It's with that hand in Wren's hair that Cam pulls him back to lean down for another kiss, his tongue stroking into Wren's mouth. Everything is silk and wet and heat and Cam is hard—unexpectedly hard. Pressing against Wren's stomach, his body seeks something more.

"Yes," Wren pulls back to whisper. Cam looks into his eyes then and feels his knees buckle from a rush of intense pleasure.

"What—" he swallows, closes his eyes and can't help crowding closer. There's no other word for his body demands; he grinds against Wren even as his mind wakes. "I don't under—*oh*—"

He stops when he feels Wren's erection against his leg. With his eyelids sultry at half-mast, Wren bites his lip. When he closes his eyes and arches his hips into Cam, something... leaves. The intensity of pleasure that has overwhelmed Cam abates long enough for his complete confusion to surface.

"Oh *shit*," Wren swears, then pushes him away, so suddenly Cam stumbles back. "*Oh shit*, you don't—"

"Wait what?" Cam reaches for him and Wren just shakes his head and sidesteps him.

"You don't know, oh my god I thought you *knew*," Wren says, closing his eyes and taking a stuttering breath. With that, the frantic wanting slowly wanes from Cam's body.

"What... I—"He can barely formulate words. "What *was* that?"

"I thought you *knew*," Wren accuses. "Have you ever—have you ever even been with someone?"

Cam feels a flush stain his cheeks. "That's—I, I mean—"

Wren pulls away. His cheeks are hectic; his eyes are wide. "I don't play with new. I'm sorry. I can't, it's a rule."

"A rule? What—" Wren turns away. "Wait," Cam says, to no avail. He watches, tingling and dizzy, as Wren walks away, light-footed and fast. *So fast*. It's all happened so fast, he feels as if he's been picked up by a tornado, turned around and utterly flattened, confused and unsure. The long room bracketed by bookshelves is empty, but the echo of Wren lingers in a wake of sibilant energy streaming through and past Cam.

CAM LIES AWAKE IN BED for hours that night, puzzled and turned on. It never occurred to him that he might be attracted to men, too. What's more confusing, he parses in the dark, is how... not-weird the idea is. Or seems. It's not threatening, even if he's never felt it before.

Then again, maybe he has. Cam thinks of his friend Adam in high school. They'd run track together and admiring Adam's body, as another athlete, had made sense to him. Adam had a sense of humor and a lightness to his personality that had drawn Cam to his friendship as soon as they'd met. Maybe it wasn't as intense or confusing as what he's been feeling for Wren, but from where he is now, Cam can see that it was attraction.

Is it his nature, buried deep, or is it just *Wren*? Nothing has ever felt like this connection with Wren, the curiosity and longing these last months, then the explosive fervor between them when Wren kissed him. Cam recalls the moments just before, staring at his notes in the library basement, confused but unable to resist his body's call toward Wren. He pictures Wren's smug expectation, his lightning eyes.

Cam rolls over; his phone tells him it's past three a.m., and he's nowhere close to sleep. The screen casts a too-bright light, piercing the dark. No matter though; Nate could sleep through anything. He's snuffling lightly in his bed. Cam breathes steadily and tries not to relive the moment, the crash of energy and desire and light between his lips and Wren's, their bodies and skin. He tries to ignore the way his skin still throbs and the unsettling desire flooding his limbs, so that he can sleep.

It's useless, resisting. It's strange too, to feel pulled toward such a concrete fantasy. His fantasies have always been vague, flashes of desire and thoughts of pleasure between nameless bodies. Cam has always wondered at his own lack of desire compared to what he's observed in high school friends or living with Nate, who brings a casual stream of women through their door and has a well-developed libido and ease with sex that Cam doesn't.

This desire is definitely more specific. Uncomfortable, but sweet. Grounding, as if—for one of the rare times in his life—he is present in his own body and the space around it. He's seldom noticed that he *wasn't* grounded. Running feels almost the same; the high that comes afterward matches the rush he felt kissing Wren.

* * *

WREN WALKS OUT OF THE LIBRARY on autopilot, not really aware of what he's doing until he's getting off the bus in his neighborhood. It's dark enough that he knows he has to be alert, but he's still in enough shock that he has to actively work to try to sense his surroundings in any way.

Nora is home, he knows. He left her there just a few hours ago, with a promise of a late night guilty pleasure *Clueless* screening. Fuck. He cannot even face her, or the sheer volume of internal *I Told You So* that will come pouring out of her. Wren grits his teeth, shoulders open the door and drops his bag. Nora's already on the couch, hair in a half-fallen bun, wearing her kitten pj's.

"I can't," he says as soon as she looks at him.

"Wha—?"

"I just said, *I can't.*"

"You can't...?" Nora says.

"Talk about it? Deal with you being smug?"

"Okay, so." Nora tries to smile at him, her *calm down it's going to be okay Wren*, smile. "We won't do any of that. How about, because you seem to be in...distress," she says delicately, "We can watch the movie quietly with no talking, or we can raincheck the whole thing?"

Wren closes his eyes and flumps onto the sofa next to her. "It's a lot easier to be mad at you when I prematurely assume what you're going to do, you know," he informs her.

"Well, yes, I would think so," Nora says with a laugh. "Why do you want to be mad at me though?"

"Cause you love me and it's easier," Wren says, shuffling so he's more comfortable and cuddled against her. She pushes him off and starts to help him with his boots.

Clueless is a magical movie, because despite hundreds of viewings, it still holds Wren's attention and entertains him well enough to give him a small buffer of time between what happened in the library and his need to process it. He doesn't talk to Nora that night, but locks himself in the hush of his room and tries to reason himself out of the recoiling internal horror he'd run from the library carrying.

Despite Cam's protests as Wren fled, Wren cannot help but believe he took advantage of Cam in an unacceptable way, without true consent. Wren breached a trust; it was incredibly foolish to assume that Cam knew what was going on and to allow himself to be misled by the strength of the connection he felt. Cam's initial abandon and then his sudden confusion is one of those gut twisting memories Wren knows he'll be actively avoiding for months. Cam had been so *open*, a flavor unlike any Wren's tasted. Cam's inside him now, bringing a deep, longing tug that radiates through Wren. His skin feels too alive and everything tingles and aches, aches from wanting but also because he *can't* have him now. It is rending, wrangling the discipline to walk away not only from Cam, but, until he can trust himself again, the game.

Wren has to forget this whole thing. Although he's built for touch, Wren's lived through enough wanting and needing and denying to know he can forget. Taking Cam, who apparently didn't know or understand who Wren is, would be wrong. It's a game for a reason: because no one gets hurt, not him or the person he's with.

Wren remembers what it was like to trust someone so much he let him in and in, opened himself with the faith that he'd never be misused. He remembers months when he waited for the right times to let Robert take him apart so sweetly. More acutely, he remembers what it felt like to have that trust broken. In the wake of broken promises, Wren refused to touch or let himself be touched intimately, to relive that vulnerability with no one to catch him in the fall.

Wren is built for touch. Affection and simple love he has with Nora, with his family; they won't break his heart.

As for the rest, for pleasure beyond what he can provide himself... the game is a safe way to feel physical release and intimacy and fun, without having to let go or risk himself. Or, at least, it had been.

"IT'S OVER," WREN GREETS HER with in the morning, thumping a box of Fruit Loops onto the table between them.

"What is?" Nora asks cautiously.

"The game. The boy," Wren says, waving his spoon. He hardly slept, he feels as if someone put his skin on inside out, and the last thing he wants is to have to talk about this.

Scratch that. The last thing he wants is to have to talk about this *ever* again.

"Wanna tell me wha—"

"Nope," Wren says, opening the box of cereal so vigorously it tears down the side. He sighs. "It won't work out, it's not gonna happen, it's over, and we're all moving on."

"We?" Nora asks.

"Yes. You, me, the fucking cereal, all of us," Wren over-pours the milk and then sighs again. Being defeated by breakfast cereal on top of all the rest is almost too much. If there wasn't so much milk in the bowl, and if he didn't care so much about his bedding, he would retreat into his cave with his cereal.

"Okay," Nora says quietly. She puts her hand on his, smiles and then hands him some napkins. "Eat your cereal so *it* can move on, then you and I are going shopping so that *we* can."

* * *

THE CHEAPEST FLIGHT HOME TAKES him to an airport hours away from home. Nebraska unfolds as the highway ribbons its way closer to a house filled with an energy Cam once unconsciously freed himself from.

His father is awkwardly silent on the drive—they both are. Luis Vargas has always been a quiet man, contained in all the ways Cam trained himself to be as a teenager.

Cam's leaving Nebraska for Chicago was an impulse that shook everyone. Cam wasn't the impulsive one. He had always been steady, nearly unchanging in the constant roil around his family.

When his plane home lifted into the air, Cam really knew in his bones that Chicago had been the real flight, the best escape.

On the drive Luis talks about his long-deserved promotion at the plant and buying a new car for the first time in his life, a small coupe. They talk about it, his father haltingly pointing out features Cam would never have imagined he would want.

At the house, he and his father unfold similar long frames.

"Everything in your room is the way you left it," Cam's mother Julie says, as soon as he walks through the door, and kisses both his cheeks. *Of course.* Because clichés have a basis in truth, and what college homecoming would be complete without a realization that one no longer fits into the husk of one's old life? "I know it's dinner and not breakfast, but I thought we'd do *arepas* tonight. Your favorite."

"Thanks, Mama," Cam says, kissing her back.

"I WISH YOU WERE STAYING LONGER than a few weeks," Julie says that night. "We miss you."

"I know," he says, smiling at her.

She's changed her hair slightly; it's shorter and lighter. Cam has a feeling of slight displacement, as if everything he's deeply familiar with, constants during his whole life at home, are slightly off-center. Not unfamiliar, but strange. The kitchen table is the same, but the chairs are different. They've recovered them.

Luis nods in acknowledgment and goes back to cutting his *arepa*, a cornmeal-based flatbread his mother made from scratch for Sunday breakfasts since Cam was a kid. There was always an array of cheeses and deli meats laid out on the table to stuff into the steaming, torn-open pockets, where the cheese melts deliciously in the heat. He hasn't had them since he left for Carlina. He opens one carefully and avoids the steam; thin-sliced asadero cheese and ham are at the ready.

"But I got a job that I could keep through the semester, and..."

"And?" she prods gently.

"I really like it there," he admits. "Not that I don't *here*, it's just different."

"I can't imagine Lex holds much of a candle to Chicago," his dad chimes in.

"Just a different pace," Cam says. It seems like betrayal, to feel hemmed in by his old home and old room and the big, empty spaces in their small town. The running here is better, true. But he just doesn't feel as awake. What was home doesn't sit right around his skin anymore.

He thinks of Wren, of five minutes in a library that felt like a supernova in an empty room.

"Do you want more?" His mom bumps his foot under the table and smiles when he nods. The foods of his childhood—hot, fresh, the perfect grit of maize flour in his mouth, these are the things he'll gorge on before he has to leave. Out of the corner of his eye, he quietly watches his parents as they gossip about news in town. His father looks a little older.

"How's Pey?" Cam asks out of nowhere. The fourth chair at the table looks empty to him. His father tightens his lips until they're thin and white.

"Oh, you know Peyton," his mother says lightly, taking another *arepa*. "Always on the move."

"Needing money," his dad chimes in.

Cam ignores that last bit. "Where is she now?"

"I'm not sure, honey," his mom says.

"Oh, well." Cam knows better than to worry, knows that his worry would only stress them further. Peyton will call if he needs her; somehow she always knows. He bites his lip and grabs the butter from across the table. Even though Peyton usually calls using what they've always called their *twintuition,* there are times he just plain misses her, and it's hard not knowing how to find her. It's been a long time since they've talked.

"I know you miss her," his mom says, covering his hand with her own. Cam resists the urge to pull away. How can she see him so transparently sometimes and not at all at others? His parents miss Peyton too, but he knows that they also feel a certain relief at the distance. The trouble she always made was harder for them.

"Can I help with the dishes?" he asks. His dad is still frowning at his plate and the tension sits like a stone in Cam's stomach. He shouldn't have said anything.

THE STARS ARE BRILLIANT TONIGHT, brighter than anything he'll see in Chicago, for which he is thankful. Peyton is somewhere under the sky, too. What does it look like where she is?

Cam has so much to figure out—enough for him to feel he's in a bit of a quagmire. If ever there were someone for him to talk to, it would be Peyton. But what would he tell her? That he kissed a boy and it felt like the Big Bang in his body? That he has no idea what that means?

He'll go back to Chicago in two weeks. And he'll do what he does best: Watch and learn and slowly figure this thing out. And although he'll make himself move past the emptiness Peyton's absence leaves here under a hometown sky, he'll pace each running step to the beat of missing her; she's always been half of a whole, and he feels her absence more here than he has in the months since he left home.

It's not just the worst memories that linger in the corners of the family home, the shouted arguments, the anxiety that coated them all whenever she ran away. Cam thinks of the thick tension he swam through whenever she returned, or the incredible sense of loss that last time, when they'd finally come of age, and she had escaped the home that had always seemed to stifle her. Peyton had been born too free, and although nothing was ever wrong, exactly, their father's rigid adherence to a certain old school culture and their mother's too-easy acquiescence had always been too much for her. Peyton had confessed over and over, curled in Cam's bed on late nights after having snuck back in, that she just couldn't stand it anymore. Cam had felt this, too, since they were kids. The difference between them lay in the fact that he'd learned to rein in that chafing need to break away, and acted with a calmer, more controlled energy.

When she left, a hasty one-line note on the kitchen table and a box of letters she'd been secretly writing Cam for over a year tucked under his bed, he felt her loss in the most visceral way, like a rending in his core.

Somewhere, Peyton breathes air he's never touched. She's got a constantly shifting life that he never really understands. But although it aches, she's there; and in moments like this, knowing that is the closest he comes to comfort.

CHAPTER FOUR

NATE HAD SET UP A SYSTEM early on, when they met. Socks on the door were too obvious, even though he thought they were slightly hilarious and had admitted he was tempted to go with a throwback system. In this day and age, he said, texts should suffice.

Cam had nodded and played along; at the time, he doubted he'd ever be in a position to avail himself of the system.

And yet... something is awake now. Concrete. Cam wonders at himself. He watches, trying to pull himself apart into threads and pieces to understand what lies below. He looks at men and at women, assessing their faces and bodies, waiting to see if something sparks in him, to see if he's just been missing something this whole time in assuming he was only attracted to women.

When he tries to examine this, he senses so much more below some surface he created inside himself: something alive and wanting and bright, something confusing and tangled. Sometimes it's too much to let himself dwell on it. It makes him feel unsteady and frightened; he's not who he thought he was, and he has no idea who or *why* he really is.

So he spends the rest of his summer working behind the register at a deli on Chadsworth, watching people come and go and quietly listening to their conversations. He comes home crowded with a press of feelings, with fleeting desires cultivated by observing faces and bodies and by small talk. He wakes in states of shaking arousal, with remnant images of bodies and hands on him, and indulges in furtive release when the intensity of layered desires begins to crest.

And he runs. He lets himself feel most alive when he runs; he can think of nothing more than the count of his breaths and the big sky above him. And when he gets home, he feels awake and incredible, strong and steady. It's almost what he felt with Wren, but safer because he understands it.

* * *

"YOU GONNA ASK HER OUT?" Nate says, as his pen taps his notebook rapidly. It's been a long day for him, Cam can tell. His blond hair, always shaggily disheveled, is in a particularly telling state of disarray. His hazel eyes are by far his most expressive feature; at this moment, they express tired curiosity.

"What?" Cam breaks out of his fog.

"You've been staring at her for a good five minutes," Nate says, tilting his head toward the girl a few tables over that Cam has indeed been staring at. The café tables in their dorm quad cafeteria are unusually empty. "Not really being subtle about it."

"Uh." Cam bites his lip. His fingers trace the grooves of the table. It's a dark wood, real wood, sealed so it shines, but textured by use over time. He's not eating anymore, and is instead trying to study while Nate eats. "It's not like that." And it's not. Well, sort of. But not. He's just wondering. She isn't beautiful, but her looks are interesting. Compelling. She's sitting with friends, and her laughter is bright; it's what drew his attention.

"What's it like, then?" Nate prods.

Cam looks up at his friend—how much he can tell him? Can he explain how he's wandered classes and streets, examining faces and bodies and trying to figure out where his desires land? He certainly can't expose more—how often he's watched for even a glimpse of Wren; his attempts to search out Wren's last name through late-night library research; how keenly his body calls for more. Wren's kiss was a flame touched to a fuse, and Cam has spent the time since then on the edge of ignition.

"I don't know," Cam says finally, miserably. Confessing this—exposing this—makes him feel small and somehow also confined in his body.

Nate gives him a long look. He does this sometimes, as if Cam is a puzzle he's trying to put together. Cam has gotten good at ignoring it, for the most part. He looks down and blindly highlights some portion of text, hoping Nate will get the message and drop it. Cam is in no position to say anything; to him, the world is just one big puzzle. More often than not, he finds himself staring at all the pieces, baffled as to what picture they're supposed to make.

* * *

"CAMERON," A FAMILIAR VOICE SINGS through the phone. He double checks the number: it's not one he recognizes.

"Peyton," he says. "Hey! You're lucky I answered."

"You should always answer strange numbers, because there's always a chance it will be me," she responds easily. She does have a point.

"Where are you?" Cam lies on his bed; there's an automatic smile on his face, a sort of sighing through his body he gets whenever she calls. No matter where they are, they always have a connection; he goes through his days always aware that she's somewhere. But it's comforting to hear her voice; it pulls him back into himself.

"Arizona," Peyton says.

"*Arizona*," he says, surprised. "What the hell is in Arizona? I can't think of anything exciting enough to bring you there."

"You'd be surprised," she says, laughing, "at the things that call me." Cam closes his eyes.

"I miss you," he says.

"Hey," Peyton responds softly, worry in her voice. "Are you okay?" It's uncharacteristic of him to be open like this. When they're together, he rarely has to say what he's feeling, but it's been a long time since he's seen her. It's hard to catch her, nomad that she is. Cam doesn't always mind, because he understands how much she needs this sort of life, flitting from one brief stop to another, changing anything she must to suit whatever calls her next.

"I think so," he says, opening his eyes. He turns onto his side to face the wall and moves his phone to the other ear. The phone's getting hot, and he hates that feeling. "I don't know."

"College being okay to you?"

"Yes. I like it," he says.

"Chicago too big?"

"No, it's just right. Besides, it's not like I'm *in* the city." The near claustrophobia from buildings and bodies feels good after the great open skies in Nebraska. "There's just something—new."

"Oh, that sounds promising," she says. "Tell me more."

"I don't know yet," he says. "I'm not sure what it is, I have no idea how to figure it out. I don't know how to talk about it right now."

Peyton hums lightly. "Figuring something out. That's gonna be a challenge for you."

"Shut up," he says it lightly, but means it to some extent. Peyton is good for him; she foils some of his personality traits—as he does hers—very well. Her impulsive personality, her instinct for change and her willingness to trust her intuition and desires are all things he doesn't have and she has long challenged him to develop.

He's still waiting for his traits of steady patience and careful observation to rub off on her, so he can't fault her for pushing.

"Well," she says, "I'll be settling here for a little while. I want you to call me when you need to talk. Or if you need help figuring out whatever it is."

Cam sighs. He knows she means it, but it's hard to trust that she's really staying anywhere, because Peyton moves on whims. She inevitably gets herself into some sort of trouble he or their parents have to help her out of, then falls off the map and into silence for long stretches.

"I will," he promises anyway, because he's never felt a need for concealment with her. He's not keeping secrets or evading right now, he's just confused. If she's where she says she'll be when he has more words, he'll call her.

"I love you, Peyton."

"I love you too, Cam," she says quietly before hanging up.

* * *

THE GIRL CAM HAS BEEN NOTICING lives in his dorm. How has he never noticed her before? Once he's recorded her in his memory, he suddenly sees her everywhere. She's curvy and quite a bit shorter than he; she laughs easily and touches casually. He observes her with friends and learns that she's not particularly social, but is always with the same two or three people. She wears her shiny, light brown hair both straight and in curls—he's not sure which is natural, because both always look styled.

"Seriously," Nate says, shoving him lightly one day as they leave the dining hall. "You are making me crazy."

"Shut up." Cam shoves back. Nate grabs his arm and starts to drag him along. "What are you—?"

"I'm doing what you won't," Nate says. He walks straight up to her. Her friend seems to be in the middle of a story when they arrive, but stops mid-sentence.

"Hi," Nate says, dropping into one of the hard, overstuffed chairs in the commons. "I'm Nate. This is my roommate, Cam."

Trapped by manners and curiosity, Cam sits too.

"Hi, Nate. Cam," the girl says, obviously amused. "I'm Maggie. This is Christine and Lauren."

A small moment of silence passes, awkward and begging for someone to navigate the graceless interruption.

"I've seen you around a lot," Cam offers, wincing when he realizes how awkward this sounds.

"I've noticed," Maggie says with a smile. Cam resists the urge to close his eyes. Maggie turns in the chair next to him. She pitches her voice lower. "I've had a small bet with myself, how long it might take you to come introduce yourself."

Nate snorts softly.

"And if I never did?" Cam asks.

"I think I might have caved eventually," she says. Then she smiles the wide, true smile he's watched for weeks. "I'll have to thank your friend some time. Although I do deduct points for execution. Awkward."

"Yes," Cam laughs, sparing Nate a glance. He's making conversation with Christine and Lauren. Cam knows it's an effort to distract them, but it's not working all that well; they're both watching him and Maggie in the gaps in conversation.

"We should go for coffee or something," he blurts. Maggie laughs and nods.

"I'd like that."

* * *

He finds her in line; he's not running late, so it throws him off to see her near the front of a long line.

"Hey," he says, trying to get her attention. She's focused on her phone.

"Oh, hi!" Maggie smiles widely. "I was just going to get—"

"Do you want me to—?"

Maggie laughs and Cam looks down. She makes this look easy without betraying a trace of awkwardness or uncertainty. He doesn't feel right in his body; he's like an imposter trying to prove something to someone who doesn't even care.

Cam hasn't seen Wren since that night in the library. He doesn't bother trying to convince himself he doesn't want to—he looks everywhere he goes.

"Let me get you your order," he manages finally. It's the polite thing to do on a first date, after all. Assuming this is a date.

"Okay, yeah," Maggie says. "Thank you. I'll go grab us a table over there." She points to a row of two-person tables by the window. "I'll have a frappuccino, medium."

Maggie is obviously a coffee drinker, although Cam bets that when she makes it for herself, she takes a lot of cream and sugar.

Cam watches her settle. She wipes the table carefully and hangs her purse from the back of the chair. He's seen her around the dorm enough to know she's put more effort into her appearance today; she's wearing a nice skirt and a little more makeup.

"Here you go." He sets down her drink. "I took a chance on the cookie." He doesn't add that he's seen her eat them in the cafeteria. That would be creepy. Her face lights up.

"Oh, yum! Thank you. Want to share?"

"Oh no, I'm good." His chair pulls out with a loud screech that turns the heads of a few patrons. *Smooth, Cam. Smooth.*

"So Cam, mystery boy, tell me about yourself."

"Mystery boy?" he asks.

"That's what we call you," Maggie explains.

Cam laughs. "That must be a theme. I was calling you that in my head for a while too. Well, girl, I mean."

"Well then." She leans forward and crosses her arms on the table. Her eyes are brown, but not like his. Hers are lighter, like milk chocolate, bright in the sunlight. "Let's uncover things." He blushes and she laughs like butterflies storming the room, beautiful and startling.

"ALL RIGHT, THEN," MAGGIE SETS her empty cup to the side. "Let's see who passes the quiz."

"There's a quiz?" Cam feigns dismay.

"Yes, of course. Don't all first dates end with a test?" Maggie looks down and bites her lip, holding back a smile. Cam doesn't think she meant to say that, but she doesn't seem to mind, either.

"I wouldn't know," he confesses. She's so much easier to talk to than he anticipated.

"Oh god, I'm your first date?" Maggie asks. "Had I known that, I would have taken you somewhere fancy." She winks and it's impossible not to smile.

"Maybe next time?" Cam says quietly. He's not sure what this means, but he likes her. That's where things usually begin, right?

"Let's see if you pass the test."

"Okay. What are the questions?"

"The usual," Maggie says. "Name, age, major, likes and dislikes, hopes and dreams, family genealogy, blood type, toenail polish color."

"Oh, is that all?" he manages through his laughter.

"No, that's just the short answer," she says, chuckling. "There's an essay due later."

"Okay," he says, "I resent the lack of multiple choice questions, but no matter. I'm sure I'll beat the pants off of you."

Maggie gasps through her laughter. "I'm not that kind of girl."

Cam covers his face, muffling his own words. "I didn't mean it like that."

"No, this is good, now I have something to put in 'hopes and dreams,'" Maggie says.

"Oh god," Cam says. He takes a deep breath and tries to manage his laughter. His sides hurt from it, which is pretty rare. "Okay, you first, since you've apparently already started."

Maggie rolls her shoulders and pretends to crack her neck. "Your name is Cameron Vargas, but never call you Cameron, Cam all the way. You are nineteen years old, majoring in environmental studies. Um, let me see..."

"You've still got the heavy hitters coming," he reminds her when she pauses.

"Damn. Well, I know you like tea," she gestures to the iced tea in front of him, "and that you dislike wobbling tables. You hope to get into my pants." She winks again and he tries to smile—he really has no idea what he wants in that regard. He tries to guide the conversation forward.

"Family?"

"Well, you told me you have a twin sister named Peyton... as far as genealogy, damn. I'm not sure I caught that part. Do we have a family tree I can reference? Is this an open book test?"

"I don't know," he says, "you made it."

"Well..." Maggie taps her fingers against the table and pretends to think. "I think you said your parents are Venezuelan? I guess the only question I'm really sure about is that your toenails are pink."

"Pink?" he says.

"Yup, cotton candy pink."

He looks away from her then, pretending that he's been caught. Outside, clouds are rolling in and the sun is fading behind them. It looks like rain. Cam had been hoping to go for a run tonight.

"So how did I do?" Maggie prompts when he doesn't look back at her.

"You'll have to wait and see." It's very bright in the cafe—at least it seems so, with the sky dimming outside. "So is it my turn? I'm pretty sure I can win this."

"Oh, we're competing now?"

"Well, what's the point otherwise?" he jokes. She makes a *you may have a point* sort of face.

"All right then, do your worst."

"Maggie Hall. Nineteen. Psych major, one older sister. Guessing from your last name, there might be some English roots to your family tree. You like your coffee sweet, chocolate chip cookies and spaghetti." He thinks back on his observations for a second. "Though I'm pretty sure you don't like the spaghetti at the cafeteria, and I have a hunch that you don't like wearing a coat if you can avoid it, because you weren't that one day it was so cold last week."

"Damn," Maggie says with a smile.

"I have no idea about your blood type and I'm going to take a shot in the dark and guess that your toenails are painted something in the purple family."

"Okay, how did you know that?" she demands.

"You wear a lot of purple." Cam explains. She narrows her eyes thoughtfully and scrunches her brow. Finally her face clears and humor floods it again.

"But not purple coats."

Cam laughs with her, then, and it's easy; it's easy and not peculiar that he knows all of this about her, and he senses that she's flattered by his observations.

CHAPTER FIVE

"WHAT KIND OF MOVIES DO YOU LIKE?" Cam drops into the chair next to Maggie, interrupting her reading. She pauses with her fork halfway to her mouth; tiny droplets of salad dressing fall to her plate. She flips her book face down and pushes it away.

"Hi, Cam, how are you today?" she says, eyebrow arching—a look that's somehow lovely despite the sarcasm.

"I am great," he says, and pauses. He really is. Usually Cam responds to questions like this automatically; people never really expect an answer other than *fine*. But it's been a good day.

"Wonderful," she says. "I like all kinds of movies. Well, no," she gestures with her index finger, "I take that back. I don't like scary suspense-type movies."

"Well, how do you feel about satire?" he hazards.

"I feel like I could manage that."

"So how would you feel about accompanying me to see *Formula Lost* tomorrow night? Nate has a date and wants us to come along."

"Ohhhh, a double date." Her eyes sparkle mischievously. "This must be step two on the dating path checklist."

"You know it," Cam says, and then—for some reason—winks. He's not sure if he's ever winked at someone. He's watched enough people flirting to know that this is something people do, but he always thought of such things—playful touches and winking, soft smiles and a certain eye contact—as deliberate. They probably are, most of the time. But it's something new for him, realizing that sometimes, energy between two people like this can just happen.

"SO WHAT'S THE STORY?" NATE flops onto his bed with his sneakers still on. Cam takes his keys from the lock and shuts the door gently; it's late. He hates when slamming doors wake him at late hours. Interrupted sleep is one of the few things guaranteed to make him grumpy.

"You just watched the same movie I did." Cam hangs his keys by the door, carefully removes his shoes and hangs his jacket over the chair in front of his desk. He tries to modulate his voice; Nate's not done anything—in fact, nothing really happened all night. But he feels on edge and has since they got to the theater. A faintly familiar buzz seems to have settled in his bones tonight. "How can you not know this?"

"First of all," Nate points out, "I wasn't paying that much attention."

Cam frowns. "Why not?"

Nate just stares at him for long seconds before seeming to move on. "Second of all, I wasn't talking about the movie."

"Huh?" Cam pops his head up, and then goes back to searching for his well-worn Huskers T-shirt.

"I mean with you and Maggie," Nate explains with exaggerated patience.

"What is this, a midnight gossip session?" Cam says a little defensively. Nate's question seems probing, though it probably shouldn't.

"Man, you are so hard to read sometimes." Nate toes his shoes off.

Cam doesn't say anything. What is there to say, really, when he can't even read himself?

* * *

"CAM?" MAGGIE SAYS.

"Hmm?" Cam squeezes her shoulder. She doesn't move, keeps her head tucked against his shoulder. After a moment of silence, she sits up, grabs the remote and pauses the movie.

"Are you—" She bites her lip. "What is this?" She gestures between them. Cam folds his hands together, something twisting in his stomach. "What do you want it to be?" he says, stalling.

"I think it's pretty clear what I want," she states.

It is. Cam has known for a while, now—the way she kisses his cheek when she leaves lately, lingering longer, her eyes on his. Waiting. Maggie's not the sort to wait for someone to make a move. She's her own person—he admires this a lot—and isn't afraid to go after what she wants. Cam senses that she is respecting his uncertainty. If that is what it should be called. Reticence? Insecurity?

"I've just never—" he starts. He sits up a little straighter, folds one knee and tucks his foot under the other. "I like you, a lot. I like being with you." Cam runs his hand down her arm, testing. Her smile is small and sweet, and she's so gentle with him. He feels strange in his skin, as if he wants that sort of carefulness, but at the same time doesn't, wants something bigger and sharper too.

"Here," she says finally, and kisses him. She kisses him slowly and confidently, but doesn't push. Maggie always smells wonderful, and when they watch movies or spend time together, the shape of her body against him is very comforting.

He cards his fingers through her hair; it slips like silk. She opens her mouth a little and it's moist and warm, so he does too.

* * *

CAM ENDS THE NIGHT WITH a kiss to Maggie's cheek, and when she turns her head for another, he leans into her mouth and tastes her lips again.

"Friends or more?" she asks when she pulls away.

"Uhh..." He feels puzzled. Hasn't kissing spoken for itself?

"I want to be sure that was—that you're okay with this. That it's something you want," Maggie says. She touches his hand.

"Yeah." He smiles. Her face lights up, delighted; it's as if he's done just the right thing, taken the next right step.

It's nice to feel close to someone like this.

"SO..." LYING DOWN, CAM STARES at the ceiling. He shapes the words he'll use, and breathes through that twisting feeling in his stomach again. It's so strange and unfamiliar, wanting to talk to someone about things inside himself. "I kissed Maggie. Well, technically, she kissed me."

"Yeah!" Nate cheers, a little too loudly for midnight in a dorm with paper-thin walls.

"Shhh." Cam waves his hand but doesn't look over. He isn't sure he can get through such a personal conversation *and* look at Nate.

"Awesome, right?"

Cam considers this. "Yeah, it was really nice."

Nate is quiet so long Cam wonders if maybe he's fallen asleep. It's stupid, trying to talk to Nate like this.

"Dude, do you really like her?" Nate finally says.

"Yeah, of course," Cam says.

Another pause, then Nate speaks again, teasing clear in his voice. "So how far'd you get? Round any bases?"

"Shut up," Cam says more easily, grateful that the conversation hasn't wandered too far into territory he isn't sure about. "To be honest, I've never been clear on what happens at each base," he admits.

"Yeah, me either," Nate laughs, "other than home plate. I definitely know that one. It's the best."

"I'll take your word for it," Cam yawns.

"For now," Nate says smugly. Cam yawns again, feeling the sleepy press of darkness. Finally.

* * *

SOMETIMES IT FEELS A BIT LIKE WORK, or a thing he hasn't quite grown into, when he's with her and she's obviously hoping for more. It's weird; he knows how guys are supposed to be. He knows Nate, and how much he wants and has sex. Thinks of friends in school, their consistent discussion and desire for it.

Sometimes, when he's with Maggie, he wonders if he was just born with something less—his desire isn't pressing, isn't urgent. It's nice, though, when he does manage to let himself go. Maggie is both reassuring and self-assured, and it's been long enough that next steps are definitely a natural progression.

"Will you touch me?" she asks one night. It's dim in her room and the TV volume is low. She's lying back on her futon, and her body is so welcoming under him. Cam swallows and lets her guide his hand under her shirt, where her skin is warm.

* * *

AFTER A WHILE, HE'S *SURE* he should feel more. How long can he give Maggie what she wants, when she so clearly wants and enjoys more than he? Nate is the only other person that Cam knows well enough to confide in, but this is not something he can talk about.

Cam watches. Nate seems to have a new girl every few weeks; Cam is regularly exiled from their room, and the library becomes his sanctuary. Linoleum and fluorescent lights, the smell of books and the quiet calm him with a grounding familiarity. Of course, he's not ready to admit how much he hopes to run into Wren there. His library visits are frequent, that hope watercolor-layered with guilt. He likes Maggie, and has no concrete understanding of what he's searching for or why he can't stop seeking that connection he felt with Wren. Sometimes, he searches campus—not just for Wren. His body seeks something hotter, more acute.

* * *

"YOU WITH ME?" MAGGIE GASPS one night, lips against his cheek, skin dewed with sweat.

"Yeah," he lies, and thinks helplessly of another moment, of pressing a small, harder body against a wall, of feeling as if he were on fire, Wren's teeth lightly biting his neck—and comes so suddenly it catches them both off guard.

* * *

CAM TWITCHES AND THEN TRIES to settle. He shuffles papers on his desk, pretends to study, looks out the window to where it's gray and raining miserably.

"Talk to me." Nate doesn't look away from their TV. He hits the buttons on his Xbox harder and winces as the zombie on the screen destroys him.

"What?" Cam puts his pencil down.

"You need to talk. I can tell. I'm your bro, right?"

"Bro?" Cam smirks.

"Shut up and tell me about your feelings before I change my mind and force you to play with me."

Cam sighs and stands. He stretches and sits next to Nate, shoving him over on the futon as he does. "I'll play anyway."

"I've ruined you with video games," Nate says.

"Yeah. I despair for my future," Cam responds dryly.

"Either that or I've expanded your horizons. Although I did hear a rumor once that they have Xboxes even in Nebraska."

"We have lots of things in Nebraska." Cam turns on his remote while Nate backtracks so Cam can join the game. "I just didn't do them. We weren't an Xbox sort of home."

"Hmm," Nate spares him a look. Cam shrugs. He doesn't talk about home much. "Anyway," Nate turns back to the screen, "Nebraska aside, you need to talk; it's killing me."

"It's killing *you*?" Cam says.

"It's hard to tell, you know," Nate jerks to the side when he's assaulted on the screen. He's very physical even when playing video games. "If it's killing you not to talk, but you know, rumor has it that it helps."

Cam swears softly when he's hit, then bites his lip and focuses. He finally responds. "I'll think about it."

"Okay," Nate says.

* * *

So far, Nate is the best thing Cam's gotten from his college experience. After initial awkwardness and feeling each other out, figuring out how to coexist in a small dorm room, Cam learned to appreciate him. Nate's a good friend; he's easy with Cam. Now that he knows Cam, he doesn't ever press too hard, but leaves the door open between them for whenever Cam does decide to talk, or for when he feels like getting up to something. Nate is a good influence in many ways; he's the reason Cam has experienced

Chicago and college in a more youthful way than he lived before.

When Cam lets loose, it's generally due to Nate's influence—recently, Maggie's as well. But Nate knows how to push without pushing too hard, mostly.

* * *

"WHAT'S WRONG?" MAGGIE PULLS AWAY from him. He chases her lips a little, and then sits back with a sigh.

"Who said anything is wrong?" He tries not to feel edgy. He's always been very adept at pulling himself in; generally only Peyton has been able to read him so easily.

"You seem distracted," Maggie says.

"Oh." Cam runs his hand up and down her arm. "I think I am. Chemistry is challenging me in a way I didn't expect." *And somewhere out there there's this guy,* he doesn't say, *who's light-boned and lithe and incredibly sexy, and it seems so wrong to be thinking of him right now, but I can't stop.*

Maggie smiles indulgently. "You don't do well with challenges you didn't see coming, do you?"

"Does anyone?" he responds, trying to change the track of their conversation.

"Cameron," she says, "lots of us."

He smiles at her. She's beautiful tonight; her eyes are bright and her hair is in loose curls. He has so much affection for her, a softness inside that's uniquely Maggie-shaped. "One of the many things you have to teach me, I guess."

She laughs, as he hoped she might, and kisses his cheek. "Between Nate and me, honey, we'll get it done."

Cam isn't sure, but goes along willingly enough.

* * *

WHEN HE'S NOT MEASURING HIS own internal state, Cam observes Nate. This is nothing new; his default setting is observation. But now he is watching for something specific.

Nate is easygoing about many things. He makes off-color jokes Cam doesn't always get, and some that he does and later feels mildly guilty for laughing at. But he's never said anything truly offensive about anyone in Cam's presence. Can he trust Nate with what's been eating him for months now? It's hard to go by the data he has; it's not as though they sit around talking about confused or gay or bisexual men.

Once he accidentally opened the floodgates with Maggie, thinking of Wren instead of her, it's been harder and harder to push everything back into the proper places. The spark of heat between him and Wren felt completely natural, in a way Cam doesn't understand. But he's not felt anything quite like it with anyone since. The closest he's come has been with Maggie, but even that is still nowhere close. Attractions have been more present in him than ever before, lately, and he's noticed with increasing frequency an especial affinity for men: a face or body that calls to him, bright flickers that still don't compare to Maggie's lasting warmth or the combustion of Wren in his arms.

Cam doesn't want to live his life missing something, but he's not sure he'll ever find something so right and simultaneously so explosive that it will be worth the risk. A sustainable heat seems to be something he should want, but looking for more when he has Maggie doesn't sit well with him.

When his defenses are down, when he's on the brink of pleasure with her, is also when he's least able to control what he's thinking; this is when Wren plagues him most. Something about picturing Wren, about wanting things he can barely name, about wondering what it would be like to be touched by him the way Maggie does, rouses him. Maggie notices changes in him. Cam assumes she attributes them to their deepening relationship.

* * *

"NATE," CAM SAYS, TURNING TO HIM suddenly. He's been unable to concentrate; this thing with Maggie has been torturing him, and he needs some perspective. "Have you ever thought about another person when you're with someone?"

Nate sets down his pen. "You mean, like, sex stuff, right?"

"Uh," Cam says, feeling heat rise in his face. "Um, yeah?"

"So, like..." Nate swivels himself back and forth in his chair. "Are you thinking about someone specific?"

"No!" Cam rushes to say. The flush deepens enough that it might actually show on his face; he's not accustomed to lying, and he has no idea if he can pull it off.

"Just other people, generally?"

Cam avoids specifying what kinds of people. "Yeah." Maybe Nate won't notice.

Nate thinks for a moment. His eyes narrow a little when he looks at Cam. Then he shrugs. "I think so? I've never really been with anyone long enough for it to be an issue."

"You think this is a relationship thing?" Cam asks.

"I don't know," Nate says. "I mean... when I'm with a girl, it's pretty much only one or two times, so you know. It's pretty—uh. Immediate."

"Immediate," Cam echoes.

"Or something," Nate kicks his desk lightly. "So when you're with Maggie, you think about other... people?"

"Not always," Cam says miserably, pushing down a wave of shame. Even after they'd started having sex, his desire hadn't increased all that much—at least for her. He's done everything he can to *not* think of a boy with delicately light skin, a shock of black hair and eyes a color he can't name, of the curve of his collarbone or the long fingers he watched for hours in a class he barely passed.

"Hmm," Nate says. He muses. "I've always kind of thought that what you think about is what you think about? That you can't always help it."

"I guess," Cam says.

"Do you want to be with her?" Nate speaks more frankly than he has before.

"I guess so?" Cam swallows. "Well, um. Yes." Nate raises his eyebrows and Cam closes his eyes. "I think so. I don't know. I really like her. It just—"

"Dude," Nate says, "I know this is, like, awkward. But you can talk to me about anything. I hope you know that. *Anything*."

Cam averts his eyes and fiddles with the cap of his ballpoint pen. "Yeah," he says. It's quiet for a moment; Nate shrugs lightly and turns back to his homework, giving Cam some space. Cam can't say the rest: that the things he desires most deeply surface when he wakes at night, aching fiercely, so close to spilling onto his sheets with half-remembered dreams of people most definitely *not* Maggie. They work in silence for a while. He startles when Nate speaks up again.

"Whatever you do, man, just be sure you're treating her with respect."

"Of course," Cam says, frowning.

"But you too," Nate adds.

"Hmm?"

"You only get one life, Cam," Nate says. "You're not me. The casual thing isn't for you. Just... be happy."

Cam smiles. Nate's not generally so serious; it's touching. With Peyton so far away and out of contact, it's reassuring to have someone who cares the way Nate does. It's not showy or stressful, it's just *there*.

CHAPTER SIX

"I've never been here before," Cam says over his menu.

"Oh, really? It's one of those native Chicago secrets," Maggie says. She's fiddling with her straw, capping the end with one finger and then drawing the straw up to watch the liquid flow out when she uncaps it. Over and over.

"You're thinking about something," he says.

"Duh," Maggie smiles, but there's something a little off about it. "Aren't we all always thinking?"

"I don't know," Cam wonders. "I've never thought—ha ha—about it."

Her laugh is familiar. Whatever oddity he sensed seems to break apart.

"Tell me another," Maggie says, after he's told her a funny story about the trouble he and Peyton used to get into when they were little. These are the things he shares about Peyton with others—the little anecdotes he can laugh over as well, like the first time Peyton had "run away," riding her bike toward the center of town at midnight with no clear plan or destination. She'd been pulled over by a police car less than a mile from the house and brought home. Compared to the other times, their increasing frequency as the two of them got older and the accompanying resentment and tension, this first always makes him laugh.

He pictures Peyton so clearly: with her twelve-year-old face set in her special brand of defiance and her hair in pigtails, caught violating curfew. He'd almost gone with her; she'd begged but he laughed her off. It was the first time they started to go different ways. Cam understood better how following impulse would only make things worse. Although he can now see clearly the divide that began to form between them that day, neither of them had understood it at the time.

Across from him, Maggie waits with her trademark smile. But funny Peyton stories are a slippery slope that can quickly slide into something shaded darker. Cam tries to twirl his pasta on his fork and it keeps slipping off, which is annoying.

"Oh, I don't know," he says. "There are lots I probably can't remember, from before I settled down a bit."

"And she didn't," Maggie guesses. "What happened, there?"

"What do you mean?" A bit frustrated with the pasta situation, he settles for cutting and eating it. He always feels guilty when he cuts it, and isn't sure if he does because it seems rude or because it seems like cheating.

"Well, Peyton certainly still hasn't settled down, right?"

He shifts a little.

"I don't mean that in a bad way," Maggie rushes to continue. "I just mean that you guys seem, from what I hear, very different now."

"I guess," Cam says, looking down. She's not wrong. He and Peyton *are* different—about as different as people can be. It's never felt that way to him, though; he's always felt like another half of a whole.

"I'm sorry," Maggie says softly. "Did I say the wrong thing?"

"No," he forces a smile. "Not at all. I just miss her."

* * *

MAGGIE IS A BIT DIFFERENT after that. The sense of oddness returns, though on the surface, everything is the same. Cam can't quite put his finger on it, but there's some undercurrent. Everything seems to hum with the faint vibration of discordant-energy.

"Did I do something wrong?" he finally asks.

"No." Maggie doesn't look surprised. "Well. Maybe."

"Oh, that's not good," Cam says. He folds his napkin carefully and puts it on the table.

"No, I mean—" Maggie sighs and looks away. "I'm not mad at you or anything. I just..."

Cam waits as long as he can through the silence that follows. "Do I have something to apologize for?"

"I don't know." She speaks slowly, thoughtfully. "Cam." She looks up at him. "Are you happy?"

"What?" Cam feels a bit confused. "Of course I am, why would you—?"

"I don't just mean with me," she interrupts, "although that too."

"Maggie," he says helplessly, unsure where she is going.

"So, I've been thinking about this for a while. And I don't know how to say it. And it might be offensive, or all kinds of wrong, but I've been having this feeling." She stops and takes a breath. "Well... I've had it. It's come and gone, and maybe it was just a small hunch, and then you seemed to disprove it—"

"Maggie," he interrupts. "What are you trying to say?"

"I don't—" She lifts her hand and lets it drop helplessly. "Cam, do you think—is there any way..."

"Any way...?" he prompts. She closes her eyes, takes a breath and then shrugs a little, settling into her body. When she opens her eyes again, there's something a little sad, or lost, in them.

"Cam, I don't know that you feel the same about me as I do about you," she says finally.

"Maggie," he starts. He has nothing to follow that with, though; how can he refute it when he's sure it's true? And how can he fail to deny it, when the implication is that he's doing the wrong thing? He cares about her. So much. After a beat, he says so.

"I know you do, Cam," she says. "But it's not the same. And—" She swallows, blinks shining eyes and then looks up, startled by their waiter bringing the bill. Cam takes it with a quiet thanks.

"How much do I owe?" Maggie asks softly.

"No, I'm paying." Cam says.

"Cam—" Maggie's brown eyes are gentle when they meet his. "I don't know that you should anymore."

"Stop it." He presses his lips together.

"Cam, when I said I care about you, I meant it," she insists. Her hand covers his and squeezes. "I care about you, and I want you to be happy, and I don't think you can be with me."

"Maggie," he says. "I *am*."

"Not like you should be," she says and takes the bill from him.

"PLEASE, MAGGIE," CAM TRIES TO take her hand when they exit the restaurant. His stomach is still knotted; his body is caught in the suspension before free fall.

"Look, Cam," Maggie says, "I think, once I have some time to get over this a little, we're going to be great friends."

"But—" Cam starts.

"That's all we were meant to be, I think." Night has come, a hush of dark cloaking the city. Her face is shadowed, but the tears in her eyes are clear. She stretches up on her toes. With her palm cool against his face, she kisses him so tenderly he can hardly feel it. "We'll talk about this more, in a while," she promises.

Cam closes his eyes and breathes; this feels terrible. He isn't just sad, but also guilty. He's let her down. And he hates that he's hurt her; it's clear that he has. Her hand slips from his before he opens his eyes. When he does, it's to watch her walk away. She's putting her purse over her shoulder, cross-body in her way, and he catches a glimpse of her tucking her hair behind her right ear. He knows so well how it smells, like coconut and vanilla, in the hollow behind her ear.

"I AM... " CAM SAYS INTO THE DARKNESS. He can tell Nate is awake. "More complicated than I realized."

Nate just snorts a laugh.

Cam closes his eyes and rolls until he feels the cool cotton of his pillowcase against his cheek. He's tangled, less sure than he was before—because he feels guilty, somehow complicit and also, for some reason, relieved.

"DUDE, WHAT WAS THAT ABOUT?" Nate asks him the next morning. Cam shrugs, and then realizes Nate can't see that when he's in the closet. He finds the shirt he's been looking for: a rich cobalt blue button-down with a light sheen to it and double pockets on the right side that Peyton gave him for his last birthday. She'd sent a huge package with all sorts of things he'd never buy for himself, as usual.

"What was what about?" Cam says, checking in the mirror the way the shirt fits.

"The crisis 'I'm complicated' shit," Nate doesn't look up; he's doing something on the computer, clicking his mouse rapidly. Probably playing Candy Crush.

Cam takes a breath. He buttons the last button. He's never worn such a vibrant color before; the man in the mirror is almost a stranger. He sits on his bed, gripping the edge with his fingers.

"Maggie broke up with me," he says.

"Oh man." Nate turns away from his game. "That blows. Why?"

Cam shakes his head, curling his toes to crack them. "She said we didn't feel the same way about each other."

"Well..." Nate starts.

"Well?"

"It's true, isn't it?" Nate says.

Cam tamps down a surge of irritation and takes a deep breath. Nate has a point, although his easy acknowledgment and unsurprised demeanor are frustrating. It's uncomfortable to know other people might see things about him so much more clearly than he has.

"I guess so," Cam says. "This sucks," he admits candidly. "I think I really hurt her, and I never meant to. I mean... I'm—"

Nate cocks his head and waits him out.

"I've been confused. And I don't know why,"

"Well, isn't that the definition of confused?" Nate asks.

"No. I mean, yes. I— I don't even know what I'm confused about. I just know that something doesn't feel right, and with her, I couldn't ever make it feel one hundred percent like I thought it should, like other people seem to—"

"Cam, man. You cannot try to figure out your shit by comparing it to other people," Nate butts in.

"Well how else will I know how to do what's right?" Cam retorts.

"By figuring out what's right for *you*," Nate says.

Cam straightens the cuff of his shirt. "You should charge me for the therapeutic services you provide."

"I will eventually," Nate jokes back. "Seriously, though—you okay?"

"Yes and no," Cam says, tipping his head from side to side. "A part of me feels like she's right, but another—"

"Hmm?"

"I think I'm just going to miss her," Cam says.

Nate smiles. "She's a great girl," he says. "She'll find a way to be friends with you."

"That's what she said," Cam says with a frown.

Nate just smiles at him and turns back to his game. Cam pulls a scarf on, knotting it carefully before donning his new coat.

* * *

"LET'S GET SHITFACED TONIGHT," NATE says, pulling up a chair across from Cam. It scrapes loudly against the tile floor. Cam winces. He hates that about this coffee shop—well, he's not really a fan of the place at all; it's sterile, with its white tiles and big windows, its regimented rows of tables that are always a bit crooked by the end of the day. The coffee isn't always fresh.

But it's cheap, it's near campus, and it's where his friends are today. And it's hot, which is welcome, with the thick January snow falling outside.

"Bad week?" Julianne smiles over her mug of coffee and the cheerful strawberry blonde swing of her hair catches the overhead lights.

"Nope," Nate says. He tilts back in his chair and drapes his arm across the back of hers. His Cubs hat is turned backwards, which makes his unkempt hair stick out in all directions under the brim. "It's just been too long since I've participated in any planned debauchery."

"Really?" Cam jokes. "I thought that's what every Sock Saturday was about."

"Har har," Nate flips him off and Cam laughs.

"What's 'Sock Saturday'?" Mic butts in.

"You know that old sock rule guys used to have in dorms?"

"And girls," Julianne chimes in.

"Yeah, I guess. You guys don't actually do that, do you?" Mic asks.

"No, no." Cam says, laughing lightly. "He just texts me the word 'socks' pretty much every Saturday. I call it being 'soxiled.'"

"I take a break every now and then," Nate says, pretending to be offended.

"Yeah, that's what Friday is for," Cam retorts.

"Well this certainly explains some things," Julianne observes.

"Oh?"

"Your excellent grades and why you are *always* at the library?"

Cam looks down, turning his coffee mug around and around on its saucer. "Yep. I do love the library." *And it has nothing to do with stupidly hoping to run into someone there,* he doesn't add.

"Okay, so, Cam's perfection aside," Nate says. "Tonight? Wild night out?"

"I'm in," Julianne says; Mic nods.

"Cam?" Nate asks in a leading tone.

"You know it's not really my thing," Cam hedges.

"No," Nate wags his finger. "What I know is that you *think* it's not your thing, but that you totally love getting crazy too. At least, that's what your actions tell us."

"He has a point," Mic smiles.

"The embarrassing ramblings of a drunken man should not be considered truth," Cam grumbles.

"Au contraire," Julianne says. "Drunken confessions are the most honest kind."

"That's a terrible line of thought if you are trying to sway me," Cam points out.

"How about this, then," Nate says, tipping his chair back down. "We're gonna have fun. You need more fun. It's on, baby."

Cam rolls his eyes but can't hide the twitch of a smile. Nate slaps him on the back, takes Cam's hand and makes Cam fist bump him.

CHAPTER SEVEN

THEY LET MIC PICK THE BAR, since he's the most familiar with the scene near campus. Cam can't claim he's completely comfortable with this group; they're Nate's friends and Cam's acquaintances, but it is a social circle separate from the one he'd briefly shared with Maggie and her friends. Mic settles on O'Leary's, which is cheap but not ridiculously busy. It's dark and close, all deep-stained wood and clusters of chairs around high round tables. Mild chaos surrounds them, but the bar rail is the busiest spot.

Cam drinks what they put in front of him. The more he drinks, the harder it is to attend to the conversation. Instead, his attention is drawn to the other bar patrons. He watches people flirt and begins to differentiate between something new and couples more familiar with each other. A woman with startlingly bright hair leans into the space of a man at her table. They seem to be out with friends, as he is, and Cam sees an exchange of energy when they look at each other. *Friends with a desire for more.*

He finds himself rooting for her.

* * *

"I HAVE SOMEONE I WANT TO SET YOU UP WITH," Maggie says breathlessly as she drops into the seat across from him.

"What?" Cam sets down his fork. "You're playing matchmaker now?"

"I think it's time," she says. He's a little surprised to find that less than two months after their breakup is enough time for this.

"I don't know, Maggie. It turns out I totally suck at the romance thing—"

"You don't," she interrupts easily. "It just wasn't right. Besides," she waggles her eyebrows, "practice makes perfect."

"Practice at what?" he asks.

"Duh." She kicks him under the table. "Romance."

She's rummaging through her bag, muttering to herself. Finally she emerges, brandishing her phone with a victorious "Aha!"

"Here, I have his number," she says.

That free fall he'd anticipated the night she left and during the days until now and for all the weeks and months since that moment in the library hits him full force. His number, she said. *His*. Maggie doesn't look up; she's pretending interest in her phone. Her cheeks are pink.

"How did—what?" he finally manages to whisper. It's so loud in the cafeteria, it's not as though anyone can hear them speaking normally, but still.

"Look, I—" she looks up. "I didn't know how to do this, I don't know that there's a right way. I don't want to offend you, and if I have I am so sorry."

"I don't know if... what I am," he says. He frowns; he's referring to her statement, but it's also true.

"Look, when we were together I saw... I don't even know. Just, things seemed a certain way. I won't lie, I did wonder a little from the start, but—I didn't know for sure. I guess I pushed it away. After we broke up, everything... the things I felt that were just off between us—I couldn't help but wonder if that's what it was." She looks at him beseechingly.

"Maggie, I can't say something about myself that I don't know," he says. When her eyes meet his he doesn't look away and the smile she gives him is gentle.

"Well, then. You don't have to do anything. But maybe this is something you could try out. He's a great guy; I think you'll get along with him really well."

"I feel a little—" He rubs his forehead. "Is this what it feels like to get hit by a truck?" He tries to catch his breath.

"Well, no," she says, laughter in her voice. "There are lots more broken bones involved in that one."

"Shut up," he jokes feebly.

"Do you need a bit?" She gestures toward her tray, as if ready to pick it up.

"No, stay." He reaches out and grabs her hand. "Just, can you stay? And I'll think."

"All right," she acquiesces. She takes her time smearing cream cheese on her bagel. It's pink, and he wonders what flavor it is. She's thorough and exact, spreading the cream cheese with an attention to its uniformity of thickness, as if the perfect spread will make the difference between a good meal and a substandard one. They don't speak. He lets himself get lost in observing her, enjoying the sense of intimacy he feels, knowing things about her that no one else in this room knows. It's not been long since she let the distance between them slide slowly into tentative friendship. Her presence feels like coming home in so many ways.

He needs a lot more time to process this new development. "Can we revisit this?"

"Absolutely." She wipes her fingers delicately and sends him a smile. His smile back is instinctual.

* * *

CAM ALWAYS THOUGHT THERE WERE three categories: straight, gay or bisexual. That's how the world works, right? Navigating some internal shift between them should be huge, right? But these labels, themselves, seem to carry a weight he doesn't feel; instead, he feels a lingering confusion born of never having questioned himself before. He doubts that Wren will be the only person to ever make Cam feel like he did—the idea is ludicrous. It was four months of something intense he could never quite name, five minutes of something life-altering, and nine months since then: more than a year of trying to find a mirror inside him with which to examine everything he'd assumed was true and no longer seems right.

Dating Maggie was something else entirely. Not a high, not a peak of rushing emotions or hormones, but something rising, something burning a little brighter. It's not as if Cam never thought he'd be in a relationship—he'd just had no idea what it would feel like. He'd had no comparison other than the world and what it said to him, despite that itch that never let him feel truly connected with himself or with Maggie. But still, she had known.

He trusts Maggie now as much as Nate or Peyton.

Cam takes a breath and opens his phone, thumbing to her number to text her. If she thinks this might be good for him, what harm can come of trying? That Maggie felt comfortable enough to address it first is calming.

The truth is, he's been more concerned with *not* being freaked out by his reaction to Wren. Questioning his sexuality hasn't felt scary, because being gay isn't scary to him. It should be, shouldn't it? But not being able to figure things out because he's so disconnected from the world and himself—that really scares him.

Cam takes a deep breath, then another, and taps out his message:

Let's get coffee and talk about it.

* * *

"IT'S NOT THE IDEA OF being gay, you know," he says, after he and Maggie have progressed through awkward conversation openers. They've never been awkward before, but right now there is a giant elephant on the table between them that they have to address, and figuring out how to ease into that seems impossible. Once he can't take it anymore, he goes with a straightforward approach.

"Okay," she says slowly, and blows on her steaming mocha. "What is it then?"

"It's not knowing if I am," he admits. "Or who I am."

"How long have you been trying to figure it out?" she asks gently. He looks down at the table and traces the rim of his mug. This sucks, because he doesn't want to admit that he'd been unsure before he met her. He never wants her to think she was an experiment.

"I think... well, I know," he says honestly, "a few months before I met you."

"Oh?" Maggie tries to hide her frown.

"I promise, Maggie, it was never like I was just experimenting or trying it out. I was confused and I was drawn to you. I liked you and I was attracted to you and I just—"

"Cam, it's okay, take a breath," she advises. He does.

"I just... I don't know anything," he finally says.

"About this?" she asks.

He laughs humorlessly. "No, about anything," he admits. "Who the fuck am I?"

"Oh, honey," she touches his hand lightly. "Cam, everyone goes through this, you know?"

"Seriously?" he snaps.

"I mean it. It doesn't necessarily have to look the same, and maybe some people haven't gotten there yet. But we're growing up. Becoming adults. Nothing looks like we thought it would when we were kids. Maybe we're not who we thought we would be, or where we would be."

"You think so?" he asks pensively.

"I do," she says with authority. "Look, it seems like you're overwhelmed, and you're processing a lot of stuff. But you have friends, and we want to be here. Nate and I want to help you."

"You've talked to Nate?" he says, surprised.

"Not about the gay thing," she says quickly, and winces. "I should reword that. It was probably offensive. But like, just about being worried about you. You've been getting more and more tense and worried and withdrawn. Which for you is saying quite a bit."

"Really?" He looks at her, surprised. "Am I withdrawn normally?"

"Oh my—" Maggie bursts into laughter, bright peals that ripple through the room. "Cam…" She shakes her head and tries to calm her giggles. "I do love you so much."

* * *

HIS NAME IS JASON BEALS. He's good-looking in a very generic sort of way, with blue eyes and brown hair; he's the same height as Cam but more muscular. Their meeting is awkward as hell at first; Cam's never been good at small talk. He needs to observe people before coming out of his shell, so he's terrible in one-on-one situations.

Jason is unperturbed by the awkwardness. "So tell me your story," he asks when they're finally seated. They're in a large restaurant off of Shawnee. The ceiling is open, with gray painted ducts and exposed pipes. Tasteful black and white photos decorate the walls. It's very minimalist and airy. Their voices seem loud in the silent room, intruding on the hush of soft-spoken waitstaff.

"That's quite the question," Cam stalls. His finger traces the leather seam along the edge of the plastic menu.

"Want to hear mine?" Jason asks with a grin. Cam finds it in himself to smile. Jason's skin appears pale in the too airy light. His shirt—maroon and white stripes in a casual polo—accentuates the contrast.

"Do we have time? Is this an epic novel with a tragic hero?" Cam jokes.

"You've caught me," Jason says and holds up his hands. "My real name is Jay Gatsby."

"Shouldn't you be floating in a pool, then?" Cam jokes and then winces. "Okay, that's a line of thought that's gonna get creepy."

"Good point," Jason says. "So should we play twenty questions or something?"

Cam feels a small pang, remembering his first date with Maggie. "Let's try something a little more organic."

"All right. Cam...?"

"Vargas," Cam supplies.

"Okay. Cam Vargas, what are you majoring in?"

"Environmental studies," Cam says. "Not through the hard science track, but social science."

"I'll be honest and admit I've never even heard of that," Jason shrugs sheepishly.

"Almost no one has; think about the various ways you can engage with environmental issues—" Cam says, before biting back his spiel. "Never mind, I can get pretty boring if you get me started. What's your major?"

"Oh, we'll come back to this, I think," Jason says. "But I'll allow you to distract me for the moment."

Prepared to listen, Cam fiddles with the straw of his Coke and settles his elbow on the table. Jason is dressed more casually than he; the polo is nice enough, but not what Cam would have worn to this restaurant. It says quite a bit that Jason chose this restaurant, though; it definitely makes an impression for a first date. Jason ordered a beer right off the bat, and he slowly picks and then peels the label from the bottle as they talk. Other than that, he doesn't fidget. He's definitely comfortable in his skin and with conveying open interest in Cam.

The restaurant starts to fill; couples and groups congregate around the tables in the middle of the floor. Many mingle with drinks in hand; their glasses sweat through napkins. A lot of them seem to know each other.

"Oh, looks like there's a show tonight," Jason says, looking over at the corner of the restaurant. Cam follows his line of sight and is surprised to see a stage. A couple of guys are setting up equipment, putting together a drum kit and hauling speakers.

"They do live music here?" he asks.

"Of a sort," Jason replies. "From the sudden influx of people who know each other, I'm guessing that we're getting a treat tonight. They never advertise these, so I've never gotten to see one."

"Who doesn't advertise?" Cam wrinkles his nose.

"The gifted," Jason says offhandedly, his eyes still on the stage; he's searching for something. Or for someone?

"Is that the name of the band?" Cam asks.

"What? Wait, no—" Jason turns to look at him. "You know, people who have gifts."

"I have no idea what you're talking about," Cam says, a bit annoyed.

"Where are you from?" Jason asks. "We might have skipped that part in our personal histories." He cracks up, which lightens the mood.

"We sort of failed at that, actually," Cam admits.

"So I'm guessing you aren't originally from Chicago. And by process of elimination, I'll exclude any big city."

"You deduce marvelously," Cam says dryly.

"That still leaves a whole lot of the country," Jason points out. "Oh god, are you foreign? You don't have an accent or—"

Cam tries not to frown. "Uh, would it be a problem if I am?"

"No!" Jason swallows. "I just didn't want to seem like I wasn't paying attention. I mean, your skin is not that—"

"Okay, well," Cam interrupts, and ignores the flare of irritation he always feels when people assume he's white. "I'm from a little town in Nebraska called Lexington City. Population roughly ten thousand. Well, take away one." He wiggles his fingers. "My parents are Venezuelan. I was born in Nebraska."

"Just a small town boy, huh?" Jason smiles and tips back his beer. Cam shrugs.

"Well, I've never been to Detroit," he points out after scanning his memory to remember the next lyric of the song Jason is referencing.

"I don't think you're missing much." Jason says.

Suddenly, the volume in the room goes up and the chatter of conversation coalesces around a blue-haired girl who makes the rounds of the tables, stopping to say hi, occasionally laughing loudly. She has a bottle of beer in one hand and a cell phone in the other. There's something magnetic about her; Cam doesn't want to take his eyes from her. After she's talked to most of the patrons by the stage, she disappears down a hallway to the left and the quality of conversation shifts back into a sort of chaos.

"Prime example," Jason points in her direction with his beer bottle. "Well-known singer underground. I've heard she mesmerizes."

"Good singer, then?"

"No, honey," Jason says and leans in for emphasis. "Like I said, she's gifted. She *literally* mesmerizes with her voice."

"O-kay..." Skepticism and confusion bleed through his voice, and Cam blinks and shakes his head. "So what you're saying is that there are... these, uh, *gifted,*" he clears his throat. "And they... mesmerize people?"

"No. Well, some, I guess. They have different abilities, some more obvious than others. But they can be pretty in-group, if you know what I mean. These are word-of-mouth gatherings, from what I understand."

"So they keep to themselves?" Cam asks. A part of his brain is whirling, watching the group of people in front of him, while another is scoffing; really, this is ludicrous.

"No," Jason shrugs. "My friend Mary says her mother was gifted. And she can sort of sense things. Not that well, but sometimes she clues into things a little more than a regular person would."

"You're saying she can read minds?" Cam says, disbelieving.

"How have you never heard of this? I mean, I just grew up knowing this. This is *Chicago*. There are like, thousands of gifted people here. There are gifted people everywhere!"

Cam thinks of home. How disconnected he had been: from his family, from people he considered friends. From the world. "I have no idea," he says faintly.

"You don't really believe me, do you?" Jason's voice is laced with wonder. "I promise, I'm not lying. Look it up—" he gestures to Cam's phone, sitting next to his glass on the table.

Frowning, Cam picks up his phone. "So I just type in 'gifted' and I'll get...?"

"I have no idea; that's pretty broad," Jason says. "But it can't hurt. You'll probably get a Wikipedia page somewhere."

"Ding ding ding," Cam says breathlessly, because there is a page. There are lots of pages. "Holy shit."

"I'm trying to wrap my head around where you are right now," Jason offers. "My brain would be exploding."

"Would it be unoriginal of me to say 'ding ding ding' again?"

"I won't hold it against you," Jason says.

"I can't—" Cam sets his phone down and closes his eyes. "No offense, but I don't know if I can even *believe* you right now. I don't think I can even process this."

"You're a processor, eh?" Jason watches him carefully. Cam shrugs.

"I guess so," he responds. There's a beat of silence.

"That's cool," Jason says. "Well, here's what we can do. We can call it a night if you need to process immediately. Or we can stay here and you can enjoy what I am told is a fantastic experience."

"Oh, um—" Cam frowns.

"I won't be offended," Jason holds his hands up. "Although I will say..." his eyes flutter down in what is not shyness so much as uncertainty and a little flirtation. "I would love to see you again."

"Yes," Cam says without thinking. He's not sure what he's saying yes to—another date with Jason, staying here, finding time to process? Jason's responding smile is brilliant.

"Want to get another drink, and we can stay?" he asks hopefully. "I've always wanted to see this."

"Yeah." Cam exhales and looks at Jason carefully, examining him in profile when he turns to signal the cocktail waitress. When Jason turns back to him with a small smile, Cam is taken by the symmetry of his face. He's really very good-looking, with lovely light blue eyes. Cam's always loved examining the shades of blue and green in other people's eyes.

Jason's foot bumps his under the table and something fizzes in his stomach. He feels a little out of his own body, and a crazy idea floats into his head that if he could lean over and trace the shape of Jason's lips, he might feel more grounded.

Cam shakes his head and smiles when the waitress comes over. He's a mess; his brain feels like a stew that's been stirred too hard. He orders another Coke and wishes he'd brought his fake I.D., because he could definitely use a beer right now.

CHAPTER EIGHT

THEY LEAVE IN A DAZE. THE AIR IS COLD, and it's dark, and they aren't the only ones stumbling out of the bar. Are they all buzzing the way he is, with a little electric fire coursing through them? He's so *alive*. Alive and turned around and in some sort of shock.

Cam had no idea what he wanted when he agreed to go on this date, but when Jason stops him under a streetlight by the corner of Oak and Second, where the sandwich cart is shut down for the night, and kisses him, Cam's chest and body loosen. It's as if he's exhaling into himself, effortlessly filling a space beneath his skin. He doesn't know if it's Jason's kiss, or the way that singer, Elise, unlocked him with just the timbre of her voice—or both—but right now, this moment, is *right*.

Other than during the aftermath of his encounter with Wren, Cam has never felt the sharp sting of desire the way he does right now, as Jason's lips close over his in a simple, radiating kiss. Jason doesn't press for more; he allows Cam to pull away easily, smiles into Cam's eyes and reaches for his hand. They walk back to Cam's dorm slowly, past the throng of bodies lining the doors of a club, the quiet refuge of a coffee shop and the echoing, darkened doors of shops closed for the night. The wind hushes through barren trees; Cam turns up the collar of his coat and tucks his chin into it, but once that's done his fingers slot back through Jason's. He can't feel the heat of Jason's skin through their gloves, but the action warms him anyway.

On the quad, bright lights spill from the doors of the dorms. Glowing windows scatter yellow luminescence like stars.

"I had a good night," Cam says inanely, once they've reached the door of his room.

"I did too," Jason says with a smile. He swings their joined hands a little.

"Even if my head is spinning and a little crazy right now," Cam admits.

"Well, I did drop a bomb on you, followed by a really fucking intense..." Jason doesn't say the rest, but Cam knows what he's thinking. That singer, Elise, had influenced him deeply. He spent the hour of her set enthralled, his body coursing with heat and yearning. The effects are waning now, and only the smallest tendrils remain deep in his belly.

"Can I see you again?" Jason asks. Another student Cam knows—Brad—walks by. Cam sees him do a double take and try not to stare. For the first time, Cam really wonders what people will think.

"Yeah," he says simply. Because he wants to, and because this feels so much easier than it had with Maggie. When Jason leans in for another kiss, Cam tilts his head back and lets Jason crowd him against the wall. It's a hungrier kiss, maybe a bit too much for the public setting; but that's even better, a dark sort of thrill. Jason takes the kiss in a way Cam is certain he's never experienced and he has to hold in a sound when Jason bites gently on his lower lip. When Cam pulls away, the small wet smack of their lips parting excites him too.

"I'll call you," Jason says with a satisfied smile. Cam can only breathe out a *yes* and fumble behind himself for the doorknob.

He finds the room bright and Nate typing away at his laptop. Cam wasn't expecting Nate to be here, much less working. His lips are tingling, still damp from Jason's mouth.

"How'd it go?" Nate doesn't look away from his screen. Cam takes a shaky breath.

"Fine," he manages. Now that he's in his room, in the safest place he has, everything seems to be hitting him at once: the date, what he'd learned about the gifted, that kiss. Oh god, that *kiss*. First, Cam had not expected it. Second, his expectations of intimacy had not prepared him for this. He'd liked being intimate with Maggie, but what he had just felt was so much more immediate and, frankly, hot.

"Just fine?" Nate turns around this time, and when he sees Cam, still leaning against the door with the knob in his hand, a wide smile breaks across his face.

"You look like you've been *well* fucking kissed, man."

"Do I?" Cam touches his lips. "Is that—is this weird for you?" Cam holds his breath.

"Was it weird for you?" Nate asks.

"Not the way I thought," Cam says. "There was plenty of weird tonight I can't wrap my head around, but it doesn't have to do with this," he gestures toward his lips.

"If you're good with it, I am," Nate says. Cam closes his eyes, breathes and then opens his eyes again to look directly at Nate.

"How is this so easy for you?"

"Because I care, Cam. Because I've known you for a while. Because I want you to be happy," Nate says. Cam nods and smiles. A deep, genuine feeling of warmth swells inside of him.

"Thank you," he says finally.

Nate just shrugs and says, "Of course," before turning back to his work.

* * *

CAM HAS NEVER BELIEVED HE has a high sex drive, especially since he's come to college, where sex is so much more visible and attainable. In high school, and after his initial arrival here, his fantasies were always generic. He's never masturbated much. Occasionally, he's wondered why he seems so much less sexual than everyone around him.

It's just been another of the many ways that Cam has felt different, a phenomenon that he's wanted to observe and understand. There are days when he wants to sit down with someone and say, *I don't understand any of this* and *it feels so right, I'm not ashamed of these feelings even when the world tells me I should be.*

The night of his date with Jason, Cam showers and jerks himself off in a way he never has before. He touches his dick softly at first, letting himself thrill at the thought of dragging out the pleasure. He cups and rolls his balls and wraps his hand around his cock, stroking himself torturously slowly. He recalls feeling overwhelmed by Jason. How very much it turned him on to have someone take the initiative and press assertively against him.

When he thumbs over the head of his dick, when he feels how much pre-come has gathered there, he shudders and leans his head against the cool tile of the shower. His thoughts wander seamlessly from Jason to Wren, and, for the first time, Cam lets himself revel. He lets himself think of the press of Wren's erection against his leg that day. Something clenches in his stomach when he pictures that cock in his hand—in his mouth.

Cam's mouth waters when he wonders what Wren's come might taste like, and how the ridge of the head of his dick might feel against his tongue; and when he does he comes hard he has to bite his free hand to keep in his moans.

* * *

DESPITE HOW BLOWN AWAY CAM is by learning about people with gifts, he manages to hold off on research until he can do so at the library. For some reason, he wants to be alone for his research—something niggles at the back of his mind and he wants space and books to figure it out.

Luckily, the day after his date is Sock Saturday; and while Nate doesn't take advantage of it every weekend, he does so this time, texting Cam a picture of ridiculous socks he must have found online, knitted shark socks made to look as though the shark's mouth is stretched around the ankles. They even have little fins. Although he's in line at the coffee shop, Cam laughs so hard several patrons turn around to stare at him

He doesn't mind spending a Saturday night in the library. It's at its most hushed then, private and familiar. He has a usual table, where Wren found him sitting last semester. Even though he knows it's stupid, he's drawn to it in the hope that Wren might want to find him there again.

After arranging himself at the table, laptop up and notebook ready, water bottle in its usual spot, Cam thinks through a plan of attack. Books would be ideal, but he hasn't any idea where to start. Sifting through the Internet will be time-consuming, but there he'll be able to easily find firsthand information and stories.

Wikipedia is a tool he always takes with a grain of salt, but also a helpful starting place because it offers summarized information and references. The article he finds on gifted people refers to two topics he wasn't expecting: mythology and concrete studies.

For now he's not interested in lore, but reality.

As overwhelmed as he was by the revelation that people with special gifts exist, the reality of this deluge of information is staggering. The list of references alone is mind-blowing. Cam has to pull away from the laptop, take out his notebook and write down questions that have nagged him since his date with Jason; he hopes to use them as tools to help guide his initial research.

Most pressingly, he wonders what sorts of abilities one can have, how the community works and how the hell he could have gone nineteen years of his life with no idea that people with such gifts existed.

His first objective is answering the last question. It takes a while, but after a lot of searching and sifting, he manages to find a semi-current map based on census results, charting population density of those with gifts in the United States. Although the population is small, it's clear from the data that a number of these people do reside in Nebraska. Chicago, it seems, has the second largest population cluster in the country. Cam knows that his ignorance has nothing to do with *where* he lived, but rather *how* he lived, burying himself from the world.

Cam thinks of the swelling number of patrons in the restaurant shortly before Elise arrived and took the stage. Jason's comments made it sound as if a community dynamic exists between people with gifts. Researching this is harder, because there's nothing straightforward about it; nothing he finds in a quick search leads him to any sort of organized community, or conversation about one. He's not sure he has enough data to hone his questions here, either, so he moves on to abilities.

It turns out that defining abilities is often murky: some primary ones are identified, and then what are called secondary and tertiary abilities. Without work and study, these are often underdeveloped, and not all choose to study the application and development of them past initial discovery.

Ability emerges between ages fifteen and twenty-five, the late teens being most common. Cam is staggered to discover that Carlina actually offers a course on the history of people with gifts.

He had obviously not perused the university course catalogue closely.

He begins to click through the list of most common abilities. *Siren Call*, which is apparently what Elise performed on Friday, is in the top five. *Bonding*—the ability to create bonds between people, like marriage but stronger, and unbreakable without release by the creator—is one that Cam finds especially intriguing.

But it's the ninth on the list that takes his breath away. *Compelling.* Cold shock washes through him when he reads the description. The niggling idea that led him here is suddenly crystal clear. What happened with Wren—that connection, that indescribably magnetic pull—*this* is what that was. Cam is suddenly, startlingly sure.

That night—that night in this library, almost exactly *here*—Wren's knowing smile and the way Cam followed without understanding why—the way Wren looked, lounging against the wall with triumph and desire in his eyes—he'd been fucking *compelling* him.

Cam remembers so clearly now that startling crash of clarity as he broke free from drowning pleasure and then Wren's exclamation, words that made no sense: *I thought you knew. I don't play with new.* What did that mean, then? What had Wren meant by "play"? And how could he have known that Cam was so innocent?

Cam has never felt embarrassment over losing his virginity later than most of the people he knows. Maybe because sex always seemed like this *thing*, this force he had never been tuned into, never wanted so badly he actively sought it out. But for days after that moment with Wren—if he's being honest with himself, months—Cam had agonized over it and wondered if Wren wouldn't have walked away if Cam *hadn't* been inexperienced. He'd had no idea *how* Wren had known, but he obviously had.

Now, armed with clear knowledge—well, speculation really—Cam has to wonder what Wren had been playing at. And playing it certainly was; Wren had said so. For reasons Cam can't begin to name, the certainty sends a deep wave of desire through him; he finds himself actually starting to harden.

The idea of being someone's plaything, of being compelled by someone else, taken out of his body, away from the constant running of his consciousness and his hesitation, is suddenly the single most erotic thing he's ever desired.

Cam checks the time and slams the screen of his laptop closed. It's only ten thirty, and chances are he's still soxiled; he hazards a text to Nate. His whole body is thrumming, and he tries to distract himself by reopening his laptop and searching the library catalogue for books, but he's hardly paying attention because his brain is swarming with these *images* and a visceral heat. Laughter spills from his mouth; for the first time in his life, Cam is acting like a completely sex-driven teenage boy. He finds it hilarious and freeing and natural.

In less than half an hour Nate texts back an all-clear. Cam collects his stuff to trek back to his room and then straight to the shower.

* * *

"JASON WANTS TO TAKE ME TO DECOY." Cam checks the fit of his jeans in the mirror, and considers his shirt.

"That'll be a change for you," Nate responds.

"Not my speed?" Cam strips off the shirt and digs through his closet for another.

"Dude, who knows what your speed really is?" Nate says, still looking down at his copy of *Sports Illustrated*.

"What does that mean?"

"It means you're figuring stuff out," Nate explains. "Let yourself be open to new things and you'll figure out what you like."

"That makes too much sense," Cam says. "Want to come?"

"And be the third wheel?" Nate says dryly. "No thanks."

"No, we can get a group of us. Maggie and Christine and the girls." Cam starts feeling a little more enthusiastic.

"Isn't this supposed to be a date?" Nate asks.

"Yeah." Cam shrugs and goes back to his closet. "I don't know. It'll just be more fun with you guys. More comfortable."

"Well then," Nate stands up. "I don't have any thrilling plans for tonight. Text Maggie. What time are you supposed to meet Jason?"

"He's coming here," Cam says, distracted. "Okay, I have no idea what I'm supposed to wear to this place. Casual? Slightly better than casual?"

Nate laughs. "God, you're getting so gay," he jokes. Cam shoves him and then laughs too.

"That's so offensive."

"Here." Nate plucks a shirt from Cam's drawer. It's a deep maroon with a shimmering screened graphic of a tandem bicycle on it.

"That's a T-shirt. That doesn't fit any more," Cam points out.

"It's tight. It's bright. Jason will totally dig it," Nate says, gathering his towel and shower caddy.

"If you say so." Cam looks at the shirt doubtfully, but trusts that Nate knows better than he what he should wear to a club.

"You look good," Jason says almost as soon as he's in the room. "Where's Nate?"

"Showering," Cam says. "And thank you."

"Anytime." Jason pulls him closer, starts kissing him slowly.

"What's this about?" Cam pulls away, unused to easy physicality. "Nate will be back in a few minutes."

"But he's not here now, and you look too good to resist."

Cam smiles, and enjoys the warm rush of flattery.

"You look pretty good yourself," he says. He does; Jason's hair is tousled and light and the buttermilk of his textured shirt seems to brighten the blue of his eyes. It was never exactly easy with Maggie, wanting touch or giving it, but it feels a lot simpler with Jason. Acquiescing to that urge, he leans in to kiss Jason some more. He's just gotten his fingers threaded through Jason's hair when there's a flurry of knocks and the door opens.

"Hey, we're ready—" Maggie stops dead. "Oh yeah. Um. Hi, Jason?"

"Hey," Jason says easily. Cam surreptitiously wipes the moisture from his lips. "What are you doing here?"

"Oh, they wanted to tag along," Cam says, wincing. He probably should have warned Jason beforehand. There's a pause before Jason shrugs affably.

"The more the merrier, right?"

"Absolutely." Maggie smiles, and it's mostly real. Cam feels a bit guilty. It's one thing for her to know he's dating someone and another to see him with someone. Especially when she's caught him in a kiss that certainly felt more passionate and immediate than any he'd shared with her. But she just rubs her hand over his bicep and winks.

"Nice shirt," she says slyly.

Cam blushes and tries to change the subject. "So have you been to Decoy before?"

"Yeah, once," Maggie says, settling comfortably at his desk chair. "It'll be an experience for you."

Cam huffs. "Nate said the same. Is there something specifically wrong with me?"

"No, honey, there's nothing wrong with you," Maggie assures him. "It's just nothing that Cam a year ago would have wanted to do."

"Cam a year ago?" Jason pipes in. "What does that mean?"

"You didn't even know me a year ago," Cam points out to her.

"Wow, hey," Nate comes through the door, hair damp and flat against his forehead. "I wasn't expecting an audience."

"We'll head down to the lobby," Maggie says. "And see you in a few. Try not to primp too much; I don't want to wait too long."

"Oh fuck off," Nate says good-naturedly. "You know you take the longest."

"Never," she says, gesturing to let Jason exit ahead of her. "I came into the world this beautiful. No effort needed."

"Absolutely," Cam says quietly, and is rewarded by a sweet, intimate smile.

CHAPTER NINE

"WOW, THIS IS..." CAM STOPS A FEW YARDS from the club. Music pours out, bass thumping loudly. They're early enough that there is almost no line.

"Told ya so," Jason drawls. Cam frowns, a bit annoyed that Jason has assumed what he's thinking. He isn't even sure what Jason is implying.

Actually, he's overwhelmed. This is *not* his milieu. They cross through the held-open door; Maggie gives the bouncer a friendly little wave and Jason gives him a nod. And maybe it's the murky dark broken by the too-bright glitter of light from a disco ball combating the frenzy of multicolored strobe lights, or the way the music is so loud his bones vibrate; maybe it's the smell of so many packed bodies, whose sweat amplifies a cacophony of perfumes and colognes, but it rubs him the wrong way, like a cat being petted backward.

"You need a drink," Nate yells into his ear, tugging on his elbow. Cam feels the annoyed look that moves over his face before he can stop it. Luckily, Nate is persistent and also mostly immune to Cam's rare bad moods.

He allows Nate to drag him to the long, sticky bar and lifts his hand with a grimace after accidentally resting it on the bar top.

Maggie shoulder-bumps him from the side; he hadn't realized she'd followed them as well.

"We'll leave in a little while if you hate it," she promises. "But let's give it a chance, okay? Have a drink or two and see if you can't just let go a bit."

Jason's hand curves into the small of his back; his body is close when he reaches for one of the shots Nate lines up on the bar in front of them. Cam makes a face but obligingly picks his up. He isn't expecting the tap of Nate's glass to his, and a little liquid spills over onto his fingers; Nate laughs, and he and Maggie do the same. With a breath and closed eyes, Cam tips back the shot.

The first shot is horrible; the second is worse because he knows what's coming. It doesn't quite burn like rubbing alcohol, so he guesses it isn't vodka. Nate must remember the horror of Cam's only previous encounter with that, for which Cam is marginally grateful. He'd be more grateful if whatever Nate has given him weren't equally disgusting. He gags and covers his mouth.

"We'll get you something else next," Jason says into his ear. "And a chaser." Cam wants to decline but thinks better of it. He will refuse the next offer.

They end up against the wall on the far side of the club. Jason seems content to wait while Cam gets his bearings. After a while, his irritation with the noise and heat starts to abate. There's something hypnotic about the lights and colors and the flickering glimpses of people dancing. Next to him, Jason moves almost imperceptibly with the beat of the music.

"You should go dance," Cam says. He has to pitch his voice louder and repeat himself.

"No, I'm fine," Jason says, smiling at him intimately.

"No, really. Go dance with Maggie or someone. I want to watch," Cam insists, and then laughs when he realizes the implication of his words. Jason shrugs, winks and holds his hand out to Maggie.

Back against the wall again, Cam absorbs the resonance of the music. He considers sitting when one of the tables lining the perimeter of the club is vacated, but it seems selfish to grab it just for himself.

Nate emerges from the miasma, two drinks in hand, one with a drink napkin wrapped around it. Cam bites back a sigh; he can't even tell the color of the liquid inside. And he can't decline if they don't give him a chance.

Nate gestures toward the table Cam has been eyeing and slides in to claim it just ahead of another guy. This seems rather rude, but it's so fucking loud Cam can't apologize. The guy just shrugs, though, takes it in stride, and turns to find somewhere else to settle.

"Home base," Nate shouts, noticing Cam's concern about hogging the table. The drink Nate hands him lights with the colors of the room; it could be anything, and when he gives Nate a questioning look, Nate beams and waves at him to go ahead. Refusing whatever it is they all want to happen tonight is starting to feel like swimming upstream; rather than argue, he takes a sip. It's fresh and cold and citrusy, with an unexpected little bite: something he can drink more slowly. Cam rolls his eyes at Nate, whose face is all smug anticipation, and gives him a facetious thumbs up.

"Hey, babe." Jason's voice, sudden in his ear, startles him. He kisses the crook of Cam's neck. Cam squirms away; he is pleasantly loose—looser than he has been—but Jason is damp with sweat and his hand is too hot against Cam's side; his kiss is too familiar. Jason ignores this and gestures toward Cam's drink. He tastes it, makes a so-so gesture and gives it back.

"Come dance with me," he begs. The dregs of Cam's drink sear with increased potency—the alcohol in mixed drinks must settle. Maybe it will settle *him*, if he takes a chance.

"I don't know how," he responds.

Jason lights up. "Come on, I'll teach you."

What the hell. It's not as though he can make too big of a fool of himself with so many people surrounding them; he's a whole lot less concerned than he might have been before having that last drink. He's been watching the crowd long enough to get the general idea that not much skill will be required to pass himself off as mildly competent. He just needs fewer inhibitions.

Jason leads him into the throng, bumping past bodies, winding through them like a ribbon being threaded through lace. Cam has no idea where Jason is taking him, or why he chooses to stop where he does. Jason's hands cups his hips, guiding him to the beat. Trying to watch him and not look around is confusing and inhibiting, but finally Cam curls his arms over Jason's shoulders, closes his eyes and focuses only on the music and the movement of Jason's body against him.

It takes a bit—maybe half a song, although it's hard to tell, the way the DJ melts them together—before he starts to lose himself. The music prickles over his skin; Cam bites his lip and presses himself into Jason's hands, incrementally more pliant and willing, when that feeling—that prickle—intensifies so suddenly it's like being hit with a bucket of cold water. He gasps when his body jolts into a painful wakening.

He's here.

Cam has no doubt. He doesn't question how he knows, he just *does*. He looks around dumbly, but too many bodies spin around him. Suddenly, all the drinks catch up to him too fast, too hard; he's disoriented and sweating. He jerks back from Jason.

"Hey, are you okay?" Jason pulls him in. Cam pushes his hands away, struggling to scan the room over the heads of everyone dancing. It's no use, not in these throbbing shadows; a small, dark-haired boy won't stand out like a candle.

"I'm fine." He turns back to Jason, trying to shout over the music and convey a calm he in no way feels. "I just need the bathroom."

Jason points toward a corner, where Cam can see the faint white glow of a restroom sign with an arrow pointed at a dark hall. Cam tilts his head to indicate he's headed there.

"I'll meet you at the table," Jason shouts.

Cam pushes his way through the throng with little finesse. There are definitely a lot more people here now than when he arrived; that feeling of *too much* presses back in on him. What's dizzying him is amplified by the needle-in-a-haystack quality of the search. There's no sense of direct pull to help guide him, just the knowledge that Wren is here somewhere.

Cam peers into faces, scans everywhere he can. At his height, he's able to see over the heads of many people, but it's just too fucking dark, and the insistence of strobe lights casts tricking shadows all over the place.

And then *it* surges, that amorphous, unsettling knowledge of being called toward something. Cam gasps and stops stock-still—and it's gone. It's gone so fast he stumbles. He spins around but sees nothing. His whole body tingles with the sort of pain that comes to a waking limb. He stands where he is, eyes closed and heart pounding, and knows it's useless to search anymore.

When he enters the bathroom, he's shocked. The floor is wet; the towel dispenser is empty. Suds linger in the chipped bowls of sinks. The walls are covered in paint and pen, words and drawings, graffiti both crude and wistful, obscene and poetic. And from the far stall come the unmistakable sounds of two people together.

Cam feels a rush of blood burning all the way to his hairline. In the mirror, he's sweaty and rumpled, hair mussed, and there's something unreadable about his own eyes. It's disconcerting; he feels so out of his element. *I'm drunk.* He waves his hands under one faucet, cursing automatic sensors, and then tries a second when the first doesn't comply. He lets the too-cold water run over his hands and wrists, and splashes some over his face. The noises—breathless and laughing and encouraging—spill from the far side of the room. Cam is fascinated by his response; he's aware and too hot and *turned on*.

Cam shakes his head and slams out of the bathroom. It takes a while to wend his way through the bodies to find his friends. It's just Maggie at the table, though, sipping something and bobbing her head to the music.

"I have to go," he says urgently into her ear. She jolts and spills her drink. "Shit," he says, groping for napkins and finding only damp ones from their beverages. He uses the few dry corners to dab at the wet splotch on her pants. "I'm sorry."

"It's okay." Her hand covers his and she ducks to look into his eyes. "Hey, are you okay?" Her smell lingers when she pulls away. Cam tries to hide the way his hands are shaking.

"Yeah, I just—I can't find Jason and this is too many people; those drinks hit me too hard," he says, wondering if it's a good excuse.

"Go outside," Maggie orders. "I just saw him, I think. I'll find him. Text Nate once you're out there."

"Okay, thanks."

Outside, the air is freezing against his damp skin, and when he gulps it into his suddenly aching lungs, Cam starts to laugh. He laughs and wanders in the opposite direction from the line into the club as he shrugs into his coat. He ignores the looks he gets and walks down the street a half block before pulling out his phone to text Nate.

Sry, but had to leave. Don't worry abt me, I'll see you at home

He's surprised to get an almost immediate response.

U sure?

He texts as quickly as his numb fingers will permit.

Yes

Cam leans against the wall. The bricks bite unevenly through the thin material of his coat. Frenetic heat seeps from his body. Above him, the sky is clouded. He doesn't move when he feels a touch on his elbow.

"I couldn't find Jason," Maggie says.

"Let's just get out of here."

"Are you sure?"

"I'll text him." Cam says, motioning to his phone. It's awful, but Cam is glad she didn't find Jason. Maggie gives him the look he's learned means she's figuring something out about him. He looks away.

"I'll do it," she says finally, and tugs the sleeve of his shirt. "You can't text and walk for shit."

Cam smiles and resists the urge to tell her about the article he read earlier in the week about the surprising number of walking-while-texting-related injuries and deaths. Lectures can wait, especially when she's doing him a favor.

AT SOME POINT THAT NIGHT Cam manages to pull some coherent thoughts together.

a) He needs to apologize to Jason

b) Which means he should respond to the texts Jason sent and

c) He has to go back to that club, because it's the closest he's come to Wren in months and he can't not chase down even the slightest lead.

Tacked onto these points is a P.S.: He has to acknowledge that he might be an asshole, because he's enjoying what he's just started with Jason, but he's willing to drop him for even a hint of that something he felt with Wren.

Nate doesn't come home that night, which is good, because Cam's been drinking and that makes it more tempting than ever to try to talk about this. Cam's not stupid; he knows that any attempt to explain some mysterious tether to a elusive boy he's said maybe sixty words to *ever* and hasn't seen in months would only seem crazy—crazier than anything he's said, foolish and downright bizarre. God, he's so strange. His *life* is. Small-town, out-of-touch Cam would think...

He's not even sure what Cam-two-years-ago would think. Because on the other side of a lot of changes and a lot—but not enough, he knows instinctively—of growing, Cam's not sure he recognizes that Cam at all anymore.

* * *

"HEY, BROTHER," PEYTON'S VOICE COMES quietly through the line. Cam yawns and tries to pry his eyes open. He feels as though he's *just* gone to sleep. And as though he ate a bag of cotton balls.

"Pey, what time is it?" he groans.

"Where I am or where you are?" Peyton laughs. Cam feels his eyes slipping shut and pulls the blankets up around his shoulders.

"I don't know where you are," he murmurs.

"Good point," she says, and sings softly, "Wake up, Cam."

He sighs and hitches himself into a sitting position. The glowing numbers of Nate's ridiculous Captain America alarm clock tell him it's a quarter past three. He *had* just gone to sleep.

"Are you okay?" he asks around a jaw-aching yawn.

"I'm not calling about me," she says.

"Hmm." The constant brightness of campus streetlights spills through the window. Cam traces the seam of his comforter. "What, is your spidey sense tingling?" he jokes.

"Absolutely."

Cam has no idea why, but the easiness of her answer, the affability and laissez faire tone of her voice suddenly *enrages* him.

"You know what," he says too loudly, "you can seriously fuck off." He hangs up the phone and tosses it onto the bed, then puts a hand to his head. *What the hell was that?* The phone rings again almost immediately.

"I have no idea—"

"Wow," Peyton is laughing, but in a shocked sort of way. "You're mad at me. I don't remember the last time you were mad at me. That was kind of... refreshing. And sudden. Irrational?"

"I'm too tired and drunk for rational," Cam explains. He thinks back on his night, and how many ways he's called himself weird in the last few hours. "I had a strange night. It's been a crazy year... so much is happening and suddenly I'm realizing I have so much *stuff*. Pey, I'm not sure I know how to handle it," he blurts. He swings his legs out of the bed and trips over his shoes on the way toward the mini-fridge. Kicking the shoes mostly out of his way, he grabs a bottle blindly and cracks it open. Lemon lime. Not the worst he could have done in Gatorade roulette. "Moving here—having Maggie and Nate to talk to is something I didn't realize I needed so much."

"Oh?" Peyton says softly.

"But they aren't you. They'll never have that... this *thing* that only we have," Cam grimaces and swallows an irrational surge of anxiety as honesty swells. "*Had*. That we had." His voice rises. "You're here and not. I never know. I tell myself you know when I really need it, but it's on *your* terms."

"Cam..."

"I'm just... god, Pey, I'm so *pissed* about this, at *you*."

"Apparently," Peyton says.

"It's not the first time I've been mad at you, you know?" Cam points out, sitting back on his mattress. It sags a bit, but he's gotten used to it.

"Oh, I know, I remember that time when we were six—"

"I don't just mean when we were kids, Pey," Cam interrupts. "I've been mad at you plenty since then."

Peyton pauses before she speaks; her breaths amplify. Is he suffering some lingering brain-to-mouth, alcohol-removed filter issue?

"Why don't you tell me?" she asks. Her voice is quiet again, this time with sadness.

"I—" Cam starts. "I'm not sure I realized it before."

"Before now?"

"I'm—I feel like..." He places his fist over his heart. "There's a lot I haven't let myself feel, for a long time." He doesn't have to specify.

"Well, I could have told you that, stupid."

"Fuck off." He laughs when he says it. The tension begins to split apart.

"Oh god, listen to that mouth; college has corrupted you," Peyton says between giggles. They both fall silent for a while.

"I miss you," he admits. "I've needed you."

"I thought I always called when you did," she says morosely.

"Like I said—you called when it was always *worst*, Pey," he explains. He tries to tell himself to test the words before they come out, but they rush out on their own anyway. "There are lots of ways I've needed you. And I miss—" he clenches his eyes shut. "I've needed you to need me too."

"Oh, Cam," her voice thickens. "I didn't think... you're always so—"

"So what?"

"I don't know when it happened, but sometime when we were teenagers, you changed. Or I did. But you… I don't know. It's not that you pulled away. But you seemed suddenly so… insular. Like you'd stepped back."

"I *had* to," he says. "I had to, I just felt like I was suffocating under it all at home; removing myself felt like breathing. I know it doesn't make sense, but… it wasn't necessarily about pulling away from you, or not needing you. You pulled away too. And over time, we changed. I've trusted that you're here for me whenever I'm at my worst or lowest and ignored that it really hasn't been enough because I love you and need you for more than that."

"Cam, I tried for a while, for the first few years. I know you didn't pull away from *me*—but you pulled away from everything and I didn't know how to reach you. What we've had—I thought it's what you wanted," she says, a slight sharp edge in her voice.

He pauses, and breathes, and frowns through the tangle of thoughts jamming his tired brain. "I think…" He wets his lips. "I'm really kind of drunk."

Peyton laughs.

"I might be too drunk for this, because maybe we're talking in circles I can't quite make sense of right now."

"Cameron," Peyton chides him carefully. "Things don't always have to make sense."

"I'M SORRY IF YOU HATED THAT," Maggie says over dinner the next night.

"I didn't." Cam sits cross-legged on his bed with a box of Siamese chicken balanced precariously on his lap. "I'd like to go again sometime."

Her hand pauses halfway to her mouth and she eyes him suspiciously; her chopsticks dangle sprouts. "What?"

"I had fun for a while. I'd like to try again."

"You hated it."

Cam rolls his eyes. He knew she'd be suspicious. He hadn't liked it all that much—he hadn't hated it, though. "I'd like to try again. Now that I know what to expect. And not to do shots."

"Point," Maggie mumbles around a mouthful of food.

"Oh, and find out what it was that Nate was giving me to drink, because those were good."

"Oh, that's a Tom Collins," Maggie supplies.

"Hmm." Cam busies himself with finishing off his chicken. The TV hums in the background while they hang out. The judges on some singing contest she likes chatter on low volume.

"Heard from Jason?" she asks. She wipes her mouth delicately with her napkin, folds it and puts it into the container.

"Just put it in the takeout bag," he says when she stands to put the container in the trash. "The room will smell like Chinese food for days if I don't take the containers out tonight anyway."

"Okay." She climbs onto the bed next to him and settles down to watch the show.

"I texted him to apologize. He said it was okay."

"That's it?"

"Yeah," he shrugs. "I don't know. I've been having a good time with him, but..."

Maggie gives him a sympathetic look he's not sure he wants to receive.

"Shut up," he says with a laugh, pushing her over. She just mock-glares and settles back down; he should know better than to trust this complacency, but he's lost in his thoughts and caught completely by surprise when she suddenly attacks him with tickles.

It's hard to be mad though, when Maggie makes him laugh harder than he has since he was little.

* * *

WHEN THEY GO TO THE BAR again, Cam is careful to go without Jason. He hasn't seen Jason in a week or so, and the only exchanges they've had are sporadic texts that have been petering out as he's responded to them more and more slowly.

"So, are you guys not going out anymore?" Nate asks one night.

"I don't know." Cam flips quickly through channels. "I'm just... looking for something."

"What?"

Cam pauses at a cooking show. "I have no idea, but I don't think he's it."

It's not that he's looking for something nebulous. He's looking for Wren. It's stupid, to expect that he'd come back to the same bar. But it's the only lead he's got. Cam knows it would be completely disingenuous to go there with Jason looking for Wren. And while he could have something concrete with Jason, Cam doesn't want to stop chasing something he's not been able to replicate.

* * *

HE KEEPS GOING BACK. AFTER the third time his request garners strange looks from both Maggie and Nate, so he starts going alone. Saturday nights he once spent at the library, studying or opening his mind to a host of things he'd never considered, he now spends in the dark, with the glitter of colored lights and the claustrophobic comfort of hot bodies.

It's actually nicer, going alone. There's a freedom in being there without having his movements tracked by eyes that know him. He moves on the dance floor in revelation, emancipated from his previous reservations. He orders his own drinks. He observes and files away information and always, always leaves every sense open for another surge of recognition, which is why Cam is so startled to find Wren the way he does. He feels nothing other than the sway of people dancing around him; he doesn't feel Wren at all. He *sees* him.

CHAPTER TEN

WREN AVOIDS DECOY AS LONG AS HE CAN, but Nora loves it here; she loves the drinks, which she claims are the best, loves the mix of music. And Matt's on management duty Saturday nights. Wren's not sure about him, but Nora seems to like him—enough to press for their visits to this particular club so she can see him even for short minutes. Wren assumes he must have a fantastic aura, or something else he can't see.

Despite what had happened the last time, coming back isn't a huge deal, not big enough to make a fuss over, when all he needs to do is be careful to close himself off; using his skill to avoid sensing Cam feels like necessity. The last time he came, he'd been drunk and loose, and that bond ripping through him, startling and hot, had been two -way. He'd known instantly that Cam could feel him too. So now he locks down inside, tries to exercise a muscle of sorts that he hasn't before. He doesn't drink, but he does dance; he's never needed alcohol to burn away inhibitions. Wren knows his body. He knows how to move it, how to use it to express the deep streak of his own sensuality. Wren is careful not to open himself to any interactions beyond touches on the floor and the feeling of bodies against him. He's not here to search for something new, no matter how hungry he feels for that sort of touch.

Wren probably won't see Cam here again anyway. Even the quick glimpse he'd caught that night, standing half behind a pillar and out of sight, had shown him how out of his element Cam was.

It's a complete shock when the lights shift and he turns and sees Cam face to face, because he *should* have sensed him. The shock roots him, freezes him so that his partner bumps him awkwardly, and keeps him there long enough to watch Cam take a deep breath and begin to work his way through the people between them.

It's hard with so many people here, but Wren tries to sense what Cam is feeling; he gets a glimmer of determination. His sensing ability is not well honed, but Cam's projecting and it pierces through him; Wren's body and senses respond instinctively. The part of himself that always desires the upper hand reacts the way it's been trained to when this much fervor is aimed at him: by pulling it in.

Cam stops less than a foot from him. His eyes are darker in the shadows of the room, and his breath comes fast and hard. Wren pulls a bit harder, until Cam is dragged into his space. But he doesn't make him do anything more. Cam's hands coming up to cup his hips do so by their own volition. Cam's breath, hot and damp, ghosts over his ear, and the words Cam speaks are of his own choice.

WREN SMELLS LIKE NOTHING CAM has ever experienced: sweaty and masculine, but also clean and light, a peculiarity that floods his brain, makes him sway and fuels a rising, uncontrollable fire. He's been looking for Wren, but never had an idea what he'd say if he found him.

He's probably as surprised as Wren when his lips find the skin of Wren's neck, when his teeth bite it lightly. Somehow their bodies are responding to the beat of the music, throbbing and sensual and encompassing, moving with it and each other.

"Wren." Cam mouths the edge of Wren's ear and feels the edges of his plug under his lips, and he can't help what happens next. "I'm not new." He pulls Wren closer with a sharp tug. His thumbs slip under the hem of Wren's shirt, feel the ridges of his hipbones through the low-slung waist of his pants. "I'm not new and I know."

"*How*?" Wren asks. Cam wants to imagine there's something breathy and needing in his voice, but it's impossible to read nuance over the throbbing music.

"Do you really want to talk right now?" Cam asks. He rubs his thumb under the seam of Wren's jeans and feels the slap of desire hit him, somehow stronger and more desperate than before. Wren's skin feels electric against Cam's mouth. Touching it feels like greed.

"Tell me what you want, Cam," Wren says—commands, sweet but steel-strong.

"Now, *now*." Cam pushes Wren back, guiding him with his body. Wren laughs and something... unclenches. Releases. Cam feels lightheaded and awed. He feels so much when Wren compels him. Even without that compulsion, the push, the drive, of *now, now, now* doesn't leave him. Wren laughs again and takes Cam's hand, pulling him roughly through the crowd.

Cam hesitates at the threshold of the bathroom when he realizes what is about to happen. But when Wren looks back at him, eyes beguiling and provocative, he pushes it down. This feeling, this thrill, brings him into his body high and fast and hard. When Wren pushes him into the stall, banging the door shut carelessly, he's laughing too.

"Do it," Cam begs. The cacophony of the music is dimmed. He doesn't need to yell; in fact he whispers low, needing, as he arches his body against Wren's. The tile wall feels cold under his shoulders,

"Do you know what you're asking?" Wren crowds closer; now his hands are on Cam's hips, pulling their bodies hard against each other.

"*Do it*," Cam says urgently.

Wren's eyes meet his, then darken a little. His lips shine with moisture and his skin seems to glow in the strange light. And then he does it, *compels* him. Cam's whole body rises to a new height of pleasure. Everything he feels—the chill of the wall and Wren's body against his, the light and the air he breathes—is a sensual caress.

"How's that?" Wren asks. Cam can't formulate a response. He doesn't think about what comes next, he *acts* what's next, cupping the back of Wren's neck and pulling him in for a desperate kiss. It's hungry and starts sloppily, but then Wren shifts, tilts his head up to meet Cam's lips better and it's suddenly *everything*, lush and slow and heady. The kiss escalates and heats until Cam isn't sure he'll be able to breathe. He breaks away, panting, eyes closed, focused on every sensation coursing and rolling through his body. He hardly feels Wren's fingers flipping his belt open. Wren's mouth is at his neck, biting and sucking and drawing whimpers from him. He's never made noises like the ones Wren's mouth wrings from him, and when Wren pushes his pants down far enough to get a hand into them, something primal and broken rises through him and comes out in a pained groan.

"Wren," he manages, and moans. Wren's hand is sure and hot, pumping fast and spreading the pre-come dripping from his dick. "I'm going to—I—"

"No," Wren uses his other hand to cup Cam's cheek. He shakes it a bit until Cam's eyes open. Cam feels the swamping rush of orgasm recede. "You'll come when I let you."

"Yes," Cam says faintly. The bathroom door swings open, music spills in and anyone coming in will *know*. He bites his lip hard to keep himself calm. Somehow the threat of being caught here with Wren makes him so hot he can hardly contain himself. Wren's eyes bore into his. His hand slows a little. Wren licks his lips, breath shaking. His cheeks are red, flushed with the heat between their bodies.

Wren puts his free hand against Cam's chest and presses him against the wall more firmly. Cam's eyes flicker from Wren's eyes and lips down to where his hand is working Cam's erection expertly. Cam's sure he's never been wet like this on his own; after a little while it's tacky, and Wren's hand catches. It chafes, but Wren's hold on him sends him pleasure signals even while he registers discomfort. Wren stops and licks his hand quickly before gripping Cam again.

Wren takes his time, rubbing his thumb against the ridge of Cam's frenulum and then over the slit, slipping down what moisture he gathers there. Then he grasps Cam in his fist and pumps him from root to tip. Every few strokes, his hand closes all the way over the head, his palm cupping and passing over it.

Cam can tell Wren is working him in more ways than one, letting him feel the intensity of pleasure and also keeping his slide back up slower, inching up by degrees until Cam is gasping and gripping Wren's shoulders, his fingernails digging into the soft cotton of Wren's T-shirt.

"Wren, please. *Please*."

"Mmm." Wren rolls his body sinuously and sensually against Cam, leaving enough room for his hand to keep pumping. "You beg so pretty."

"Oh *fuck*," Cam manages weakly, his head falling back when the pleasure crests hard and fast and wrecking through him. He comes and comes, crying out and thrusting his hips up into Wren's hand, gasping as a horse does after a hard race. His orgasm lasts and stretches until he finally becomes incrementally aware of his surroundings. Wren's forehead grinds against his collarbone, and his chest heaves along with Cam's as they gasp for breath. Cam can feel a faint vibration running under his fingers; he can't tell if Wren is shaking or laughing or on the verge of orgasm himself.

"Let—" he tries, voice hoarse and weak. He runs his hand down Wren's arm, over his stomach and down to the button of his pants. The door to the bathroom opens again, and this time with louder voices, more than two.

"N–no." Wren takes his hand gently. "Not here—"

"But—" Cam recoils when Wren pulls his hand away from his softening cock, which feels more sensitive than he can ever remember. He's felt Wren's erection against him—initially, when they'd been kissing, and just now as their bodies were plastered together.

"Don't worry." Wren kisses him softly, confident and sly. "I'll take care of it."

Cam frowns; disappointment is cold in his body. Wren smiles, and Cam calms and acquiesces. Distantly, he notes that Wren is doing it again. It's different from the pull of desire and heat.

"Can I see—will I see you again?' he manages. Wren gently tucks him back into his pants; at Cam's words he looks up, surprise clear on his face.

"You want to?"

"Are you kidding?" Cam says. "Why wouldn't I?"

Wren averts his eyes and shrugs. He takes a breath and after a moment draws himself a bit taller. "I'll think about it," he says.

"How will you know where to find me?"

Wren's hand sneaks around to Cam's back pocket to pull out his phone. He frowns when he gets a lock screen and holds it out for Cam, who manages to unlock it with unsteady fingers. Wren works fast; Cam barely hears the chime of Wren's phone—he must have sent a text to himself.

"I have your number," Wren says.

"Okay," Cam says, dazed. He doesn't want to leave, not when Wren's eyes are still so dark, when his body still seems to be vibrating against Cam's.

"Go," Wren commands, but softly. Cam obeys and knows it's because Wren is compelling him. He stumbles out and avoids the eyes of the man leaning against the sinks waiting for a free stall. He washes his hands quickly and opens the bathroom door into the chaos of the club. Eyes half blind, senses oversaturated, he makes his way out of the bar and into the night.

WREN'S GOT HIS PANTS OPEN before Cam has made it out of the bathroom. One part of his brain is occupied with compelling Cam out of the club, as far as he can project. But most of his mind and body is focused on the rush of power, the sense of control and the pure erotic stimulation of Cam: Cam's smell; his long dick, so hard in Wren's hands; his pleasure ebbing and peaking at Wren's command; the intensity of his orgasm and the noises—*fuck,* the noises he made.

Wren comes in seconds, one hand shoved against his mouth to keep it muffled. When it's over, he sees a perfect ring of tooth marks where he bit down.

The taut string of desire he felt from the moment Cam's lips grazed his neck relaxes by fractions.

Wren leans against the opposite wall of the stall. He cleans his hand automatically with toilet paper, closes his eyes and tries to center himself. Exhaustion begins to set in; it's not just post-orgasmic lethargy, but the drain of his energy; he exerted so much to compel Cam. Manipulating someone lightly is one thing; Wren's skill with this is very well developed. But Cam's energy had a will of its own. It had taken a lot for Wren to control the pace of his pleasure.

Wren waits until the last person exits the bathroom before stepping out himself. He feels his feet rooting to the earth, which he knows means he needs to sleep and recharge.

Home is far away, and Wren almost falls asleep a few times on the bus. He staggers through his door, falls face down on his bed and passes out in seconds.

* * *

CAM DOESN'T REMEMBER GETTING HOME. He doesn't remember talking to Nate; from Nate's questions the next day, it sounds more as though he was talked to *by* Nate.

"What was your deal?" Nate says. He's trying to balance on one foot while putting his jeans on. Cam can tell by his lack of balance that Nate is hungover.

"What do you mean?" Cam stretches and thinks vaguely about breakfast. He's ravenous.

"You were in a zone last night, man," Nate responds. He tucks his wallet into his back pocket and gives Cam an expectant look.

"What?" Cam runs his fingers through his hair. It's getting too long. It's so thick that if he doesn't get it cut regularly, he gets overnight tangles and mats that are extremely annoying.

"Are we going to eat or what?" Nate says impatiently.

"I didn't realize we had plans."

"We don't. But I'm hungover and either you are or... something. I can tell."

Cam turns away and searches for a clean pair of jeans in his dresser. He doesn't want Nate to see the face he's making. How on earth will he explain what's going on? Went on. Will hopefully keep going on, and on, and on. He struggles to remember what he told Nate about his plans for the previous night.

"Um," he says, trying to cover his uncertainty with an overzealous search for a T-shirt.

"Where did you go, anyway?"

Cam takes a chance. "The library."

"I didn't even soxile you, man," Nate mourns. "That's just sad, Cam. What was your deal, then?"

"Found something that blew my mind," Cam says absently. *Did something*, is more like it.

"I'm starving." Nate shoves him toward the door as soon as Cam has his shoes on. "Tell me about it on our way."

"Where are we going?" Cam snags his wallet.

"Thai," Nate says.

"What the hell? It's—" Cam checks his cell and groans when he sees a missed call and some texts from Jason.

"It's—?"

"Ten," Cam manages distractedly.

"That only means we're late for our date with the perfect hangover food. Even if yours seems to be a boringly intellectual hangover."

Cam shakes his head and sticks his phone back in his pocket. He'll have to figure out what to do about Jason later.

"SO WHAT BLEW YOUR MIND?" Nate says around a mouthful of noodles.

"Hmm?" Cam tunes back in. He's elsewhere: the shimmer of gold threads in Wren's deep green T-shirt and the strip of luminescent skin between the hem of his shirt and the distressed denim of his low-slung jeans; the black Converse shoes he'd been wearing. His black hair had been styled differently: mussed, with frosted tips. He can almost feel his lips, plush and wet from Cam's mouth.

"What the fuck were you studying? You're not even here." Nate snaps his fingers to get Cam's attention.

"People with gifts," he responds automatically, scrabbling for anything that might work.

"Gifts?" Nate makes a face.

"What? I'd never heard of them before," Cam defends himself.

"Seriously?" Nate is systematically separating the broccoli from the rest of his dish.

"Am I the only one? I don't know!" Cam says.

"Dude, is this another Nebraska thing? That can only be an excuse for so long."

"First of all, no it's not a Nebraska thing. But secondly, have you ever been to Nebraska?" Cam asks flatly. Nate shakes his head. "Then really, you have no idea. I can use the Nebraska card any time should I need."

"Well," Nate points out logically, "unless we're talking about Carhenge."

Cam laughs and leans lengthwise across the seat. His stomach is too full, and he's tired and distracted. He wants to be left alone with his thoughts so he can relive the night before: from the loud music and discomfort of light sweat in the sweltering club to the reality of having sex with a near-stranger in a bathroom.

Eyes closed, Cam represses the shiver of desire that rises at the thought.

"So what's the deal? Just looking 'em up?"

"I don't know," Cam says. He pushes his plate away and takes a last sip of his Coke. "You know me."

Nate tilts his head and considers him before shrugging and pushing his own plate away. It's clean, minus the tiny pile of reject vegetables. Nate checks the time and stands.

"Got to go—promised Ellie I'd meet her for coffee."

"Ellie, huh?" Cam says with a smile.

"Shut up," Nate grumbles.

"No, really. That's the third time I've heard the same name out of you. Got anything to share?"

"Like I said," Nate says, handing his credit card to the server at the front register, "shut up."

Once home, Cam gathers his stuff to shower. He takes his time soaping up in the steaming water, closes his eyes and relives Wren's touch and the spiraling heat, reveling in the dual layers of his own pleasure and what Wren had given him.

Wrung out from the shower half an hour later, Cam collapses on his bed. He can't stop thinking about it. He really doesn't want to, either.

He falls asleep with his phone in hand, feeling stupid for hoping Wren will text him soon.

CHAPTER ELEVEN

IT TAKES WREN THREE DAYS of vacillating to make up his mind. It's not that he's never played with someone for a longer period of time; that's usually what he does. But something—something he can't put his finger on—that lies between him and Cam makes him hesitate. It's not a bad thing; he doesn't sense anything that makes him feel threatened, just unsettled. There's a tenor to their connection that lingers, maybe because it feels like *theirs*, rather than *his*. The fact that he'd been unable to sense Cam in the club unnerves him.

On the second night after it had happened, lying on the couch watching a show with Nora, she interrupts his thoughts.

"Wren," Nora says, sleep threading her voice. "You need someone."

Wren doesn't dignify that with an answer. Instead he cuddles closer to her, pulls the soft crocheted throw his mother made him when they moved into the apartment closer to his neck and sighs.

"Don't get me wrong," she continues. She's playing with the ends of his hair; the sensation cascades through him pleasantly. "I love hanging out with you, but you've been an octopus all summer, and it's only getting worse."

"I have to get what I can," Wren says. He yawns. It's late. "I get so much less Nora time when you're out with Matt."

"Mmm, do I detect jealousy?" she asks. He sits up and lets the blanket slip down, dislodging her hand when he turns to face her.

"Not at all. I'm glad you've found someone you like," he says. "I just miss—"

"Yeah," Nora interrupts. "But that's why I said you need someone. Because I know you, Wren, and I know how important touch is to you. I don't know if you get what you need when all you do is play, but you haven't even been doing that for ages now, and you've pretty much attached yourself to me any time I stop moving."

"I'm sorry, it's probably annoying you, isn't it?"

"No." Nora smiles and then sinks down, tucking her head onto his shoulder. "It's just the same old conversation. I want you to be happy. And I want you to know that even if you don't want to, or can't see it, you have needs you're not meeting the way you're living now."

"Nora," Wren says, whispering into her hair. He doesn't want to have this conversation, not when he's so tired and knows deep down that she might be right. He smiles. "I'll find someone to play with, and you can have some peace of mind." He doesn't need to tell her that maybe he already has.

"That's not what I mean, and you know it." She pinches his side, making him giggle and squirm away.

"Well, the rules demand that's what I do."

"Ugh," Nora says. "I hate your rules."

"So you've said, honey," Wren replies. He pulls the blanket back up around them and buries himself in the hum of the show they've been mindlessly watching.

He's fighting inevitability. Wren avoided Cam from a sense of responsibility and respect: both because Cam didn't know what was happening and because of his own rules. But Cam knows, now.

He's not new, and the taste of what they had isn't nearly enough to satiate Wren's hunger. He refuses to let himself consider what Nora had said, because if he goes forward with this, it can't be about anything more than the game. He's not sure of his footing, which is unsettling, but he wants more. So, as he does best, Wren makes a plan. And then he slowly crafts a text.

LIBRARY, TONIGHT. 10. YOU KNOW where

Cam is in bed drowsing when he gets the text. It's already nine p.m., and Tuesdays are the longest days of his week. One hour hardly seems like enough time to get ready; he just has to shower and find clothes, but he wishes he had a lot more time to mentally prepare.

His closet is a mess; he's been so lost in the aftermath of being utterly wrecked by Wren that he's let his careful order go; it's been hard to care. But it is annoying right now, when he needs to decide what to wear. He resists the urge to ask Nate for advice. Maybe he should dress to impress; but in his experience, the context for dressing to impress involves job interviews and weddings, not a potential rendezvous in a public location with a man capable of commanding his desires and actions.

Perhaps this is not a completely productive line of thought if he needs to focus.

Simple but good is probably best. He himself finds tighter shirts, pants and rich colors attractive. His newly discovered penchant for cowl-neck and slim sweaters probably won't work here. Not if he's going for a repeat of their last encounter. Cam knows there's no guarantee that's what will happen, but he can certainly hope. And dress for the possibility. He doesn't own pants anywhere as tight as what he's seen Wren wear, but he can do a flattering shirt. It's cold enough out that he can't justify something short-sleeved, so he opts for a soft Henley shirt in an olive green that Maggie had insisted highlights the caramel of his skin.

"What are you doing?" Nate says around a mouthful of chips. "Finally reorganizing?"

"Was the mess bothering you?" Cam turns from the closet. The pile of discarded and dirty clothes mingling on the closet floor is pushing into the space on Nate's side of the closet.

"Naw, you know I don't care. I've just been wondering how long you could stand it. Not your style, man."

"True," Cam acknowledges. "No, I'm getting dressed. I'm gonna go to the library."

"What exactly is at the library? It's like you're in love with the place. And it's already nine," Nate points out.

"I need to get more research done. I thought my project was due next week but I was wrong," Cam lies easily. *And just where did that skill come from*?

"Uh, all right." Nate doesn't sound convinced, but a glance at the clock shows Cam it's actually a quarter past, and he still wants to shower. Ignoring Nate—he really doesn't want to answer questions or have to lie again—he rushes out with his stuff.

When he gets back to the room, Nate is occupied with watching some greatest moments of pro football thing on Sports Center. Despite an upbringing immersed in college football-crazy culture, Cam's never been a fan. He tries to take extra time with his hair without being obvious. When he picks up his phone to pocket it, he sees another text.

just to talk. then we'll see

What does that mean? Cam sends back an *ok* so that Wren knows he's gotten the messages and is coming, and before Nate can say anything else, he slips out the door.

* * *

WREN GETS TO THE LIBRARY with twenty minutes to spare. It gives him time to settle and to think. Unfortunately, the more he thinks, the more his body buzzes with hunger and impatience. He knows he needs to lay out what is going to happen for Cam, but isn't quite sure what will happen after that. Should Cam say no, Wren feels as if he might still be hard to resist. Which is just not acceptable; he won't compel anyone without consent, *ever*. Nor is he willing to try being with anyone outside of specifically designed play.

"Hi." Cam comes around the corner of the stacks, breathless. His hair looks different—not neatly combed to the side, not damp with sweat. It looks like a richer brown, paired with the green of his shirt, and it's lifted a bit and styled for height. Wren's mouth waters, which he thought was just a figure of speech. Cam's lips draw his attention—and then his eyes, which are on the edge of troubled and deep with questions.

"You came," Wren manages.

"I—" Cam comes closer, and then, to Wren's surprise, kisses him. Takes his face between the palms of his hands and kisses him. The kiss is not soft or laced with the uncertainty Wren had read; instead, it's surprisingly confident.

"Wow." Wren pulls back and catches his breath. "That... I... wasn't—"

"I'm sorry," Cam whispers.

Wren doubts very much that he is, considering that he's crowding closer, kissing the corners of Wren's lips and across to his ears. Wren shivers and tilts his head for more before he thinks better of it. A sensation of drowning in pleasure covers him, something delicious and heady and *dangerous*.

"No, no—" Wren gently pushes Cam away with hands on his waist. "We need to talk first."

"I know." Cam pulls away. His lips are wet. "Or I don't know—I've never been like this before; I apologize."

Wren smiles and bites back the return confession on the tip of his tongue. He can't say things like that and maintain the distance and dynamic he's looking for.

"So," Cam says, looking around. "If we're just talking, why are we here and not sitting?"

"Call it nostalgia," Wren says coyly. He runs a finger up the defined muscle of Cam's forearm where the sleeve of his shirt is pushed up and lets himself bleed a little of what he's feeling into Cam. Cam's eyelashes flutter, and when Wren uses that finger to trace a circle inside the tender crook of Cam's elbow, exerting a little more energy and pulling on the reservoir of desire pooled inside Cam, he revels in the hitch in Cam's breath.

"How can I just talk when you—" Cam traps Wren's finger with his free hand.

"Because I get to," Wren says simply. "That's what we're here for. You want more."

"Absolutely," Cam confirms.

"There are rules," Wren says. He leans against the wall and deliberately relaxes his body in a way that draws Cam's eyes. "They're non-negotiable. It's how I play."

"Play?" Cam repeats faintly.

"That's what I do. That's what this would be."

"Okay," Cam agrees. Wren wonders at his fast acquiescence. "What are the rules?"

Wren swallows and licks his lips.

"First: You tell no one. Ever. If you do, it's over."

Cam nods, unfazed.

"I'm in charge," Wren continues. "I can end it any time."

"What else?" Cam says quietly.

You make me everything. You let me own you.

"You understand what I can do, right? What I'm capable of?"

"I think so," Cam says slowly.

"I'm going to use you, Cam," Wren says sweetly. "I'm going to make you use me. I'm going to make you want things you never thought you would."

"That sounds—" Cam takes a deep breath.

Something dark and hot curls in Wren's belly. He can feel how much Cam wants this. "You need to think carefully," Wren warns him, "and understand what you're signing up for."

"I—" Cam pushes Wren back against the wall and leans in to whisper kisses and words, nipping at Wren's lips. "I know, *I know*."

Wren kisses him back, really kisses him for the first time. He wants to see Cam on his knees. Wants to see him slicked with sweat, on his back, begging. Wants to watch the flex of muscles along his back and the line of his spine while Wren fucks him senseless. Wants, wants, wants so much.

"You should have questions," Wren points out, breathing the words heavily against Cam's lips. "Aren't you a little scared?"

"Of what you can do?" Cam whispers. His fingers are wrecking Wren's hair. "No."

Wren takes a deep breath and pulls himself in and together, and then gives Cam the same, cools him and draws him back. Cam is so open, so fucking open, as if he's left all of his doors ajar and is just waiting to let Wren in. The feeling of potency rushes through Wren like a crackle of lightning rolling across the sky.

"If you ever really don't—I'll know. I've done this, I know how. I can tell the difference between a no you want me to push and no you don't."

"I can't imagine ever feeling that," Cam admits. He smoothes his hand over his chest and tugs his shirt straight.

Wren smiles. "You'd be surprised at what I'm capable of, Cam," he says. "Don't underestimate me."

Cam looks at him seriously. His eyes are slanting and warm, dark chocolate in the too-bright library lights.

"I can tell you're calming me down," he points out.

"If you really let me in," Wren says, "you won't always be able to tell."

Cam swallows and closes his eyes. "Yes." Wren can feel the rising desire to touch him seeping from Cam's body and pushes back harder. "I want that."

"Good," Wren says, running one finger over the plush swell of Cam's lips. "You can't think straight right now, you know," he points out with wisdom born of experience. "I'll contact you tomorrow."

"Okay." Cam seems dazed.

Good. He likes his boys off their feet, so to speak. He presses a light and teasing kiss to Cam's lips.

"Good night." He keeps Cam where he is, standing between rows of musty reference books long left to solitude.

"I HOPE YOU KNOW WHAT your aura is doing," Nora points out from her perch in front of the TV. She's watching *A Few Good Men* for the millionth time. He has no idea what draws her to it so often.

"Nora, mind your own fucking business," he snaps.

"I'm not even offended," she sings, "because I can see the sexual tension all over you."

"I swear to god," Wren snarls.

"Relax," Nora bites back. "I can't help it. It's huge. I don't know who the hell he is but he's got you *goooood*."

"You have no idea what you're talking about." Wren takes a deep breath and dismisses her comments.

"I know, I know," she says flippantly, waving her hand. "You've got him; you've got the whole thing under control."

Wren wrangles himself together and turns on his heel, smartly closing the door behind him.

Meddling friends who can see more than they should be able to are the fucking *worst*.

* * *

THIS IS ME CONTACTING YOU.

Cam smiles when his phone vibrates. He's in Environmental Economics; he attempts to respond surreptitiously under the desk. It's a small class, only about twenty students, and he knows he's being obvious. But he doesn't want to wait.

This is me saying yes.

He reads Wren's text again, then again. Its tone is different. Or maybe Cam wants it to be.

He's spent the last day in such a heightened state of awareness and arousal and longing it's a wonder he's managed to function during classes and social interaction.

Then we'll start slow, Wren responds. Cam puzzles over that. *Cherrie's. Nine, tonight. Assuming diner food is ok. Can you?*

Cam squints at the phone. Just what does that mean?

Still, he doesn't hesitate. *Absolutely*.

WREN IS WAITING FOR HIM at a table all the way at the back of the restaurant. The place is dim, and a little ragged in a broken-in way. Cam's never been here. It's late. Are they supposed to be eating? Not that it matters; he's been too excited to eat, and still is.

"Hey." Cam stands awkwardly by the booth and smiles at Wren, conscious of how foolish he must look. Wren props his chin on his hand and examines Cam carefully. He does the same. Wren's hair is different again, the lighter tips he'd sported last week are now green. He's wearing what looks like a cowl-neck scarf, with a hood that rests against his neck. It's midnight blue and overwhelms his face. He looks younger.

"Sit." Wren gestures gracefully, with a small, secret smile on his face. Cam works his way into the deep red, cracked faux leather booth. The table wobbles; he thinks of Maggie.

"How are you?" Cam starts politely.

"Hmm." Wren leans forward, crossing his arms on the table. "I think we should talk about *you*."

Cam bites his lip and looks into Wren's eyes. They're such a startling deep jade, and the connection he feels momentarily unsettles him.

"I'm hoping to be really well soon," he surprises himself by saying. Wren makes him feel like someone new: more daring, more open; ready for things he can't even name.

"Is that an explicit yes?" Wren asks.

"Yes," Cam responds unequivocally.

"Excellent," Wren says. He fixes that stare on Cam again; suddenly Cam feels rooted to his seat and can't take his eyes away from Wren, can't imagine wanting to. Feeling exceptionally exposed, Cam struggles against the sudden increase in his breath rate. Wren's stare renders him useless and naked.

"Go outside, to the left, behind the building. Wait for me," Wren commands. Cam obeys without a second thought.

CAM WAITS FOR WHAT FEELS like forever. The sky is clouded over, so he doesn't even have the few city stars to contemplate. Instead, he focuses on the muffled noises of the city around him. Breathing slowly and steadily, he looks around. Behind the restaurant is a small parking lot with an "Employee Only" sign at each space. It's dark; the streetlight is out, and with every breath he feels the frigid February air freezing in his nostrils. Whether he's shivering from anticipation or the cold is irrelevant.

Finally he feels it, something tight curling inside him. Wren comes around the corner.

"Good," Wren says. He runs his hand through the hair over Cam's ear; shockwaves pulse through Cam at the touch. He leans in and makes a small noise of pleasure.

"Tell me what you like," Wren says. His finger trails down the tendons of Cam's neck to the hollow between his collarbones.

"That," Cam says softly. "You touching me, god, it's—"

"I know that," Wren's voice is laced with amusement. "I mean before this. With whomever else you've been with."

Cam hesitates—telling Wren these things feels more like exposure than anything physical.

"Tell me," Wren sings softly, placing his open hand on Cam's chest, over his heart.

Cam has to reply, now. It's a little uncomfortable, recalling moments with Maggie in this context, but he does it. "My neck, my hips. And the obvious places. I fantasize about feeling out of control. Not having to think about it too much—letting it be instinctual. Making the person I'm with come."

"Ohhh." Wren leans in and starts on Cam's neck. "That's gonna be a hard one."

"What?" Cam's got a fistful of Wren's shirt in his hand. His eyes close as he sways into the pleasure. "I don't get to—"

"When you earn it," Wren breathes against his ear.

"*Oh shit.*" Perfect, perfect words to settle who is steering this.

Wren reaches up and tugs Cam's head down for a kiss, and then another, fierce and wet and overpowering.

"I can feel it, god, it's like setting you on fire when I say that," Wren says, a little wonder in his voice. "It's so easy to read you."

“That’s n–not,” Cam shudders in a breath as Wren guides Cam’s hands under the hem of his shirt. Wren’s skin feels incredibly soft under Cam’s fingers; his belly is flat and smooth. “Usual?”

“Not this easy. *Fuck,* you’re so open to this.” Wren pushes him against the wall, and a strong sense of déjà vu comes over Cam.

“Yes, *yes, yes,*” he chants in a whisper, aware of the possibility of being discovered. His hands move up to expose more of Wren; his index fingers glide over Wren’s hard nipples.

“*Ah, ah, ah,*” Wren says, pulling away. Cam swallows his disappointment.

“Please let me touch you,” he begs.

“Oh, I like that.” Wren tugs on his ear playfully. “Get on your knees.”

Cam does, without a thought.

“You may touch me gently,” Wren says quietly. When Cam’s shaking fingers go to the button of his jeans, Wren moves his hands away gently. “Not like that, over my clothes.”

Cam exhales, and then begins to touch. He starts where he wants to most, cupping his hand around Wren’s erection, held tight in his pants. The pants are thin, made of some sort of synthetic material. Wren feels *right* in the palm of Cam’s hand; feeling this—a man so hard and so perfectly shaped for the cupped give of his palm—is something he’s been imagining. Things hadn’t progressed quite this far with Jason, but he’d wanted it. Cam moans a little and then puts his face against Wren’s hard-on, rubbing his lips over it as if he could taste it, greed filling his mouth. His hands span Wren’s hips and move down, his thumbs following the path of Wren’s groin and down the insides of Wren’s thighs. He applies a little pressure and Wren steps apart and spins so that he’s leaning against the wall he’d had Cam pushed up against.

“*Oh.*”

Wren's sighed satisfaction is faint. Somewhere he registers that his knees hurt, but it's nothing compared to the pleasure of feeling the curve of Wren's body under his hands. Heat seeps through Wren and slowly into Cam. He brings his hands up and rubs his thumbs up the length of Wren's cock with confident pressure.

"*God*," Wren says, a little louder. Cam's body feels like a humming live wire, barely held in check. "All right," Wren says, pulling him up. "That's enough of that."

"But—" Cam tries to kiss him, to touch him anywhere he can, and Wren stops him with a look.

"I'm going to make you come now," Wren informs him matter-of-factly. "You're gonna come in your pants and I'll make you walk home wet and knowing it was me that did it and that I can make you do it anytime."

"You can't—I'm—" Cam feels the spiral of heat inside him spike; he's overcome and owned, and it's delectable.

Wren puts his hand on Cam's cheek and focuses his eyes on Cam's. When Wren's hand travels, it does so slowly. He pulls up Cam's shirt and digs the crescent of his thumbnail into one of his nipples; not too hard, but hard enough for Cam to feel a tiny, pleasurable pain that makes him cry out. He bites his lip and tries to keep quiet.

"No, no," Wren says, smiling, "I want you to make noise. I want you to know that anyone could come and see this."

Cam groans loudly, helplessly, and then Wren's hand is there, holding his dick and squeezing hard through his pants and when Cam's eyes flutter shut, Wren tells him to open them. Obedient and pliant, he does. He manages to focus on Wren's eyes, and the pleasure peaks so quickly, so explosively, that Cam cries out and shudders and has to hold on to Wren to keep himself upright.

"Feel good?" Wren asks smugly, an intense focus lacing his smile. Cam manages to nod weakly. "Excellent."

And then it's so fast: Cam's head is still spinning inside out when Wren kisses his cheek lightly and then turns and leaves.

"What—?" Cam has to lean against the wall to try to find his balance. The sensations of pleasure and helplessness Wren implanted in him ebb slowly; a keener awareness of where he is and what he just did comes over him.

He should be ashamed or embarrassed to have done something so public, to have enjoyed feeling used and commanded. But instead Cam feels elated and expansive, electric and hungry for more.

CHAPTER TWELVE

All it takes is one look. "What happened?" Nate asks.

"How..." Cam responds vaguely.

"To your pants?"

Cam looks down and sees that he has stains on his knees. He's grateful he took the time to wipe himself sort of clean before coming in. It was one thing to walk home feeling the wet reminder of what had happened, and another to face Nate. He hadn't thought about evidence of his having been on his knees, though.

"I dropped my wallet," he says stupidly.

"Seriously?" Nate seems a little annoyed. "If you're gonna lie, at least do it well."

Cam knows he doesn't even remotely have the energy for this, so he just shrugs and starts getting ready for sleep. He needs the dark; he needs to sleep off the weight of this before he can start the next day with a semi-clear head.

* * *

The weeks following that night are erratic, to say the least. Cam never knows when Wren will call him. He never knows where they will meet until Wren tells him. Wren seems to know endless deserted spots in the library; sometimes all he does is text Cam call numbers and times. And unless something incredibly urgent is happening, Cam obeys. Wren doesn't have to compel him to come, because he is a burning bright flame and Cam is a helpless mess of hunger, a moth incapable of resisting the light.

It's not until their third encounter that Wren touches him the way Cam fantasizes he would, reenacting that moment in the club. Only this time, it's in the dead quiet of the library. The sound of his zipper, drawn down agonizingly slowly, seems to Cam like the powerful bang of a gunshot, and he has to grunt with the effort of not coming.

Wren does that. He has the power to magnify every touch, to draw so much from Cam that, every time, it's a complicated balancing act of nearing and coming down. Sometimes Cam manages to control himself; at other times, Wren has to hold him carefully with his eyes and command him to breathe through it.

Every time this happens, Cam has to push down his sense of embarrassment about being so quick to come. This time, Wren laughs and bites the hinge of his jaw, slowly pulling Cam's dick out of his boxers, barely pushing the flaps of his jeans open and down until his dick is all that's exposed.

"Don't worry. I fucking love it," Wren says. His fingers dance over Cam in the lightest tease. "I love how much you want it—"

"You," Cam breathes out on a moan. "I want *you*."

Wren's hand pauses for the slightest moment. He blinks and something flickers inside Cam. Wren shakes his head and then looks back at Cam; he grips him with a sure, searing hot hand; his thumb presses almost painfully against Cam's slit. Wren smiles wickedly, brightly, licks the smear of pre-come off of his fingers and kisses it back into Cam's mouth. The slightest tang touches Cam's tongue—this is something he's never tasted before. Wren exhales, runs one finger down the shaft of Cam's suffering erection and breathes against his lips.

"Come."

And Cam does.

* * *

"TELL ME," PEYTON SAYS WITHOUT preamble. Cam sighs. He's looking for a pen, and the homework for his Urban Structure course mocks him from his desk. He's behind in several classes; he's even skipped a few. Wren's siren call is so much more potent than any of Cam's concerns about school.

"I don't know what you're talking about."

"Shut up, your voice is totally transparent," she says.

"I said *hello,* Peyton." He tosses his bag down on his desk. How could all of his pens have magically disappeared?

"Okay, so I'm guessing a little. But you've been quiet. What was the point of yelling at me and having me create a special *Cam only* email address if you're not even using it anymore?"

Cam swallows. Guilt pops up in his stomach. "You have a point."

"Aha!" she crows, "I knew it!"

Cam starts rooting through Nate's desk drawers, which are haphazardly packed with random crap.

"So tell me," she presses.

"Peyton." He takes a breath. "I can't. I really can't right now."

He hears her humming, and then a heavy silence.

"Are you in trouble?" she says finally.

"No, I promise," he says. "I've just also promised I wouldn't talk about it. For now." He has no idea why he's tacked on that last sentence; as far as he knows, the command has not been lifted, and he can't bear the idea of a time when this will be over and he'll be able to speak about it. That wouldn't feel like any sort of freedom.

"Pey," he says softly.

"Yeah?"

"I love you."

There's a long silence after that. He doesn't know the last time they said it. It's just known.

"I love you too," she responds softly. He exhales and they both hang up.

* * *

HE BEGS FOR IT SEVERAL TIMES. With kisses pressed to the corners of Wren's mouth, with fingers slipping under the waist of Wren's pants, with one leg between Wren's, grinding hard while he pants against Wren's skin.

"Let me touch you, *let me*," he says over and over. "Let me see you. Let me make you come."

But Wren just smiles and twists away or pushes him back with his power. "In time."

* * *

"NATE IS GOING HOME FOR the weekend," Cam says as soon as he sees Wren. He wants to say it before Wren can reach into him.

"Good for him," Wren says with a laugh.

"Can you come over?" Cam stays a few feet back, as if it will help. "Please. I want to take time."

"You want me to work you over longer?" Wren is definitely amused.

"Maybe if I have you long enough, you'll let me—"

"Oh, Cam," Wren says, shaking his head. "I have you, you know that, right?"

Cam's mind blanks a little, and he's drawn into Wren's arms like a magnet.

"Yes," he says finally. Wren holds his hands in a tight grip, holds his eyes in an unblinking stare.

* * *

"I SAW JASON YESTERDAY," MAGGIE says out of nowhere as they are shopping for clothes. Cam puts the T-shirt he'd been contemplating back on the pile on the table. Above them, a song currently in heavy rotation on the radio blares, swear words and all. Chicago is so foreign sometimes.

"Oh?" he manages. He tries not to flush. He spots a table of slim-fit plaid button-downs; the mannequins next to them wear wide-necked sweaters in jewel tones. Cam starts sorting through the shirts. He's tired of dressing in plain, nondescript clothes. He finds that he *wants* to be noticed. A pattern is developing in what Wren has let slip about what he appreciates on Cam. It's rare to get him to say anything like that. He's always manipulating Cam so deftly, he doesn't often talk about what he wants or likes, much less let Cam touch or give him pleasure.

Cam's pretty sure that Wren gets off on that, though. He's as much as admitted it whenever Cam has really pressed for reciprocity.

Still, Cam aches to touch him when they're not together. There are so many ways in which Cam has not yet been with someone; despite the intimate nature of his relationship with Maggie—even moments he'd had with Jason—what Wren brings to him in comparison is so much sharper. As if the pleasure of being with Maggie was muffled under a layer of snow. Wren, though… letting Wren have him is like turning on the sun.

Wren's touch rolls through him like electricity charging in roiling clouds, comes over him like pounding sheets of rain during a fast-moving storm. He drowns in it gratefully; he lights up and comes and comes, as if Wren is drawing him completely inside out. He walks home stumbling through the residual charge, ions and atoms dizzily bumping into each other, in a leftover high.

He wants very badly to return some of that pleasure to Wren. The thought leaves him dizzy and desperate. Cam can't compel Wren, though he knows very well that Wren manipulates *him* into sex in places he'd never normally have it. Makes him louder, more shameless. Gets him on his knees, or propped on the edge of a sink in a bathroom. Leaves him helpless in dirty stalls and dark halls. And there are times when Wren touches him, especially right before orgasm, that fill him with so much desire and pleasure it seems he'll simply combust.

Cam wants to give, to experience everything he fantasizes about. He loves being used and made, but he also craves something else. Closeness. That draw he's felt from the start. Since that first look in the classroom he's wanted to feed the part of this connection that is more than just sex.

"Cam!" Maggie snaps her fingers in front of his face.

"Sorry—" he clears his throat and looks around, trying to push down his thoughts of Wren.

"Jason?"

"Oh yeah," Cam says lamely.

"He told me you just dropped off the face of the earth," Maggie says. She's a little irked; her arms are crossed and her eyes are doing a *thing*.

"Have I told you, you look adorable today?" he says, apropos of nothing. She does. Her hair is tamed into soft curls, and she's wearing a sweater in a lovely coral that accentuates her curves.

"Don't change the subject, Cam," she sniffs.

"Sorry, I don't mean to," he says. He really doesn't. "I'm just everywhere right now."

"Cam, I'm gonna be honest, okay?" she says. He sets down the shirts he's picked out to buy. "I thought you'd been acting unusual and sneaking around with Jason this whole time."

"Why would I sneak around with Jason?" Cam asks in wonder.

"I don't know. Are you embarrassed about us seeing you with a guy?"

Cam laughs, incredulous. "You've seen me with him already. Why would I be shy? Besides, that's not quite what I meant."

"What *did* you mean, then?" Maggie asks. Cam sighs.

"I don't know. Why assume I'm with Jason? Have you seen me with him recently?"

Maggie's eyes narrow just a bit. She's lined them with dark purple that makes them look a deeper brown. "You've been sneaking around. We've noticed it. What else are we going to assume?"

Cam looks around; the store is starting to fill up. "Do we have to do this here?"

Maggie rolls her eyes and swishes away. She stands in line for the register with the basket of clothes she's picked out digging into her forearm. Cam takes a few breaths, picks up the clothes he's chosen and joins her.

"Please don't be angry," he says quietly. "Let's go to coffee, and we can talk."

"You won't lie, change the subject or evade?" she says testily.

"No." He feels a pang when he realizes that continuing to keep a secret might technically be evading. He'll be up front with her about the fact that there are some things he can't tell her. There's no way he's going to test Wren's rules and risk ending this.

FROM THEIR USUAL TABLE, CAM gets a coffee sleeve to stick under one of the legs so it won't wobble, then watches Maggie order coffee. The sun is just breaking through an oppressive blanket of clouds. It's been a depressingly dark day, with the hush of impending snow muting even the rattle of bare branches. The glow of sun darting through, a warm finger of light briefly touching the asphalt of the busy road, lifts his spirits.

"Thanks for taking care of the table," Maggie says. She sets his coffee in front of him carefully.

"I know how it goes," he smiles at her. It's nice to have a *thing*, something routine and steady. Cam's been surprised to learn how much he values the extremes of controlled, predictable and safe moments, and the crashing highs of unpredictability and recklessness. For the first time in a long time, he recognizes the twin half of himself—so like Peyton—that he locked up years ago.

"Jason has no idea what's up. He said you stopped contacting him." Maggie cuts to the chase.

"I didn't know how to—" Cam starts.

"No one does; it sucks, but it sucks more to not do it and leave someone hanging," Maggie chastises. Cam looks down guiltily and picks at the edge of the paper sleeve around his coffee cup. He takes a sip and winces when it scalds his tongue.

"Point taken. I'll message him."

"And now you'll tell me what is going on," she prompts. "Because it's clear as day that something is."

"Maggie," Cam starts and then sighs. "I can't tell you."

"You promised not to evade," Maggie hisses. An older couple has just taken up residence at the table next to them. Cam rolls his eyes. Of course. A whole empty coffee shop and they choose *that* table.

"I'm not evading. I'm being honest. I promised... someone. That I would keep a secret."

Maggie looks at him for a long time, and he tries to maintain eye contact.

"Are you okay? Are you safe?"

"I—" He looks at her like she's a little crazy. "Of course. What does that even mean?"

"Cam, you have no idea what you're doing half the time," she points out. He feels a spear of anger flash through him.

"Don't treat me like I'm dumb," he says.

"I'm not," she says wearily. "At least, I'm not trying to. But you came here just... totally clueless. About what you were doing, about you. It's a process to figure yourself out, you know. For all of us. I just feel like with you..."

"With me?" he snaps.

"You were so closed up. So detached. And suddenly it's like... realizing things about yourself opened these doors. I want to be sure that you aren't doing anything that's risking or compromising your safety just because it's new and—"

"Maggie," he interrupts. He's so pissed he has to clench his fingers together. "I don't want to be an asshole, but I am really close to telling you to shut up."

"Cam," Maggie tries to take his hand. "I'm saying this because I love you. I *love* you, and sometimes when you love someone it means telling the truth to protect or care for someone, even when it's hard. Or you risk making them mad."

Cam takes a deep breath. The sleeve around his coffee is nearly shredded. He's pulled the cardboard until it ripped, leaving the ribbed inside exposed and ragged. His leg bounces at triple speed.

"I'm not in any danger," he says finally. He's taking risks, he knows. But he *wants* to. Now that she's said it, he wonders if the chase, running after and trying to bottle that incredible high he gets from Wren, is part of opening those doors. Peyton has never closed herself off from anything she really wants. She spent so much of their youth being wild and unpredictable, and their home life reflected that turmoil when their parents didn't know what to do or how to stop her.

"Maggie," he says slowly. "I know you are saying this because you care. And I hear you. But I don't think I can talk about it right now. I need to calm down and think about this."

Maggie nods. Her eyes are brighter, shimmering with unshed tears. He's not sure of their source, anger or hurt, but he doesn't ever want to make her cry. Cam flips his hand over and opens it, wiggling his fingers in invitation. Small and warm, soft-fingered, Maggie's hand fits perfectly in his.

"I love you too, you know," he says.

CHAPTER THIRTEEN

"OH," CAM MANAGES TO SAY. His hands are buried deep in Wren's hair, and he tries not to pull on it while Wren's mouth trails down; he's already kissed all over Cam's chest, biting and working his nipples until they're swollen and too sensitive. Cam's pretty sure his neck is marked up too. But there's no part of him that cares right now, and, since Maggie and Nate know something is up, he feels less pressure to hide. Wren's mouth is dangerously low, now, licking the vee of Cam's pelvic muscles; his hands slowly inch Cam's jeans down. His chin is close enough to bump the head of Cam's cock, and it takes everything Cam has not to push Wren's mouth to where he wants it the most.

Wren loves to tease him and has done nothing but the last few times they've been together, coming so close, then pulling away and forcing Cam into orgasm with barely a touch of his fingers. The last time, Wren took long minutes to lap Cam's come from his fingers and belly without ever touching his dick. It was infuriating and intoxicating at the same time.

"You can pull my hair, you know," Wren says with a self-satisfied smile; his eyes burn fiercely when he looks up at Cam.

"*Shit*." Cams head thunks back against the wall.

"God, you want it so bad," Wren murmurs, and moves his mouth down to the top of Cam's thigh. He inhales sharply at the crease of Cam's groin, as if Cam is something delicious, as if Wren wants to consume him. Cam feels close to hysteria.

"You said you'd know when it was too much," Cam gasps.

"You aren't saying no," Wren points out, then runs one finger up Cam's dick. It throbs heavily.

"What if I did?"

Wren stops and closes his eyes. When he opens them, it's with a determined and focused look. "I can feel it, you know?" His hands span Cam's hips and he pushes them back until Cam is braced against the wall. "I don't care what your mouth says, because everything inside you fucking *wants* this so much. Even the teasing."

"God," Cam groans loudly. He's completely forgotten where they are. Luckily it's a slow night at the library; he didn't see a single person when he came in. "I'll beg; I will, just please."

"You could beg so beautifully if I made you," Wren says, his voice laced with dark amusement. As if Cam is a pleasing toy, as if he isn't writhing on the edge and so desperate he wouldn't stop Wren if he chose to blow him in the middle of a packed stadium.

Is this dangerous? The question reverberates heavily into his chest, long enough that even Wren must sense it, some stuttering lack of surety.

"Do you want me to stop?" Wren asks for the first time, sitting back on his legs where he's kneeling on the scuffed brown linoleum.

Cam shakes his head. The fact that Wren sensed it is all the assurance he needs.

"No," Cam says, his voice low and thready, "I want you to put your mouth on me, please, fuck, *please*—please."

"Mmmmm," Wren's hand circles his dick and tugs on it lightly, quickly, leaving Cam gasping, head arched back. When he opens his eyes the fluorescent lights waver and hurt, imprinting behind his eyelids. Wren's head is in his hands before he can think about it, his fingers pull Wren's hair taut, and Wren moans lightly, high and broken, a cut-off sound like nothing Cam's ever heard.

"Yes," he breathes, because this is what he's wanted more than anything: to make Wren helpless, to break him down until his body is covered in a sheen of sweat and he writhes with the pleasure Cam gives him. It's not much, that one little moan, but it's more evidence of pleasure than he's gotten from Wren before. He pulls harder and Wren's fingers dig into the meaty flesh at the back of Cam's thighs, pulling him closer before he finally, *finally* takes Cam into his mouth.

* * *

CAM IS TWITCHING ON THE EDGE of sleep when a snatch of his conversation with Maggie comes back to him. Despite the chill, Nate had inched the window open for fresh air. Cam can feel storms coming, and ahead of them March winds sweep over campus, occasionally gusting through the two-inch gap with a hollow, aching sound. This once sounded like loneliness to Cam—or what he understands now was loneliness. For years, it had just felt like some unfinished hollow place that he had filled with running, letting the rushing high of a hard run swamp it when it was at its worst.

He doesn't feel like that so much, anymore. The cavern is filled from so many cups, pouring in a coming home to his connection with Peyton; the sweet tenderness of Maggie's gentle hands and insistence; the laughter and simplicity of his friendship with Nate and, in the best way, with the scorching shock at every touch of Wren's body to his.

No, the wind tonight is soothing, reminiscent but good, a reminder of growth. Still, one particularly sharp rattle brings him from the knife's edge of sleep. *Jason*.

Fuck. Maggie had left him with no question that he ought to let Jason know something, anything. She had been completely unsympathetic to Cam's uncertainty about how exactly he was supposed to handle the situation or what he should say, and she had a point.

"Do you think there is any way I actually knew what to say to you when I did it?" she'd pointed out, only the slightest hint of upset lacing the question.

Cam shrugged. He felt tiny and sad when he thought of how hurt she'd been, even though he knew he would never have hurt her intentionally. Being so blind for so long... well, there's nothing he can do about it now, other than to be the best friend he can to her, and to anyone else he might have unwittingly affected.

This probably includes Jason. Cam reaches over to his nightstand, unplugs his phone and burrows under the covers with only his arms peeking out.

Are you awake? he types, before he can overthink his approach.

You live! comes the immediate response. Cam exhales; Jason's playful, quick response makes him feel even shittier.

I'm sorry, he replies.

There's a long pause.

I'm not sure if that's for the silence, or for what's coming next, Jason finally replies.

Despite his feeling terrible, Cam's eyes had been starting to droop. *Would it help if I apologized again?*

Depends on what for, is the cryptic response.

Cam frowns.

"What the hell are you doing?" Nate's voice pops out of the darkness, startling Cam into dropping the phone.

"Huh?" he says.

"Fuck, Cam, it's three in the morning," Nate doesn't wake well at a normal hour; three a.m. when he'd been sleeping soundly isn't any better. "Make your phone stop fucking buzzing."

Cam switches his phone to complete silence. "Sorry," he says. There's no further sound from Nate other than the deepening even breaths that signal his heavy drop back into sleep.

A string of texts has come in from Jason during the exchange with Nate.

You're a cool guy. I like you, but I get it if you weren't into it or something else happened

And I figured you're new to this whole thing

But seriously, at least tell the next guy when you're done

Cam bites his lip.

Maybe Maggie does have a point. Wren's not dangerous in any way she might have meant or worried about, but Cam has to admit that he's definitely influencing Cam's whole life. And not all of those influences are positive.

Just sated from being with Wren, skin still sticky with the imprint of Wren's fingertips and tongue, it's easy for Cam to promise himself a little more discipline. No more dropping classes and friends and blowing off phone calls from his mother.

I know it's inexcusable. And stupid to apologize now. But fwiw, I am sorry.

Jason doesn't respond. Cam can't lie to himself and pretend he's on tenterhooks waiting for absolution over the next few days, not when his resolve to manage his life and fit Wren in is completely blown to hell the next time Wren texts him. But it is a relief when Jason does text him a week later, a simple *All right* offering an acknowledgment of Cam's apology, if not acceptance. It's a small measure of karmic retribution, medicine he's glad to take.

* * *

"CAM." MAGGIE DROPS INTO THE CHAIR next to him with a mild *whoomp* sound. "What are you doing?"

His whole table is strewn with papers and books. Eyes aching, half blind from an attempt to squash as much reading into two hours as possible, Cam glances at her.

"What does it look like?"

"It looks like madness." Maggie pokes at a haphazard stack of papers, article after article on environmental law precariously balanced.

"I have an exam today in a few," he says, bending back to his reading, hoping she'll get the hint.

"I've never seen you this stressed about a class before," she says.

What's given me away? Looking down, he realizes that his shirt is buttoned wrong, and wrinkled. There is a ketchup stain on the knee of his jeans and, now that he's surfaced, he's pretty sure his hair must be sticking up all over the place from when he buried his hands in it while hanging his head over his books.

"I—" He closes his eyes. They're dry and throbbing. "I'm a little behind."

"Cam—"

He really isn't in the mood for the warning edge in her tone. "Maggie," he says, taking a breath so he doesn't snap at her, "not now."

"But—"

"Not. Now," he says between his teeth. "You're free to quiz me tonight or anytime today past six, okay?" He knows he deserves it; part of him recognizes that he needs it, and hopes that a lecture will wake him up from the fog Wren has him in.

Maggie isn't pleased; her lips are tight and white. She makes a show of pulling out her phone. "I'll pencil you in," she snaps and leaves. Cam sighs raggedly and turns back to his books. He's really not doing well enough in this course to go after her and apologize right now.

Suddenly his phone starts to ring, the sound muffled from wherever it's marooned under drifts of paper. He locates it eventually under his textbook and the notebook he had stacked under that.

For the first time since this race started, with Wren barreling faster and faster through his life, Cam turns off his phone without looking at the screen. It could be anyone, but Cam can't risk knowing it is Wren; even though he knows that Wren cannot actually compel him through the phone, Cam also knows there's something so addictive about Wren that he has no faith in his power to resist.

WREN PULLS THE PHONE AWAY from his ear, stares at the screen where his call seems to have been dropped and frowns. He presses the call button again, but this time it goes straight to voicemail.

He doesn't leave a message. It's not the first time Cam's not picked up immediately. Wren puts his phone down and forces himself to turn back to the dinner he's throwing together, shaking the vegetables in his pan before they can burn. It's early—only five—but it's been a day. He's wound tight and wonders how soon Cam will return his call; the longest he's ever gone is about half an hour. It was totally forgivable—he'd been in the shower; he wasn't dressed or properly dried, of course; and as soon as he'd seen the missed call, he called Wren back. The image of Cam naked and shower-wet is a powerful antidote to any negativity. Actually, that image is working for Wren right now.

Still, a glass of wine with dinner is more than welcome. The scent of ginger pork stir-fry fills his tiny kitchen. Maybe he'll make Cam wait a little, too: sip his wine slowly and read, taking the time to savor every bite of his dinner, drawing it out and keeping Cam guessing as to when Wren might call him back.

IT'S A WONDERFUL PLAN, INSOFAR as half of it works. Wren does enjoy his dinner and savors his wine—a lovely bottle his parents bought him on their last visit as a gift for his birthday. But Cam doesn't call back. As the hours tick by, Wren finds himself drinking another glass to soothe himself until Cam does call; his skin feels too tight and he's on edge. After that glass, he has another to calm him down when he starts to feel annoyed, and the last glass, the dregs of the bottle, is to help him forget because the silence from his phone feels more and more like rejection, and rejection is something Wren promised himself he'd never let another man make him feel.

Nora comes home to find him limp on the couch, covered in tortilla chip crumbs, *Cupcake Wars* blaring on the TV.

"All right," Nora says. He ignores her; either she'll read him or will just know; it's pretty obvious he's a mess. "Let's get you to bed."

Wren makes a face, and then scoots to make room at the couch near his head. She sighs and picks the empty bag of chips from his chest, attempting to brush the crumbs off of him and into her hand. She dumps them into the bag and settles down, pillowing his head on her lap. Wren closes his eyes. Her skirt is an incredibly soft cotton; her fingers are perfectly gentle threading through his hair. He closes his eyes; her nearness and kindness and the safety of being with someone who knows him—one of the only people he feels this safe with—brings him near to tears. He burrows a bit more.

"Do I have to talk about it?" he mumbles.

"Not if you're not ready," Nora says. Wren swallows the hard knot of tears in his throat and exhales, breathing deeply, slowly.

He's overreacting and can't bring himself to stop, but at least now he doesn't have to talk about it.

Wren wakes the next morning with a headache from the wine and a crick in his neck from sleeping on the couch. His mouth feels as if it's been lined in cotton batting and his eyes water from the assault of sunlight pouring through the window. He sits up slowly, with one hand shading his eyes the other braced on the couch. The screen of his phone is too bright when he thumbs it open to read the time and check if he has any messages.

He doesn't.

JERKING OFF IN THE SHOWER almost seems like a good idea. Even through the hangover, Wren considers it. Cam could probably not care less, but it seems like a sort of *fuck you* to do it without the rush of heat fucking Cam brings. He'd be getting off out of messed up spite, not because Cam is brought him to pleasure.

In the end, the hangover and the sour taste in his mouth at the thought of Cam stop him. There's no way not to think of Cam, not when he is somehow the only thing Wren sees when he closes his eyes to fantasize.

Wine always brings him the worst hangovers; his eyes are bloodshot and his bones ache, even after his shower. Going back to bed sounds like the best idea; burrowing in his covers and the soft familiarity of his room, his private refuge, would be so welcome. But he has a class, and Wren is a responsible student.

Bagel in hand, phone held indecisively in the other, Wren heads for the door. When he checked to gauge if he had time to sit down and eat after his shower, he'd seen a message from Cam, *finally*. He'd managed to ignore it while dressing, choosing a soft gray shirt with a row of horizontal buttons at the collar and ragged jeans. He's feeling disheveled and doesn't mind dressing as he feels. Also, they're comfortable clothes. Wren could use some comfort.

Sunshine stabs at his eyes when he exits his apartment. Wren curses and digs through his bag for sunglasses. He rarely wears them—they make his eyes feel funny—but right now, that can't be worse than this. It's not until he's in class, notebook laid out carefully in front of him, that Wren gives in to the urge and opens his phone. He finds two simple messages.

I'm sorry

and

Call me when you can?

Wren deletes them, wondering why Cam wouldn't just call him, before shutting down that line of thought: under that wondering is a small desire for something from Cam. Some sort of pursuit.

He shakes his head and lays his phone flat. There is no way he's going to allow himself to think or feel that way, because it tips the balance. Wren's not going to tolerate Cam breaking the rules, much less himself. No matter how much he wants Cam—how often and how deeply—Wren's rules exist for a reason; and if last night is any indication, he might be in over his head.

* * *

"I NEED ADVICE," WREN SAYS. He's at the door to Nora's room; though it was open, he'd knocked softly.

"All right." Nora sits up on her bed and crosses her legs. She pats the comforter and smiles.

"But I need you to—" Wren hovers in the doorway. "Not do the thing."

"What thing?" Nora's hair falls forward when she tilts her head.

"Where you think you know what's best and try to get me to see the light, or whatever."

Nora frowns and shifts. “What’s going on, honey?”

Wren perches carefully at the edge of her bed. Her duvet is embroidered with a lovely design: pale Japanese blossoms dripped along the contours of her bed. “I…” He thinks about what he’ll say. What advice he needs. He finds he doesn’t know. Nora can’t give him advice without being influenced by what she thinks he needs, because she never stops telling him to try again or that she knows he’s lonely.

The last few days have done nothing but prove how lonely he is, yes. But they’ve also cemented his belief that this means he needs to tamp down this thing with Cam.

Only he can’t really bring himself to end it.

“You know what?” He stands up. “Never mind.”

“Wren, honey,” Nora says, taking his hand and tugging him back down.

“I don’t think… I don’t know what to ask right now anyway,” he says. Nora watches his face for a bit before shrugging.

“Want to watch a movie?” she asks. He nods, grateful that she’s able to find ways to comfort him. “Come cuddle.”

Nora sets up some pillows next to her at the headboard. She picks through what she has on her laptop and queues his favorite—*Benny and Joon*. She lies next to him; her pillows smell like mint and tea tree oil and *her,* and when she nestles in next to him, pulling a blanket over them both, he turns until his cheek is pressed against her shoulder.

CHAPTER FOURTEEN

THINGS WREN IS GOOD AT: writing, comforting people and creating and maintaining order. He knows how to create what most people find intangible or might not notice. He's excellent at making spaces that convey comfort or ease or retreat. He can soothe and give pleasure in equal measure. And he knows how to place everything in his world in a way that feels safe for him.

What he's doing with Cam doesn't feel safe or ordered, which is a red flag. But after a few days, Wren doesn't want to stop, tells himself that is just the point: It's not that he can't stop, he simply doesn't *want* to. That means he needs to work harder at maintaining the upper hand. Right now he just has to reestablish his role and put this all to rights so that he and Cam can carry on the way he intended.

Six, upper east by the agriculture books, he texts Cam.

Okay, Cam responds immediately, which is pleasing. Then, *Thank you*, which sits strangely, because it feels sexy but somehow unsettling. That thank you should be everything he wants, right?

"YOU MADE ME WAIT," WREN says without preamble. Cam's eyes are hooded and at Wren's words he looks a little troubled. Still, his hands reach for Wren unerringly. When his thumbs wind into

Wren's belt loops to pull him in, Wren doesn't bother to repress the shiver rolling through him.

"I had—" Cam starts.

"Shush," Wren whispers, lips already millimeters from Cam's.

It's not only hunger that slams through him then, and not just hunger that he bleeds into Cam. Still, Wren has a plan, and he's going to execute it to the letter.

"THAT WAS—" CAM PULLS HIS shaking fingers through his hair, gasping as he comes down. Wren's hands work to tuck Cam back into his jeans. Arousal and a desperate need for completion are wrecking him. It's hard to see straight, and harder to hold on to the steps he was going to execute to shape this encounter the way he sees fit.

"We should talk," he says. His voice is gravelly and unsteady, and Cam's hand on his shoulder is searing hot.

"Um," Cam blinks, "a good talk?"

Wren laughs with only a trace of bitterness and just says, "A talk."

They find a secluded table. Cam pulls out a chair for Wren, then one for himself.

"I made rules," Wren starts.

"Yes," Cam agrees.

"If you don't follow them—"

"Did I break a rule?"

"Did we agree that I am in charge?" Wren says with a dangerous sweetness.

"Yes, and that's—"

"So when you didn't return my call..." Wren raises an eyebrow and waits for Cam to rise to his lead.

"I wanted to," Cam starts, looking troubled. "But I'm falling behind in school and I—"

"Oh, I didn't ask to hear excuses," Wren cuts in. Cam bites his lip and looks away, and a cresting surge of frustration rolls through the room and straight through Wren. *Fuck*. It's a lot easier to balance this when he doesn't actually care that much about whom he's playing with.

"If I don't do well in school, I'll have to figure something out. I'm here on scholarship, and if I lose that... I am *not* going back to Nebraska," Cam says stubbornly, and Wren has to work hard to suppress the surprise that wants to show clearly on his face. Oh, the things he doesn't know about Cam! He's hungry for them, even when he knows he has to shut that curiosity down.

"I do suppose that if you have to drop out of school, this—" he gestures between them, "might be harder to do."

Cam nods. His fingers are splayed wide on the table. Wren picks at the remnants of a sticker that had been plastered to it.

"Give me a schedule of when you're free," Wren concedes. He hates making concessions. "When it says you're free, you're free, do you understand?"

"Absolutely," Cam says without hesitation.

"You're gonna tell me what you want. Make me a list. We'll see from now on if you can be good enough to earn those things," Wren says.

"I could just tell you right now, because the thing I really want—"

"No," Wren interrupts softly, hungry eyes searching Cam's. "I want a list of your fantasies. Even the ones you don't know if you really want but that linger in the back of your head." Wren tilts his head and smiles; it's not a comforting smile but a coaxing, deliciously dirty one. "Even the ones that make you feel unsure and slightly ashamed." *The ones tucked into your heart*. "The ones that will be hardest." Wren really knows now that having this control seems like owning Cam.

"Where do you live?" Wren asks, and tries to ignore the way Cam's face lights up. Cam digs through his bag until he finds a pen, a bright green one decorated with Hulk stickers. He searches out a semi-dry napkin and writes his address on it. He has to go back over the lines several times before it's actually visible.

"Can you read that?" he pushes it across the table to Wren. Wren holds back a smile.

"You went to the trouble to find a fancy pen," he laughs, "but not a piece of paper?"

"Oh." Cam shrugs. "My friend gave this to me as a joke."

Wren smiles wider and shoots him a wink. "I'll see you later," he says, subtle notes of temptation and challenge in his voice.

THAT NIGHT, IN THE COVER of an empty room, Cam sits to work on his list. It starts simply, because what he's wanted is simple and immediate: to get Wren off. Cam's craved this for as long as they've been together. Well, not *together,* Wren would never use that word. Whatever he would call it, Cam has never let himself think beyond the most obvious methods of getting Wren off: with his hands, his mouth, or even just by rubbing against him the way that Wren does for him sometimes, rolling his thigh steadily, sinuously and hard between Cam's legs. Once, he ordered Cam to ride it, to rock himself against Wren's stillness until he came, jittering and off balance.

What would that be called, though? There's a name for everything, Cam knows. It's just a matter of learning. Trepidation—or something like it—follows the movement of Cam's finger over the wheel of his mouse. He touches it to bring up the screen of his laptop and tries to think of a good phrase to search for what he wants.

Cam has never been much of a porn watcher because it just never felt right; it turned him on but he was disconnected from what he was seeing, as if distant from pleasure. Maybe this was because he'd been watching men and women together. After he met Jason and kissed him, he'd tried other kinds of porn a few times. But nothing matched the feeling he was seeking, a replication of that stolen moment in the library with Wren. For the most part, after that, Cam had stuck with what his brain supplied him.

He can't manage this search without coming across porn. Apparently, the word for what he wants is frottage, which is just ridiculous. He writes it down anyway. Nate isn't due home for a while and Wren obviously expects more than three items on his list. He doubts that any of them are boundary-pushing. And Wren seems to need more from him, seems to be seeking something specific.

Porn of all kinds filters through his computer in the next hour. Some acts he never even knew existed. Rimming, felching, fisting—all these things make his cheeks darken so much he's afraid he might overheat, even if he doesn't particularly want them. Cam can't begin to unpack his reaction to these things; partly because they're embedded in videos containing other sex acts that he discovers really, really turn him on.

At ten to two, with Nate due home very soon, Cam's body is helplessly throbbing for release. Some things he's been watching—like fingering and anal—he now desperately wants to try, but he can't take the time to test whether fingering feels good right now, and he has an idea that Wren wouldn't be okay with receiving. If it were him—well, *when* it is, because even though Cam feels uncertain, the idea of having Wren do it to him makes everything he has stand to attention—if it were him, he imagines, he'd feel very vulnerable. Most of the men in the videos he's seen actually go *soft* before it starts, only regaining their erections after a little while. Cam isn't sure why, but even that appeals to him.

He writes his list in order of things he's most comfortable with and wants the most, down through the harder things to write. Wren had told him to write everything, so, with a few deep breaths, he does. Once he's written the last—rimming—he's shaking.

There's really no time for Cam to linger when he finally has to jerk himself off and it's a risk to do so with Nate so close to home, but Cam pulls his cock out of his pants and sets a fast pace from the start. It's not a new realization anymore, how much the threat of being seen or caught turns him on. Turns out that works when he's alone, too.

Cam comes mere minutes before Nate's arrival. He's cleaned up and sitting limp in his desk chair, still breathing hard, when Nate gets in. The room probably smells of come, and his face must still be red, but Nate ignores it. Nate's a pretty sexual person, so Cam is almost positive the shoe has been on the other foot.

* * *

Is he gone? Wren texts the next afternoon. Cam had emailed him the list, as well as his schedule. He's hopeful that the list means they're going to progress to things that involve some nudity on Wren's part—something he'd really rather do where they have privacy and time. With that in mind, he'd added times when Nate wouldn't be home.

Yes, Cam texts back with tingling fingers.

He showers quickly, trims and grooms and styles the way Maggie has coached him to. Even though he hopes to have to take them off, Cam chooses the tightest jeans he has and a shirt that shows off his biceps. If he were going out, he might pick something new from his wardrobe, something more structured or daring. With the promise of privacy and time, Cam wants something he can take off easily should he be so lucky. As much as he's here for Wren to play with, he's going to be sure to do everything he can to try get his own way, too.

When Wren breezes in, not bothering to knock, Cam's already caught in his web. Wren's gotten so used to Cam, so adept at compelling him, that he can do it from greater distances now. Cam starts stripping as soon as the door is closed; it's the first thing Wren tells him to do. He has a bit of trouble with the pants. Wren doesn't move at all while he struggles out of them. He takes off his boxers as well.

"Good boy," Wren purrs, still standing by the door when Cam is finally free of them. "Lie on the bed."

Cam's head spins a bit—this feels like going zero to sixty in no time flat—but the driving *do, do, do* chanting in his blood is what he listens to.

"Spread your legs a little." Wren finally moves, setting his bag down and stepping toward the end of the bed. Cam has to battle an upwelling of uncertainty and embarrassment. "No, no," Wren murmurs. He makes sure to connect with Cam's eyes before bringing his enjoyment, his excitement to the surface. And so Cam easily spreads his legs as far as his hips and the bed allow.

"Touch yourself, just a little," Wren says. His eyes travel down Cam's body and Cam can almost feel it, a sensual caress from his neck to his hard dick.

Cam palms it slowly, lightly. He's never been naked like this before, on display and in such bright light. With Maggie it was always in the dark. Foiled against Wren, who is wearing a black double-layer hoodie with a complicated network of zippers and light green, skintight pants, Cam is doubly conscious of his own nudity.

Wren says quietly, "Now your balls." Cam blushes furiously but cups them and rolls them experimentally. "Perfect," Wren breathes, something nearly reverent in his voice. He sits at the end of the bed and crawls between Cam's spread legs. Wren sits back on his own legs and just watches. Cam's hand starts to work the way he wants it to, over the head, fingering the glans, collecting droplets of pre-come; he feels himself throb against the heat of his palm. He brings his other hand into play, tugging and tracing his balls.

When Cam starts to breathe harder, Wren gives him a devious smile and begins to touch him as well—not his dick or balls or even up near his groin; instead, Wren's fingers travel over his ankles. Down the ticklish arches of his feet. Behind his knees, which tickles, too, but also sends hot pinpricks through his body. Cam arches a little, beginning to push up into his hand. He starts to lick his palm to ease the friction, but Wren stops him.

"Tsk, tsk." He wags his finger playfully. "Not yet. Don't want you too close. We're just warming up."

Cam slows his strokes. Wren puts his hands against the insides of his knees and pushes so that they're spread farther and up in the air. Cam gasps; he's so exposed like this.

"You love it," Wren tells him, and suddenly Cam wishes he could do more, spread himself farther and let Wren see everything and anything he wants. When Wren's finger traces up his crack, Cam has to close his eyes. He's never, *ever* touched himself there. Since making his list, he has hoped Wren would be the first to do it; even if it were to feel good, touching himself this way, Cam hasn't wanted to risk it being weird or *not* feeling good when he knows Wren will make it incredible.

"Hold your balls up," Wren commands. Cam does. Wren shifts around; Cam's eyes are closed, because he's sure that if he looks at Wren, he'll never be able to hold on to the orgasm they're both working to keep at bay.

"There's not enough room," Wren complains. "Lie sideways with your ass at the edge of the bed." Wren's not wrong; he's quite a bit shorter than Cam, who barely fits onto the dorm-issue bed. He has no idea what Wren's going to do, but he obeys blindly. "Keep them spread." Wren nudges Cam's legs until he is holding them up with hands behind his knees. Cam opens his eyes in time to see Wren steal a pillow and settle on his knees on the floor.

"What—" Cam has to stop to swallow. "What are you going to do?"

"You gave me a list," Wren says lightly, almost impishly. "I figured we'd start with the hardest and see if you can be a good boy about it."

"Holy—" Cam gasps, because Wren doesn't give him any warning before spreading Cam's ass cheeks and sealing his mouth over Cam's hole. "*Oh god,*" he moans, completely off guard and a little trepidatious. "I don't know..."

"Quiet." Wren pulls away and lightly bites the sensitive inside of Cam's thigh. "You trust me or you walk away. Those are the rules."

"But—" Cam stops. Wren has started again without waiting, applying tiny, light licks to the rigid edges of his hole, and it feels *so good*, so incredibly good; nerves he's never known he has are lighting up like Christmas lights all over his body. Some part of his mind tumbles with anxiety and constant worry—*is it gross? Do I smell weird, taste weird*? He had no idea Wren would do this, start from the end of the list, and he wishes he'd had an extra hour—or three—to *prepare*.

"I know you like this," Wren says against his skin, his mouth and breath moist and warm. "*God*, I can feel it." He noses up the length of Cam's erection, suckling at the head a little while his thumb presses lightly against Cam's hole. Suddenly a hunger Cam has never imagined consumes him; he wants something inside him. Wants *Wren* inside him where he feels suddenly empty.

"Oh, f–fuck—" Cam arches and tries to grind down onto Wren's finger, body caught between opposing poles of need, wanting to thrust further into Wren's mouth but also to push down onto the sweet tease of the finger barely breaching him. "Please, *please*," he begs.

"Please what?" Wren says, pulling off of his dick. His enjoyment is obvious, the teasing clear in his voice.

"More," Cam gasps.

"Well, I do have a list to work through," Wren taunts before removing his thumb. He presses it against Cam's perineum and closes his mouth against his hole again, burrowing into the divide between his cheeks. He keeps Cam on the edge and guessing, going from hard and fast licks to light suckles and flickers of his tongue. Pleasure rolls through Cam like storms roiling, swamping him until he almost can't breathe. His asshole begins to pulse, and it's incredibly strange but so pleasurable to feel himself open so easily for Wren's finger.

"Can I touch myself?" he manages to ask.

"No," Wren says, almost absently. "You're going to come like this." Wren's thumbs dig his cheeks open even farther; his hands grip Cam so hard he hopes he'll have bruises. Wren hums, licks over Cam sloppy and fast and then, without warning, stiffens his tongue and probes until he's breached Cam's hole. He massages the supple give of Cam's ass and presses and presses until he's further in, a thing Cam would never have thought someone might *actually* do and that feels like nothing he has words for.

"Come now," Wren says with steel and confidence, then pushes his thumb in and Cam does just that, crying out loudly, pulling his legs back as far as he can to milk just a little more, as much as he can, out of his orgasm.

When it's over, Wren helps him ease his shaking legs down, then nudges and helps him move until he's properly on the bed.

Cam keeps his arm over his face; there's something free-falling and strange and incredible about this moment of coming down. He loses himself in it, letting himself bask in a way he's never been able to before. Everything is usually so rushed and furtive, risky and *public* that Cam has to scrounge for the strength to pull himself together. He's aware sometimes of Wren gently nudging him in those moments.

Right now, though, the silence is almost complete but for their breathing. Floating in this silence is a luxury, new and now, deeply needed. After a moment he hears the whisper of tissues being pulled from a box. Wren perfunctorily cleans him off.

"Sorry," he croaks. Wren's hand pets his shoulder briefly, and Cam finally lets himself open his eyes. He blinks against the bright lights. Wren looks... different. His eyes are wide in what seems almost like surprise. His lips, darker than Cam's ever seen them, tremble. Cam doesn't need any of Wren's abilities to catch that Wren is overwhelmed. The only thing Cam knows how to offer is what he himself would want.

"Kiss me?" he asks.

Beautifully, Wren doesn't resist. His clothes are rough against Cam's skin; all those zippers are so cold where Cam radiates heat. When Wren drapes himself on top of Cam, his body is heavier than Cam had imagined. Wren kisses Cam softly, seeking something, and Cam wants to believe it's from a feeling of closeness, something sweet like the gratitude he feels right now. He cannot believe he just did that—that he let Wren do that. Hulled and shaking, Cam lets his hands wander because even after that perfect storm of pleasure, there is an itch under his skin for more.

"Cam." Wren pulls away from the kiss when Cam's hands start to struggle with Wren's shirt and its endless supply of zippers. "I haven't—"

"Please let me," Cam entreats. "You wanted me to be good, right?" He teases, "Don't I get a reward?"

"That orgasm wasn't enough of a reward?" Wren's eyebrow arches, a fleeting, crooked smile flickering across his face.

"You saw the list," Cam's voice is huskier than he knew it could be. His eyes follow Wren's mouth. "You know what I want most." He pulls Wren down and in by his hips until they are flush. "And I can tell you want it too."

Wren looks away; despite that, he grinds down a little, as if he can't help his body's reaction.

THIS IS NOT THE PLAN. Using Cam's list his own way, on Wren's own terms, was. The things Cam wants most—simple things that made Wren squirm when he saw how many are things Cam wants to *do to him*—are all meant to be teased out, to be held aloft.

Wren is not stupid; he knew how much rimming Cam would turn him on. But he's always been able to count on his own very well-honed self-control and has never doubted it. Then again, he's never had Cam, cracked open and soft everywhere, nakedly vulnerable with those deep cocoa bedroom eyes, persuading him to give in. He never suspected Cam could be like this, so easy in the aftermath, so open and sensual. Wren can't remember a time he felt like that. No, he won't let himself remember.

Cam's fingers slide around until they cup Wren's ass and his fingertips dig into the crease between Wren's cheeks and thighs; he leans up to kiss the corner of Wren's mouth carefully and traces his tongue gently across Wren's lower lip. Wren sighs into it, sinking into the lush warmth of Cam's mouth, because *this* his rules allow. Kisses, he's bargained for. Cam's fingers explore him carefully, down the fabric of his pants over his thighs and under his shirt to map the dip of his spine. It's not until something too hot and needful spikes inside that Wren is even aware that he's moving, rolling his dick against Cam's thigh. His breath shivers out around a helpless whimper; it's so *good*. It's been so long since he let someone be like this with him. And it's not been hard, after so long, to convince himself that he can do just as well for himself as anyone else can, which is a fucking delusional lie, Wren realizes with startling clarity, when he starts to really pump against Cam.

"Let me touch you," Cam breathes into his ear, and nips gently at the edge of his earlobe. His hands span Wren's waist, and *oh* he feels so *small* in the wide span of that grip. Excitement shoots through him and he groans. There's something in him that revels in the loss of control. He's not exactly helpless, but suddenly he just doesn't care to fight it anymore. Wren rides that surging wave, nodding and exhaling a broken *yes*, crushing his mouth back over Cam's.

He knows it will hardly last, he's so close. But he manages to pull back enough to let Cam's hands work his pants open, then almost cries out when one snakes in and grips him. It's awkward and a tight fit between their bodies, but it doesn't take more than two thrusts into Cam's fist for Wren to start coming. He bites down on Cam's lip and moans into his mouth, working his hips in corkscrews.

"Oh *fuck*," is all he can manage once he's rolled off of Cam and onto his back, gasping like a fish out of water. When he opens his eyes, he finds Cam propped up on his elbow, watching him, taking him in from head to toe. Wren smirks; Cam's gaze keeps straying to his softening cock, still peeking out of his pants.

"I've never been with a guy like this before," Cam says sheepishly when he realizes he's been caught. Wren sits up abruptly, Cam's words striking him like ice water.

"You said you weren't new," he says tersely.

Cam sits too, more calmly. "I'm not. I've had sex... with a girl. I dated a guy but... I found you again, before things got that far."

"That's…" Wren scrubs his hand over his face and then realizes he's still partly undressed. He gets himself together, and his clothes, pulled into order, encapsulate him like armor.

"I didn't lie," Cam says quickly, resting his hand on Wren's shoulder. "What was I going to do? Find some guy to fuck so I could tell you I wasn't new to two kinds of sex?"

Cam has a point. But still, it doesn't sit right with him. It's like taking something, being Cam's first and manipulating him—whether with permission or not—when firsts should belong to someone… special. "I don't want to take anything from you," he says finally. Cam cocks his head and looks at him questioningly. "I mean," Wren clarifies, "like that. Relationship things or, like, first time things."

"Wren, I don't care about that," Cam explains. "That's never been a thing I've thought about."

"Cam, I don't get the feeling you thought about this kind of stuff that much to begin with," Wren shoots back.

"How would you—?"

"I just sensed it, okay?" Wren snaps. He's not sure if reading Cam from the get-go could be seen as a violation of his privacy—Wren tries to be very careful about that—but from the start, it had been almost impossible to ignore Cam's energy.

"Maybe you're right," Cam says after a while. He situates himself so his back is against the wall and looks at Wren candidly. "You made the rules, Wren, and I agreed to them before this really started. This is what I want." He takes Wren's hand and puts it on his chest, like Wren had before. "Can you read that?"

And he can, it's so clear, Cam comes through to Wren with no static when he tunes in. Wren closes his eyes and counts the beats of Cam's heart and breathes in time; for a crystal clear moment, he feels incredibly connected, dialed into a feedback loop of something *right*.

Wren snatches his hand back and straightens his clothes, rolling quickly off of Cam's bed. He feels scared and out of control and messy inside. "I have to go; I have work," he says, exiting the room with a slammed door before Cam can say anything more.

CHAPTER FIFTEEN

IT TAKES A WHILE FOR CAM to put himself together after that. He's never done well with emotional whiplash. While Peyton's erratic moods and behavior had never been directed at him, they had always dominated the family home, filled every room with edges and foreboding. Never knowing when Peyton might butt up against their parents or school or any sort of authority, when things might go from calm and predictable to the special tornadoes they all made of their emotions had always been more stressful to Cam than her actual behavior.

Being with Wren is an awful lot like being sucked into those winds. Cam isn't lying when he says he doesn't care about the idea of firsts. He does, however, care about the fact that he'd let himself be so open, so unfettered and utterly naked for Wren—fleetingly, *beyond* sex—only to be left alone and confused and frankly, angry.

It's incredibly hard to think clearly when you're naked with the residue of come on your stomach, ass still fluttering from the sensation of someone's mouth against it. Cam has never in his life dreamt of feeling how Wren just made him feel. And he hates being angry. Rather than focus on that when he knows he's being dangerously irrational, Cam forces himself to take yet another shower and gather himself.

By the time Nate gets home, Cam feels put back together and almost ready to analyze what the hell just happened.

WREN SHAKES THE WHOLE WAY home. He stumbles into his apartment, which is thankfully empty, and only when he takes off his shoes does he realize he's left his bag at Cam's.

"Fuck, fuck, *fuck*!" Wren threads his fingers through his hair and tugs, kicking the base of the door. He checks; his phone is still in his pocket, thank god. But there are other things he needs, books and notes for class, his wallet, his fucking *wallet*. What the hell is he going to do?

Wren slams himself into his room, frantically scrounging around his desk until he finds some spare cash. No matter that he has no need for it right now; until he can figure out what step to take next, the safety net of not *absolutely* needing his bag is a tiny comfort.

Wren flops onto his bed. It smells wonderful under his face. It's too early for dinner or sleep, and he's too raw for conversation or interaction. Instead he just tries to let himself drift in the comfort of his little cave. He rolls onto his back and appreciates the cocooning affect of the half-canopy sweeping from the ceiling to the wall, where it cascades behind his bed. Something about the fabric partly surrounding his bed makes it feel safe, close and comforting.

After a while, Nora lets herself in. Other than noting her arrival, Wren isn't focused on much more than trying to hold it together. Little reminders of Cam invade his senses; his stomach feels grimy with come, and the faintest wisps of scent, Cam's natural smell, linger on his clothes. If he let himself imagine it, Wren might still taste Cam in his mouth.

What persists, though, is that split-second connection that had hummed through all of his bones and into his chest and landed deep inside his most private, yearning self. Wren has to bite back tears and will himself not to go there mentally. He just isn't strong enough. He's not.

CAM NOTICES WREN'S BAG ON his way out to dinner. It's been a few hours—long enough for him to calm down and to start to assess what might have just happened. The thing is, he's not sure what Wren is emotionally capable of. Because once he's removed his own feelings and insecurities from the situation, it's suddenly very clear to Cam how scared Wren is. Of what, exactly, Cam's not sure; but now that he's perceived the fear, he's entirely sure of its truth.

"What's that?" Nate toes the strap of the bag when he notices Cam looking at it.

"A friend left it," Cam says absently.

"Are they gonna come get it or meet us for dinner?" Nate asks, pulling the door open and waiting for Cam to make up his mind.

"I just noticed it, honestly," Cam says. "I'll text and see what they want to do." He purposely avoids saying *he* because he's not ready for Nate to start asking questions.

"'Kay." Nate locks the door behind them and Cam strides away. He'll text Wren soon enough. Wren still needs time; Cam's not sure why he knows this, but he is sure of it.

* * *

WREN CAN ONLY HOLD OUT for a day before he has to get his bag. It has his schoolbooks in it, and his calendar, which he's always found easier to keep on paper than in his phone.

He refuses to go unprepared. They had an agreement, and a deep connection wasn't part of the rules. He needs to remind Cam that he's—they're—there for a specific reason. He needs to walk in and control the situation. Make Cam remember what this is about.

Wren is at his desk, toying with a mechanical pencil that refuses to work properly while he sketches out potential game plans, when he feels Nora enter the apartment. There's no noise, and she doesn't call out; but he feels something desperately sad permeate the walls and his skin and his heart.

He approaches her closed door cautiously. They've both been careful not to read or absorb each other; living with someone and maintaining privacy is hard when both have gifts, but they've managed pretty well. Wren has *never* felt her emotions so clearly before.

"Nora?" His knock is almost inaudible.

"Come on in," she calls. He opens the door to find her cross-legged at the head of her bed. Her hair is down, a mess of tangled waves hiding her face; she must have had it up in a bun.

"Can I sit?" Wren proceeds with caution. There's so much hurt radiating from her, it's hard for him to breathe.

"Yeah." She looks up. Her eyes are red and wet; her cheeks are dry but for tear tracks.

"Honey, what—" he tries to scoot in to hold her, but she just shakes her head and cranes her torso away.

"Wren..." She takes a deep breath and looks down. "I know we don't ask each other, but could you..."

"What do you need?" he asks.

"Don't read, but can you make this go away? For a bit? It's..." She starts to cry; it's impossible not to want to hold her. Wren bites his lip. She holds her hands out. "It's too much."

"Of course." Wren folds her hands in his; they're cold and small and he has to push back at the furious crest of pain that transmits through the touch. He closes his eyes, breathes deeply and pushes it back, wills it from her body. It takes a while, and a lot of effort and concentration. By the time he's managed it away, he's breathing hard and a headache is forming at his temples.

"Wren, you can..." Her eyes are open, the palest blue he's ever seen. "You can stop, I know it's a lot."

"No, *no*." He's not willing to just take something away. The loveliest aspect of his gift is what he can give, how he can make other people feel good. He takes a shaking breath, pulls from his core and slowly, achingly, fills her with comfort, with rest. With love.

He holds her there, through the increasing buzz of pain in his head that spreads into his chest and seeps into his bones. He washes her in comfort until she's nodding off. With what strength he has left, he arranges her comfortably and covers her with a blanket, saturating her with love as she slips into sleep so that she may dream in peace and wake up easily.

AFTER THAT, HE HAS TO SLEEP. His class and work shift and fucking bag all have to wait, because what he's done for Nora has been an incredible strain on his resources. Emotionally, taking in her pain was brutal, too. Not knowing what happened nags at him sorely, both during his twilight nap and waking hours, but he knows that questions will only shorten the lifespan of the comfort he gave her.

Wren wakes after a four-hour nap with incredibly sore muscles and a headache hangover. Nora is still out cold; his prolonged state of curiosity only makes him more irritated. The list of potential plans and outcomes on his desk mocks him. Cam has texted him twice—once to inform Wren that he has the bag, and once more recently to ask if everything is all right, since Wren was supposed to pick it up hours ago.

I'm on my way.

Wren knows it's a mistake, because he's carrying something ugly inside, and there's a possibility it will spill over. But there's also an aching, sharp energy in him that he's sure Cam will fix, that being with Cam will calm.

"WANT TO TALK ABOUT WHAT—"

"Shut up and take your clothes off," Wren interrupts him. Cam just raises an eyebrow and does what Wren needs. Not wants, but *needs*, he knows.

"Now what?" Cam asks quietly, standing naked by his desk. His cock is soft and he's lightly covered with sweat. He hadn't expected to find Wren waiting by his door when he came back from his run. "You realize I'm filthy right now, right?"

"I don't care." Wren makes an aborted gesture with his hand before taking a deep breath and closing his eyes. "Actually, if you must know, I like it."

Cam smiles and leans back against his desk, jolting a little when the cold wood presses against his naked ass. "So?"

"So sit back a little more and spread your legs," Wren commands. His face is closed off, the smile having dropped away once he spoke again. Cam swallows and does exactly what Wren asks; without saying so or acknowledging it, Cam knows he's giving Wren something too.

"Touch yourself," Wren says, and so Cam does.

"Are you even going to kiss me?" he asks quietly. Wren just stares at him. The only change in Wren's expression is the tiniest twitch of an eyebrow.

"Not right now," he says after a long minute of watching Cam stroke his cock torturously slowly. "How fast do you think you can get off?" he asks conversationally.

"I have no idea," Cam answers honestly. "Are we testing this out?"

"I'm curious about something, is all," Wren says.

"Care to share?" Cam closes his eyes briefly and centers his attention on his body.

"Get off as fast as you can," Wren says. "Without me."

Cam puzzles over this before realizing that Wren means *without being compelled*. Which is *so* not a problem. Wren might be able to bring him higher than anything he's felt before, but the desire he carries inside for Wren doesn't ever *need* that help.

His balls are velvet-soft in his cupped hand, and in the other, his dick feels long and sensitive. Cam has only to focus on the recent memory of Wren's tongue and finger edging into him to bring himself right up close to the edge.

"So fast," Wren murmurs, and, through the haze of his own pleasure, Cam sees a little wonder.

"'Cause it's you," he manages. Wren's eyebrows narrow immediately, and just as quickly he pushes Cam into an orgasm so hard that Cam almost loses his balance and falls over.

"Fuck," Cam gasps. It's over so fast, it's brutal and somehow unsatisfying. "What did you—"

"That's what you want, right?" Wren says. Cam shakes his head, feeling stupid and addled. Why does Wren sound so *bitter*?

"No, no, I— I want... what about you?" He swallows and Wren just shakes his head. He picks up his bag, which is still by the door, and turns to leave.

"Don't worry about it," he calls over his shoulder, pulling the door open without a care that Cam is naked and in full view of the hall. "I'll call you later."

And with that, he's gone.

THAT UGLY BALL OF EMOTIONS he carried to Cam eases through Wren on his way to class. His arousal fades quickly, and he has to ignore the niggling feeling that leaves an acidic taste in his throat. Cam's energy and willingness to please can be a balm, a dangerous nectar calling Wren until he's helpless. His worry for Nora, his anger and confusion are less painful now. But something's still off.

"LET'S GO OUT TONIGHT," WREN bursts through the door. A week of carrying ill-fitting skin and anxiety has crested until it's almost unbearable now.

"Tonight? Wren, it's a Tuesday," Nora responds.

"I don't care," Wren replies, shrugging off his bag and rolling his shoulders. "I feel like I need to work off some energy."

"What kind of working off?" Nora asks, her face drawn with suspicion. Wren glares at her and turns to fiddle with his hair in their hall mirror, spiking it a bit, making it messier. He narrows his eyes at his reflection. He definitely doesn't look the way he's feeling.

"I'm calling Brokk and sending out the word," he calls over his shoulder. He starts flipping through his closet for something—he's not quite sure what he wants but he's feeling edgy and wanting something sexy and confident. He wants something that will fuel this itch. He wants to make mistakes tonight.

Brokk agrees to call their friends, and they settle on a time and place. In his small bathroom, Wren darkens his eyes with liner that makes the green of his irises appear almost iridescent.

"You look like you're ready for trouble," Nora observes when he comes back into the living room. He's wearing a complicated black shirt with straps and buckles and blood-red skinny jeans it's taken him ten minutes to squeeze into. He's broken out his rarely worn, steampunk-inspired boots; they give him an extra inch of height and their heft feels grounding. Confident and untouchable and excited at the prospect of making someone want him despite his inaccessibility, Wren squares his shoulders, breathes deeply and loves the calm before the storm of the power he has and uses.

"Are you coming?" Wren pulls the basic necessities out of his wallet, license and debit card, and squeezes them into his pocket. He badly wants Nora to come, and to distract her from her own reeling heartbreak.

"I'm not sure I want to bear witness to this," Nora says. "Don't you have a thing going?"

"Nora, you don't get to tell me how to live," he responds. "I made the rules. There's no fidelity clause when I play. You *know* that."

"Wren," she says softly. "You don't seem like it's just play. It doesn't feel like that when you come back from him."

"Stop. Fucking. Reading. Me." Wren has to take a deep breath to modulate his voice. Nora is the last person he wants to be unkind to. She still won't talk to him about why Matt broke up with her, or what happened, but instead insists that he stop coddling her.

"I'm *not*," she yells back. "I know you. I *love* you. It's plain as day even without your aura."

"Fuck it, I don't need this," Wren opens the door with an angry flick of his wrist.

"No, come on, please," Nora wraps a hand around his arm. "Don't leave angry. I'll come with." He sighs and stares at the wall next to her head. "Wren, I promise I just want what's best for you."

"Nora, I just need you to drop this. I know you think I need 'true love' or some bullshit. But I don't. That's more dangerous than anything I'm doing tonight. Leave it alone."

She just looks at him sadly. "Okay, come on," she says finally, tugging at his arm. "Help me pick something out."

Wren shuts the door quietly and nods. That uneasy stirring inside feels sharper and it takes more effort for him to tamp down his distress.

WREN DANCES WITH ALL THE pent-up sex he's been strapping down, losing himself in the steady, hard throbbing of bodies and heat and music. He opens himself and takes in the energy of the room. It's a tangle of fear and desire, annoyance and anger. Wren wants it all. He wants something on the edge of insanity, wants to lose himself in it. He lets boys tug him by his straps into closer dancing that's really more like grinding with intent.

Then there's a boy—sensual and dark-eyed and tall, with strong hands that pull Wren in by the small of his back—who starts kissing under Wren's ear. When he feels the shaking exhalation Wren lets loose, he starts biting a little, pulling him further in, spanning his hips, and they're both hard and together and surrounded by people on all sides. He kisses Wren with an open, wet mouth and for an intense moment, with that incredible flash of need inside, Wren thinks he can do it. But when he pulls back to whisper the words in this guy's ear, he notices for the first time how similar he is to Cam, and how he's replicating something he wants from someone else.

"*Fuck,*" Wren shouts to be heard. "I'm sorry." He pulls away and tries to ignore the frustrated frown on the other guy's face. "I can't do this. Wrong reasons." He hopes this will be explanation enough. Nameless boy gives him a resentful look and turns away. Wren fights his way through the throng of people with shaking legs and a pounding heart.

This is so fucked up. He is so *fucked*.

He exits the club; he's sweating and shaking and, for some reason, irrationally angry. It's a walk to his apartment, but he needs the dark, close air around him. The clouds completely obscure the stars. He feels anonymous but burning too bright.

I could fuck anyone I wanted, he texts Cam before he thinks better of it. It's a long time before he gets a response.

I suppose you could

Fuck this. What? *What's that supposed to mean?*

It means you made the rules. I don't have to like all of them. Do you want me to say I don't like it?

Wren takes a ragged breath. This conversation is straying dangerously into territory he's been avoiding.

I have to go, he responds, after a long minute of trying to talk himself down from a jittering high he can't explain. His phone buzzes before he can pry it into the incredibly tight pocket of his uncomfortably tight jeans.

You can always come here. If you need something

I'm not your boyfriend Cam. Don't treat me like one. His fingers fly over the screen so fast he almost sends a message full of autocorrect typos.

I'm not stupid. I know what you want this to be. I meant sex Wren. If you need someone to fuck

Wren bites his lip. It's so fucking tempting. He needs it, hard and fast and on his terms. And safe. God, Cam makes him feel so ridiculous and disjointed. Makes him do things he resists, or wants to resist.

Nate out?

Yes

Wren closes his eyes, takes ten deep breaths and tries to think clearly. But all he sees is Cam, and all he wants is Cam, and there is a restlessness in his body he knows won't quiet.

I'll be there in 15

CHAPTER SIXTEEN

"WHAT—" CAM ANSWERS THE DOOR to get a handful of Wren, sweat-damp, his hot searching lips already opening Cam's with a desperate kiss. Wren kicks the door shut behind them and begins attacking Cam's shirt, wrestling it off in seconds. "What's gotten into you?" Cam gasps, and pulls away.

"Shut up and fuck me," Wren says. He works his way down Cam's neck and chest, biting his nipples until Cam is whining into his hair, where he's buried his face. Wren smells so good—male and sweaty and like rain and grass.

"What the hell is this shirt?" Cam tries to get his hands inside it, but all the buckles on the outside seem to be binding Wren into it. "Why do your shirts always come with so much hardware?"

Wren smiles impishly and lies back on Cam's bed. "Take my boots off," he says. Cam kneels by the bed and works them off slowly. It takes him a minute of searching to figure out where to start. Wren's outfit, difficult as it is to remove, is an incredible turn-on. He looks fierce and confident, sexy and untouchable. And only Cam gets to touch.

Assuming he can get any of this off.

"Ah!" he finally finds a zipper hidden under the row of buckles. Once Wren's feet are free, Cam runs his hands up the insides of his legs and thighs, using his strength to pry Wren's legs apart, even when Wren resists a little.

"Good luck with the pants," Wren laughs. Cam crawls up on the bed and bites Wren's lips, licks them and breathes against the moist heat of his mouth.

"I have confidence, after the shoes. However... shirt?"

Wren pushes lightly on his shoulders and runs a finger over one of the buckles. "You have to undo me," he says. A small frown passes over his face when he says it, then flickers away.

Cam wants nothing more than to undo Wren. He works the straps loose slowly; they both seem to be past the frenzy of Wren's entrance. He moves on to Wren's belt, leaving the shirt open but still hanging from his shoulders. Their movements and the moments pass as if they're suspended in molasses. Together they work Wren's pants off, inch by inch. Just getting the pants past Wren's cock is a challenge because it's so hard and presses against his zipper in the constricted space. They both sigh in different sorts of relief when it's free and Cam noses it through Wren's underwear, inhaling the the utterly male smell of him. He's wanted this, wondered about it for a while, but wondering is nothing like having, not like the dizzying knowledge of how close he is to the reality of the fantasy.

He mouths over the cotton of Wren's briefs until Wren pushes him away, squirming and laughing. "Get them off, then you can get me off," he says.

They both push them down, and then Cam gently guides Wren out of his shirt. It clanks when it hits the floor and it occurs to Cam that he's divested Wren of what amounted to a suit of armor.

"You now," Wren commands.

"Can I..." Cam pauses, then traces his finger up the flushed red skin of Wren's erection. "Blow you? First?"

"*Fuck*," Wren groans. He covers his eyes with his hand. "Okay. For a bit," he concedes.

Cam doesn't want to start slow, even though he has no idea what the hell he's doing. He takes Wren in in one movement, as deep as he can, choking himself a little in the process.

"Slow," Wren tells him, and Cam feels Wren settling him, loosening the frenzy in his chest. Cam closes his eyes and pulls off by tiny increments. He takes a deep breath and kisses along the length with open-mouthed kisses and suckles at the tip. Wren is bitter on his tongue. Before very long Wren is pulling him up with impatient hands.

"No, no, too close," Wren pants.

"Can you do what you do to me? Calm yourself down?" Cam asks. Wren shakes his head and pulls Cam even closer, kissing his lips and cheeks and pushing Cam's pants down far enough so that their cocks can brush together.

"Hold on," Cam says, laughing. He pushes his pants all the way off and covers Wren's body with his. He props himself up on the bed with his elbows bracketing Wren's head. Wren is so small under him, compact and lithe and so, so sexy. His eyes glitter, new-grass green.

"Come on." Wren pushes his hips up, rolling his body against Cam's.

"Wait, lube," Cam says. He moves to pull away.

"No, like this," Wren says. There's a note of desperation in his voice. "I need to feel you. I want it rough." Cam groans, buries his face into Wren's sweet-smelling neck and then lets go, rubbing himself against Wren fast and hard. He takes Wren's hands and laces their fingers together and presses them down into the bed. He swallows Wren's whimpers, tastes his lips and tongue in sloppy kisses, listens with wonder as the tone of Wren's noises sinks lower and lower until they're both grunting. It's something animal and wild, them humping each other so desperately until Wren arches up against him, bucking against Cam so forcefully he almost rolls off. He moans so long Cam can't believe it, coming between their bodies. His come creates a wonderful slippery mess; Cam rubs himself through it, grateful for the slide. Wren wrests his hands free and grabs Cam by the ass, hitching him up and against his stomach.

"Look at me," he growls and Cam feels the punch of pleasure Wren gives him, sending his orgasm through him like seismic shocks until he's sure he's coming out of his skin with it.

"*Fuck, fuck, fuck*," he cries out. Later he'll know there is no way his hallmates didn't hear them. Perversely, he's kind of proud.

"Holy hell," Wren pants, weakly pushing Cam off of him.

"What you said." Cam stares dizzily up at his ceiling. He wants to tell Wren how incredible this is; vaguely he wonders, as he has before, what it would be like to come with Wren without being pushed.

At some point—he has no idea when or who does it—their hands are clasped tightly between their bodies. Once he's aware of it, he's careful not to move or draw attention to it. Energy circulates between them.

They're both almost dozing off, filthy and naked and sweaty, when the trill of Cam's phone jolts them. It's Peyton's ring tone, and he answers automatically, reaching over Wren's prone body to get it.

"Pey, it's one in the morning," he says in lieu of greeting.

"What can I say, I was feeling the love," she responds. Wren gives Cam a strange look. He pulls his hand away with a jerk and starts to sit up.

"No," Cam says, putting his hand on Wren's stomach.

"No, you're not feeling it?" Peyton says. Cam shakes his head and swallows.

"Sorry, no, I'm distracted. Where are you? Can I call you back at this number?"

"Ohhh, Cameron has someone thee-re," Peyton sing-songs.

"Shut up," Cam's face is flushing.

"Say no more. Call me later. Enjoy yourself," she says with a laugh.

"You didn't have to get off the phone for me," Wren pushes Cam's hand off of him and grabs some tissues.

"Don't worry about it. I wouldn't have answered, but I never know when Peyton will call next," Cam shrugs and takes the handful of tissues Wren hands him. Wren cleans himself without looking at Cam and starts to swing his legs out of the bed.

"Don't go yet," Cam says quietly. He risks a hand on Wren's shoulder.

"What, you think you'll be up for a round two?" Wren says over his shoulder. He looks back with a coquettish expression. His eyeliner is smudged and his cheeks are still a frenzied red. Cam wants to say, *It's not just sex* and *Hold my hand, please*. But that's not what Wren wants to hear and Cam wants to keep him close any way he can.

"I'm beat. But maybe if we take a break..." he leaves off suggestively. Wren takes a deep breath and then carefully lies back.

"Won't Nate be back?" he asks.

"Good point," Cam picks his phone back up.

"What are you doing?" Wren turns onto his side, fluffing Cam's pillow under his head.

"For the first time in two years, I am soxiling him," Cam says with a laugh. "I've never gotten to. Oh the power," he jokes. Wren smiles and it's the first one Cam's seen that looks true and easy.

"Help me find a good picture," Cam puts his head close to Wren's on the pillow and holds the phone up for both of them to look at.

"Of what?" Wren tilts his head to see.

"Socks," Cam says.

"What the hell, socks?"

"You know how people used to do the sock over the door thing as a signal?" Cam asks.

"Oh, yeah," Wren says.

"So Nate thought it was hilarious, but wasn't going to do it. So he started texting me the word 'socks,' and eventually we started calling it 'soxiling.' Or 'Sock Saturday,' because that's usually when I get booted. Then he started sending me pictures of funny socks."

"Hey, I have a question." Wren half sits and looks at Cam seriously. "Have you, like, come out to anyone?"

"Well, they set me up with Jason, so yeah. I mean," Cam shrugs, "I didn't come out and say the words."

"Hmm." Wren lies back down. Cam is searching for the right pair of socks when Wren stops him. "Those."

"Rainbow socks?"

"Make it official," Wren says.

"What, should I add 'Hey I'm gay' or something?" Cam jokes, copying the picture and dropping it into a text.

"If you want to. I don't know. I... when I finally came out, there was a lot of power in saying the words. It was..." Wren squints as if he's struggling to find the words. "Really affirming and liberating."

"Hmm." Cam lowers his phone for a minute and thinks.

"I probably shouldn't assume anything," Wren rushes to add. "I mean that you're gay or bi or anything."

"I think I'd say I'm gay," Cam says. He looks over at Wren seriously, examines the light flecks of gold in his eyes. "I haven't said anything to Peyton. Or my parents."

"Who *is* Peyton, anyway?" Wren asks.

"My twin sister," Cam says. Wren's eyebrows shoot up.

"Twin?"

"Yep," Cam says.

"Do you think she—they—will have a problem with it?"

Cam thinks for a moment. "Not Peyton. Knowing her, she already knows. She's always been better at figuring me out than I have." Wren snorts softly and Cam shoots him a questioning look. Wren just gestures for Cam to continue.

"I'm not... I don't know, when I was figuring this all out, I wasn't ashamed or afraid or necessarily worried about if I was gay. Am. It feels... right. My parents, though..."

"Are they conservative?" Wren asks.

"Well, we're from nowhere Nebraska. I really have no idea how they'll react, but I doubt it will be pleasant." Cam bites his lip and takes a deep breath, pushing that away. He's got Wren in his bed, talking and open-limbed and easy and he wants to capture it, stretch the moment as long as he can before Wren backs off. He tilts the phone back so Wren can see and types, *You've been soxiled. Oh and by the way, I'm gay.* This makes Wren laugh, and Cam laughs too. It does feel a little liberating; not because Nate doesn't know, but because he's not yet said the words to anyone, and it feels a little like coming home. Like rooting inside himself in a space he's never seen before.

He puts his phone back down on the nightstand and settles against Wren on the bed. "What about you?" he asks, breaking the silence.

"What about me?" Wren says, yawning widely.

"Your family. How did they react?"

Wren stiffens slightly and there's a long pause, and Cam can tell that he's somehow overstepped or drawn attention to the comfortable moment they've just shared.

"You know," Wren says, rolling up and leaning over Cam, trailing his fingers down Cam's chest, "I think we've done enough talking for the night." He starts to kiss slowly over Cam's pecs. Cam swallows the pang of disappointment and puts his hand gently on Wren's head, feeling the thick mess of his hair through his fingers.

"Well—" he starts to say, and then Wren exhales and kisses his navel and floods Cam with a desire so thick he's shocked into stillness and oversaturated in sensation. "Fuck," he says softly as the sliver of disappointment melts away. Helplessly, he arches into Wren's touch, begging for more.

* * *

"SO, A LITTLE BIRD TOLD ME that Nate got an interesting text," Maggie says over the rim of her coffee mug.

"Was the little bird actually a big-ass bird *named* Nate?" Cam shoots back.

"I cannot reveal my sources," Maggie intones, and smiles. She sets her coffee down with a grimace after a quick sip. "Why did we pick this place?"

"I'm trying new things," Cam says.

"Apparently," Maggie says. There's a trace of sarcasm in her voice. Or something like that.

Cam frowns while he tries to figure it out. "Are you upset about it?"

"Well the coffee is terrible, but the view is nice." Maggie gazes out the window; this café does have a lovely view. He's passed it countless times but only took notice recently. On a run the other afternoon, he took the time to really look at things he's passed sightlessly for months, bringing all the colors and shapes into sharp, clear relief where they used to be watercolor-blurry.

"I meant the text," Cam says patiently.

"Maybe?" Maggie shrugs.

"Maggie," he says, taking her hand gently, "It's nothing you guys didn't know. It was mostly a joke." He thinks back to the moment he'd sent the text. "Well, and..."

"And?" Maggie prompts. She's crumbling her biscotti absently and watching him intently. Cam thinks of Wren's advice, of feeling liberated. Of himself and years closed and empty and disconnected.

"Maggie, I'm gay," he finally says, his eyes steady on hers. He's shocked when they fill with tears. "No, no, don't cry, I'm sorry—"

"No," she says fiercely and shakes her head. Her fingers grip his like a vise. "Don't say sorry. I'm proud of you. That's all."

"Maggie," he says helplessly.

"I really love you, you know?" Maggie manages to say. One tear spills over and he catches it with his fingertip. "I'm sorry it didn't work out, but I'm... I'm so happy to see you like this. *You*."

Cam takes a breath and looks out the window. The sun is coming and going behind scattered clouds. Rays of light touch the pavement and buildings dramatically. Everything moves as it should.

"So what prompted you to say it to Nate?" Maggie asks.

Cam considers how to say something without telling her anything. "You know I said I can't say anything," he starts.

"Well it's not a secret that there is someone," Maggie points out. "You kicked Nate out to have a lot of sex."

"How do you know it was a lot?" he says with a smile.

"A lot of great gay sex," Maggie teases.

"Shut up," Cam blushes.

"So—"

"He was talking about when he came out. And how liberating it was just to say the words. And I've been thinking... about how I was for so long. Being me, as you said."

"Yeah," Maggie says softly.

"You... Nate... just stuff. I'm just... so much," he trips over his words. He has no idea how to articulate how much this new life has changed him. The room brightens suddenly with spilled light, shining over Maggie's hair and highlighting her smile.

"Stuff." She picks up her coffee and wrinkles her nose, but takes another sip. "That's just it."

Cam takes the coffee out of her hands and stands up. "Let's go get something good," he says.

"Perfect," she says and follows him out.

CHAPTER SEVENTEEN

"I'M HAPPY FOR YOU, WITH all the sex and all," Nate says Saturday afternoon, "but can I bring Ellie here tonight after our date?"

"Yeah." Cam shrugs easily. "I don't have plans." *Yet*. He shoots Wren a quick text, just in case, because Wren doesn't like to be surprised.

I have a thing tonight, Wren texts back immediately. Cam is surprised to feel a pang of jealousy in his stomach.

Have a good time, he texts back, trying to appear nonchalant.

Study group is never a good time, Wren sends back, and the answer calms Cam. Would sending a smile back send the wrong message? Fuck that. He does it anyway. He's not the one with the problem connecting. Maybe slow and steady and persistent will wear Wren down.

Saturday night studying at the library holds a lot less appeal when he has less to research and no hope of Wren coming in. He texts Maggie, but apparently she has study group too. Cam frowns—is he the only one who doesn't have exams soon?

Boring, he texts her. *You know you'd rather hang out with me.*

You are fun, she texts back, *but so are good grades.* She has a point.

Is there anyone else he can cajole into hanging out? It's weird; a year ago he wouldn't have minded the solitude. Now, he'd love company, but there are not many people he feels comfortable texting out of nowhere. Most of his friends, other than Maggie and Nate, are really their friends and his acquaintances. He considers going for a run, but that won't work when he can't come back to the room. Not that he could run that long, anyway. He tosses his phone on the bed with a sigh.

"Everything cool?" Nate asks. He's picking up his half of the room, which makes Cam smile. Not only has Nate mentioned Ellie several times, a complete anomaly for him, but he's also putting in *effort*. Cam doesn't say anything, though. There's a fine line with Nate as well.

"Oh yeah," Cam says. "Just figuring out what to do tonight. Apparently everyone has study group. Who has study group Saturday nights?"

"This coming from the guy who used to spend every Saturday in the library voluntarily?" Nate observes.

"Touché," Cam says. "And shut up. I'm awesome."

"Never doubted it," Nate says. "Seriously, are you okay with me booting you for the night?"

"Definitely," Cam says. "I'm a big boy. Maybe I'll go see *Frostbite Bay*. No one else seems into seeing it."

"That's 'cause it sounds super boring, dude. Can't you go do a normal thing and go see something with explosions or hot chicks?"

Cam laughs, and although it takes Nate a moment, he does too. "Well, okay, hot guys maybe."

"I guess I'm just boring at heart." Finished with studying, *unlike some people,* Cam packs his books into his backpack carefully.

Nate shoots him an unreadable look and shrugs. "If you say so."

Cam opens his mouth to ask what that means, and then lets it go. Everyone thinking they know more about him than he does is getting old. It makes him feel supremely stupid.

You're not answering your phone

Cam looks down at the screen of his phone. It's Peyton, but he really doesn't want to interrupt himself.

At the movies

With mystery date?

No, on my own

Boring

Cam sighs.

Why does everyone think I'm boring?

I don't. That just sounds like a boring Sat. night

I was rather enjoying it until you started harassing me

Cam flips his phone over and tries to refocus. His phone vibrates with a new text.

Whatcha watching?

Frostbite Bay

Oh, good one! Saw that the other day, she responds immediately, which makes him smile. Peyton is the least boring person he knows—well, maybe second least boring, now that he knows Wren—so her endorsement makes him feel a bit better about his Saturday night choices. *I'll let you watch then, now that I approve*

Cam smiles wryly and sends her a wink before focusing on the movie.

"Still soxiled?" Maggie's voice comes over the phone. She sounds a little worn.

"Yes," Cam sighs. He's been wasting time at the coffee shop for an hour now hoping to get the all-clear from Nate.

"Well, we're all tired of studying. One can only study philosophy for so long."

"That sounds horrible. And you all say I'm boring," Cam says.

"You voluntarily went to see a movie about Iceland," Maggie points out.

"Anyway," Cam changes the subject. He's finished his coffee and is debating another. It's late enough for more caffeine to be a bad idea, but he's bored and fiddly and tired. "What's up?"

"Where are you? Not the library again, I hope."

"Shut up," he says lightly. "The library is awesome. I am an intelligent, articulate individual thanks to the library."

"You're so full of shit," Maggie says. "Anyway, you want company? A few of us are wired but done with this, and I know you aren't home."

"That would be great," Cam says gratefully. "I'm at Roast, wanna meet here?"

"Hold on," she says. She must be pulling the phone from her mouth, because she sounds farther away. "You guys wanna meet a friend of mine at Roast?" He doesn't hear the response, but she says, "Yep, we'll see you there in a few."

"How many? I'll grab a bigger table," Cam offers.

"Five? I think five," she says.

"Awesome. See you soon." Cam hangs up and eyes the room. The café is half full, but the scattering of customers makes it hard to find a table for six. No one seems inclined to leave and, although he waits a few minutes, no one does. He gives up, stands and pulls a few tables together. It's loud and earns him a few glares, but he just shrugs and carries on.

"YOU SEEM TO BE MISSING A FEW," Cam points out when Maggie tumbles in with two other people in tow. One introduces himself as Steven (not Steve, he clarifies severely). The other, Nora, is tiny, barely five feet tall, a lovely girl with an odd mix of facial features that somehow work magically together. Cam blinks when she smiles at him brightly.

"The others are coming along—Wren had to stop for cash," Maggie says; Cam blinks and tries very, very hard not to gape.

"Say what?" he manages. Nora, who had been pulling up a chair, gives him a strange look. Pasting on what he hopes appears to be a somewhat normal facial expression, Cam follows with, "How many? I want to be sure we have enough chairs." It's a lame excuse, but he's thinking fast. How many Wrens can possibly be attending their school? Maggie says something and he nods as if he's listening, then takes a deep breath and calms enough to pay attention.

"Cam," Nora asks, "are you a student here too?"

"Yes, I'm in environmental studies."

Nora is still looking at him intently. She takes inventory of his face and clothes, but in an unfocused way. Her gaze trails up above his head. He does his best not to stare back at her, because there's something unsettling about the way she's examining him. After a long, slightly uncomfortable pause, her face clears and she smiles.

"That sounds interesting. I've never met anyone in that program. What are you hoping—" she's cut off by the ring of café bells signaling someone's entrance, and Cam doesn't have to turn to know it's Wren. He's never been more thankful for advance warning, or for his ability to put on a stoic face. He'll have to write Peyton a thank you letter for all the chaos she put him through when they were kids. At least because of that storminess, especially during their adolescence, he'd learned to create a shell around himself that projects calm.

Wren settles kitty-corner from him. There's no hitch in his gaze or discernible change in his expression—it's really impressive. Wren probably had a little warning, though; Wren told him that he's gotten very good at sensing Cam's energy from a distance. Cam shakes other guy's hand—Logan—and then Wren's when Maggie introduces them. It's easy to act as if he's never met him—easy because they're both pretending, and because Cam only needed a moment to know that blowing this would make Wren run away.

It's really fucking challenging, though, to suppress his reaction to the bolt of energy that runs between their hands when they shake. Cam sees a fraction of his own disturbance in the slight dilation of Wren's pupils. Otherwise, he's excellent at containing his reaction. Cam doesn't do that badly either, other than the slight tremor that runs through him. But when he glances at Maggie, who knows his face better than anyone else, all he sees is amusement. She gives him a little thumbs up that's not nearly so subtle as she probably imagines, as if she thinks he's just checking Wren out. He rolls his eyes as she'd expect him to, and next to Wren Nora suddenly bursts into laughter.

Wren gives her a dirty look and she just smiles, keeping her eyes on his for a long beat. Wren turns away from her. "I'm thirsty," he says, and stands suddenly. "Does anyone want anything?"

"Yeah," Maggie says, standing too.

"Oh, I can get it," Wren assures her, but she just shakes her head.

"I don't know what I want," she explains.

"I do," Steven says. "Just medium coffee, black, one sugar." He speaks briefly and Cam tries not to stare. Steven is remarkably monochromatic, down to his oatmeal-colored T-shirt and faded, loose jeans that do nothing for him except help him blend into the wall.

"So," Nora says, interrupting his thoughts, "I was asking about your major."

"Oh, it's a pretty boring story," he hedges. "What about you guys? Philosophy or something?"

"Philosophical Perspectives," Logan pipes up. "It's one of those electives you have to pick to fill a requirement."

"That sounds..." Cam tries to think of something less rude to say than *That sounds boring as hell*. And they call him the boring one!

"Boring as hell?" Logan says; Cam has to laugh.

"Are you a mind reader?" he jokes.

"I wish. I'd just read the professor's mind and not have to study for this fucking test."

"That's a good point," Cam says.

"Does it even work like that?" Steven says.

"What?" Cam asks.

"Does mind reading work like that? You know. For *them*." There's something a little ugly in the way he emphasizes the last word.

"Like what?" Nora looks up from where she's been unwrapping a brownie she snuck into the café in her bag.

"You know, just being able to see into people's heads?" Steven clarifies. "That creeps me out. Never knowing what the hell those people might be able to do. Where they could be."

Cam frowns. "Gifted people aren't that common, population-wise. I'd never even heard of them before I came here," he says.

"Did you live under a rock?" Steven asks.

Cam shrugs. He's not about to explain himself or his history to this guy. Maggie's back, with a hot tea in her hands.

"So how are you now an expert?" Steven probes.

"When Cam doesn't know something," Maggie jumps into the conversation, "he researches it."

Cam cringes internally because that makes him sound lame, but smiles self-deprecatingly. "Guilty as charged."

"Hmm," Steven says. "You know, a lot of people don't think *they* should be allowed to just wander around unknown or unrestricted."

"Personally, I don't think there's anything to worry about."

"That's because you're not from here," Steven argues. "This city is like, gifted Mecca. There are so many of them here, how could you not worry? Think about how dangerous it really is. They could do anything if they wanted."

Nora has been following the conversation with narrowed eyes; she seems about to say something when Wren jumps in.

"Who could do anything?"

"People who have gifts," Nora supplies, and smiles when Wren's face tightens.

"Cities like this offer protection," Wren says. "There are safeguards and regulations that protect everyone."

"That's what you think," Steven says derisively.

"Oh, it's much too late for this," Nora interrupts. "We were talking to Cam. Getting to know him."

Cam feels put on the spot but goes along. Wren doesn't ask him personal questions, as a rule; Cam often wishes he would, or that Wren *wanted* to, because he wants to know everything about Wren. "Well, you'll all really know how boring I am when I explain. I'm in environmental studies, kind of on the policy track?"

"What got you there?" Nora asks. The strand of hair she's twirling has hints of blue.

"Oh, it's complicated. I grew up surrounded by farms. Talk about climate change and farming practices and government stuff..."

"He's so articulate, isn't he?" Maggie jumps in and rescues him.

One good thing about Maggie is that she is never quiet for long, and as an added bonus, she knows Cam more than well enough to know this whole story. Maggie's interruptions, funny quips and interjections work beautifully. They open the conversation to the rest of the group so that Cam is participating in a conversation, rather than delivering the world's most tedious monologue. It also allows him to observe. Observation is second nature to him, and he's never been able to observe Wren when he isn't engaged in class or focusing his energy on Cam alone.

He's able to deduce that Wren and Nora are good friends long before Wren reveals that they are roommates. Clearly, Wren dislikes Steven, a sentiment Cam can't help but share. Steven is hostile and rude in a very passive-aggressive way, as well as bigoted. Even unflappable Maggie is struggling with him. Why on earth have they included him in a study group?

"So you all have an exam Monday?" he asks during a lull in the conversation.

"No," Logan says, "these are class-assigned study groups for weekly presentations. We do have an exam Wednesday, though."

Cam grimaces sympathetically.

"I have no idea what we were thinking, choosing this one as our elective," Nora adds.

"You mean, other than because we needed one and could take this one together and we ran out of time to be picky because we put it off?" Wren says.

Nora's been slipping him bits of brownie; Cam is fighting the urge to smile like a fool because it's frankly adorable, the way Wren nibbles them slowly, careful not to scatter crumbs.

It's almost midnight, and with the exception of Steven, Maggie has them all laughing when Cam's phone chimes. He's a little disappointed it isn't Nate.

So? Did you like it? Peyton asks. Cam ignores the message with a pang; it would be rude to text her right now. When he looks up, Wren is watching him—he looks away before their eyes can meet.

"Nate?" Maggie asks, trying to see over his shoulder.

"No, Peyton," he says, pocketing his phone.

"Has Nate even texted you yet?" she asks.

He shakes his head and, at Nora's questioning look, explains, "Nate is my roommate."

"Is he okay?" Wren says. It's the first time he's addressed conversation to Cam directly, and there's something amused in the look he gives him. Cam is much too discreet to tell a tableful of people he doesn't know that he's been kicked out so that his roommate can have sex.

"He's fine."

"Sexiled." Maggie raises her eyebrows suggestively, tilting her head at Cam.

"Maggie," he hisses, smacking her lightly on the arm with the back of his hand. Wren and Nora both laugh, though, and Cam is utterly distracted. He's never heard Wren laugh—not like this. He sounds so real, less other, more... regular. More like any other guy and not some unattainable, otherworldly creature. Cam can't help but laugh too.

"Where are you gonna go tonight?" Maggie asks. He shrugs. "Come over and crash at my place," she invites. "You know Christine won't mind." She won't. But he's never felt comfortable with her since the romance with Maggie ended.

"Sure," he says, only a little reluctantly. "Unless Nate texts me soon."

"It is pretty late for your roommate to still be doing it," Steven says, apropos of nothing, which makes Cam stop to stare at him and sets off more laughter from Wren and Nora, who are sharing a case of the giggles.

"Is there a curfew on sex I'm not aware of?" Nora asks between laughs. Steven frowns. *He probably has no idea. Anyone with Steven would be bored into sleep or annoyed into leaving before anything might happen.* Cam shakes his head and catches Maggie's amused expression—either she's thinking something similar or knows Cam is.

"Yes," Logan jokes, "midnight. By rights, you should have had your room back about fourteen minutes ago."

"Wow, it's late," Nora checks the time on her phone. "Ugh, I have to work tomorrow. So do you," she says to Wren. Cam tucks that away—that Wren works, and that it's a job that requires him to work Sundays.

"Don't remind me," Wren moans. He stands, smoothing the line of his pants—a mustard yellow Cam had no idea anyone could pull off—and adds, "I'll be right back." He inclines his head toward the men's bathroom.

"So," Nora leans over the table and addresses Maggie. "I've been thinking, would you want to hang out sometime? Maybe go shopping?"

"That sounds great," Maggie says. "I'm always down for shopping. Lately all I've had is Cam to drag around, and he's so resistant to letting me dress him up."

"Har har," Cam says. He stands to take their mugs to the bus bin and tries to wrap his mind around this new development. What if they become friends and hang out more than just for shopping? Would there be a way he could manipulate that, somehow working himself into a new group of friends that would include Wren? He shakes his head before his thoughts can spiral too much further.

CHAPTER EIGHTEEN

"YOU'VE BEEN IN THAT STUDY GROUP all semester?" Cam tries to ask casually as he and Maggie head to her apartment.

"Yeah," Maggie says, "and if I had known you were going to develop a crush like that, I would have figured out a way to introduce you sooner."

"Me and Steven?" Cam jokes. "I fear our love would never work out."

"Eww," Maggie shudders. "No. There is something off about him. And he's an asshole."

Cam thinks of Steven's pointed remarks about gifted people and grimaces.

"Don't play dumb," Maggie continues. "You know I'm talking about Wren. Super hot, huh?"

Cam tries to think of a way to answer without giving her any ideas. Knowing Maggie, she'll start campaigning for him to take Wren on a date, or worse, try to work on it from Wren's angle during study group.

"Yes, he's hot," Cam says. Sticking closest to the truth might be best.

"You should ask him out."

"You know there's a thing," Cam reminds her, blithely glossing over the fact that the *thing* happens to be *with* the man in question.

"I—" Maggie looks away, and Cam tugs on her hand to get her to continue. "I worry about you. Should I be worried? That you won't talk about it?"

"No," Cam says. "I promise, you shouldn't." He could say something to assuage her concern, but he leaves it at that.

"SO..." NORA DRAPES HER SWEATER over the back of the couch and turns to give Wren a *look*, her eyebrow arched and a slight smirk on her lips. The apartment is dark and chilled and Wren is tired, tired in his bones. His brain is oversaturated from studying and addled from having to maintain a straight face all night. Hiding his reaction to Cam filled him with the oddest mix of sensations: regret and longing and fear. Wren's not even sure what he's scared of anymore, there's so much.

"I'm tired," he says, hoping that it will give him a stay of execution, so to speak, from having to talk to her about this. "And a little pissed, because lately all you do is read me, when you know we have a deal."

Nora sits on the couch and pats the cushion next to her. He sighs and follows, picking up a gold-accented throw pillow and holding it in his lap like a shield. Their furniture is soft, plush and welcoming; the couch is a deep burgundy. It's hard to appreciate when he's so tense from all the complicated threads binding and tangling him up.

Nora confesses, "I won't lie, I was reading him. When you came in, his astral body did the most magnificent thing—it *pulsed*, almost magenta. His physical auric body was just a lovely swirling red, a true red."

"So?" he says defensively, picking at the seam of the pillow. He's never been able to keep up with all the nuances of reading. Mostly he's interested in defending himself from her ability to do it to him.

"Yours did it too," she says matter-of-factly. "And also, after you sat down for a bit, it waned. Went lemon yellow." She says this last loaded with certainty and innuendo, as if he'll know what it means.

"What the hell does that mean?"

"It means you're scared. It means you don't know if you can control something. And I have a pretty good guess what that is," she says. She has put her hand on his arm and he has to will himself not to snatch it away.

"Why do you think that has anything to do—"

"I'm not dumb, Wren. I know you're playing with him. It was so clear," she says, shaking her head. Then she says softly, "Are you going to let yourself be scared your whole life, Wren? Don't you want more?"

Wren closes his eyes and lays his head back. He feels a swell of just too much throbbing in his chest. "Stop," he begs. "I can't do this, it's too much—"

"Honey." She pulls him into a tight, sweet hug and he lets himself be held, lets the tension shudder out of him with each trembling breath, tucks his cheek into her neck. She's so tiny, but she holds him just the way he needs most, as if her arms are strong enough to keep him from quaking apart. "I just want everything for you."

"I do too," he says, battling tears when he finally admits it for the first time in years. "I can't stop being scared, though. If I say the words. If I let myself believe. Want."

In the silence of the room she sways him a little, runs her fingers over his head and lets the quiet cradle them both. Thankful and spent, Wren lets the silence seep into his head and heart and roiling stomach until the anxiety is almost gone. Nora doesn't push him, doesn't challenge him or make silly promises about not getting hurt again.

* * *

THE THING ABOUT NORA IS that she understands him, but also can't help but meddle. Empathy for how he's feeling, she has in spades. Desire for something else for him, unfortunately, is something she can't seem to control. And it helps her, distracts her from her own problems, which makes it hard for him to get too mad about it; all of which means that in the next few weeks, he's surprised more than once by Cam's appearance at social gatherings.

Maggie, he suspects, is in on it too. Over the course of the semester, he's learned to like her—to be honest, he can't imagine anyone *not* liking her. She has wonderful energy. She's funny and open and lovely. Now that things have changed and her friendship with Cam has been revealed, Wren wants to dislike her, because as time passes, it's obvious she's in cahoots with Nora. He's reasonably sure that Maggie is clueless about what's really happening, but that doesn't mask the fact that she *wants* something to happen between him and Cam.

It's obvious. And Wren doesn't doubt that Cam sees it too, though they don't discuss or acknowledge it, ever. Wren lies in bed at night, every night, and talks himself out of Cam. Steels himself and figures out a hundred ways to cut off something that now feels intractably rooted in him. He remembers everything he can, the details, makes himself look at pictures of himself, so young, with Robert, his smile wide and sure. So in love. Although it pierces, each memory a bit of shrapnel, he does it over and over to remind himself that this is how love ends.

But erasing Cam never works.

WREN WITH OTHER PEOPLE IS enlightening. It takes him a while, every time, to loosen a little, especially the first few times, when he and Cam are genuinely surprised to see each other. It doesn't take long to catch on to Nora and Maggie's meddling, and it's clear that Wren doesn't appreciate it—he's got an excellent poker face, but sometimes the smallest flash of annoyance or worry flickers there. When it comes to observing Wren, Cam has made a concerted effort to be watchful of everything he can.

"Here," Nora says now, passing Cam a drink. The bar they're in is packed, and eight of them are squeezed into a booth meant for six people. Wren is across and down by two people—too far away to hold a conversation with, but close enough for Cam to catch snatches of Wren's conversation with others. Wren, after a few drinks, is spellbinding. His hair falls into his face a little in the heat of the bar, and his cheeks go a lovely crimson as he unknots a little with each drink. Smiling and unselfconscious laughter brighten his face into something so young and soft, it makes Cam yearn in patterns he never imagined for himself.

"Thank you," Cam smiles at Nora and sips the drink. It's strong, and he has to work not to grimace.

"Too much?" she asks.

"I'm just not used to this," he admits.

"Here," Nora abducts a soda from Brokk, her and Wren's large and intimidating friend who is their designated driver. Nora empties half of Cam's drink into hers and then pours some of Brokk's soda into Cam's glass; Brokk doesn't notice, he's so busy flirting with Christine. Cam sips gingerly.

"Better?" she asks, and he nods.

"I owe you," Cam says, reaching for his wallet.

"Don't be silly," Nora bumps his shoulder with hers. "Get me later."

"It's nearly two," Cam points out. The room lists gently. His muscles feel lax in a lovely way; everything is smoother, easier. He watches Wren without subtlety; every now and then their eyes connect and Cam knows that Wren's also been drinking too much and is starting to let his guard down.

"Another time, another place," Nora sings. Cam smiles.

"You are—" he starts, and then loses his train of thought. She laughs and sips from his glass easily.

"You too, darling," she says.

THE ROOM HAS TILTED DANGEROUSLY by the time they're ready to go. Bills are being hashed out. Maggie and Christine have already left, citing work the next day. Cam hasn't any work to do on Sunday, only some studying. He doesn't mind waiting with everyone and hopes for a moment, even a few seconds, with Wren. Wren—who has slipped away. Cam curses, and then offers Nora some money.

"You don't owe this much," she points out.

"Don' worry," he says. He frowns and tries again, this time making an effort not to slur. He stands, suddenly needing to use the restroom.

Only he doesn't need to use it. He just needs to be there. *Wren.* He's being called.

Drunk, but basically aware, Cam exhales a light "*Oh*" and follows where he's being led.

"DON'T TALK," WREN GRABS CAM by the lapels of his button-down shirt. He has to steady Cam when he trips a little; Cam is drunk, stunningly yielding and sending off waves of desire. Cam's eyes, such a lovely almond shape, are dark, slumberous and sensual, and Wren *aches*. Cam bites his lip, takes Wren's face in his hands and just looks at him, their faces so close they'd hardly have to move to kiss. He doesn't speak, but the look they share says so much. Wren swallows something down and closes his eyes.

"Turn." He manhandles Cam, pushing him against the tile wall of the stall. Cam's hands splay against it; the exquisite, smooth rich gold of his skin is stark against the cracked white wall. Wren pushes his forehead against the dip of Cam's neck and cobbles himself together, works Cam's belt open with slurred fingers and fumbled movements.

"Oh, god," Cam whines when Wren's hand finds him roughly.

"Shut up," Wren says. He means it as a command, but it comes out sounding broken. He's so weak like this, laced with alcohol that has unleashed something lighter than the darkening desire he's let himself feel for so long. He puts his hand over Cam's mouth and shudders when Cam bites down. Wren jerks Cam off quickly, grinding against him, breath huffing short and hard. He soaks in Cam's pleasure, opens himself to it in a way he rarely does, and when Cam's knees buckle, his body dependent on Wren to keep him up, they both come hard and wrecked and utterly in sync.

CAM HAS BARELY GOTTEN HIS SHAKING, buzzing limbs together when he realizes that Wren is gone. The wall under his hands and cheeks is slippery—he recognizes with a start that it's wet from his sweat. His pants are a mystery to his stupid hands, and putting himself together takes longer than it should.

"Bar's closing!" An impatient voice follows the bang of the bathroom door opening. It slams shut again. Cam washes his hands quickly and avoids his image in the mirror.

Everyone is gone when he stumbles out. Nora and the rest must have assumed he'd left.

In some ways, Cam feels as if he has.

* * *

CAM DOESN'T SEE OR HEAR from Wren for a long time after that. It's enough time for Cam to feel it, wretchedly, in his bones, enough to finally find words for what's happening to him. Wren is a beautiful enigma, a bright light that's blinding and sudden. In his absence, everything around Cam seems like waning phosphorescence.

Nate is a presence he senses but doesn't engage with. His classes are shadows, hours he has to endure, and when summer comes, he barely feels the transition. He and Nate, Maggie and Christine choose to rent a run-down house near the college until they graduate, and the room Cam now shares with Nate is bigger, which they both appreciate. With slightly more space—a living room and a kitchen and their own bathroom—Cam also has much more time to himself.

Every moment he can steal for himself, he spends remembering the littlest things, like the whimsy of plugs Wren chooses to wear; one time he'd forgone them completely in favor of a single octopus adornment that had curved along the length of his ear. Cam remembers the chaos of Wren's hair, so black it's like ink and Cam can hardly believe it's real. He treasures the closest moment they've shared, Wren's encouragement when Cam finally chose to claim what had been deep and undiscovered in himself for so long.

* * *

BY EARLY SUMMER, CAM DOESN'T WANT to admit he might have given up; he's had no way to connect with Wren other than the phone, and his calls and texts have gone unanswered. The only thing that's kept him going is an amorphous sense of a tether that hasn't loosened. There have been days when he wonders if it is deluded hope, and others when its shape is so solid in his chest, he knows it is real. Then suddenly, during the second week of June, Wren's silence ends.

Want to revisit something? Wren texts late on a Friday night.

Of course, Cam responds so quickly he's a little surprised to have avoided typos.

Find me in the library tonight

Where?

I'll let you figure that out

Cam stares at that last one, then laughs. Wren has made himself a treasure hunt, and Cam knows exactly where X marks the spot.

"YOU'RE FAST," WREN SAYS. HE'S cross-legged on the linoleum floor between rows of musty books. The bright florescent lights shine over his hair; he's wearing distressed jeans he must not care much about, since he's on the floor, and a loose purple shirt.

"Dare I say you're predictable?" Cam kneels in front of him and doesn't say *I missed you.*

For a moment they just stare at each other. Wren's eyes are one of hundreds of shades of green Cam's never seen. He read once that neither blue nor green eyes are the result of pigmentation, but rather a lack of it, and that depending on light conditions, the color of lighter eyes can vary greatly.

He hopes he'll get to spend a lot more time cataloging the shifts in Wren's eyes.

"You know I'm not," Wren responds softly.

"I know what you want, now; is that evidence?"

"What do I want, Cam?" Wren tilts his head. Cam lets himself smile. Moves slowly but deliberately until he's straddling Wren's lap without putting too much weight on his legs. He snakes his fingers through Wren's hair. Their lips are so close when he whispers it.

"*Me.*"

WREN KISSES AND KISSES CAM. Kisses him dozens of ways. He stretches his legs out and feels the seeping cold of the floor begin to warm, coaxes Cam closer until their bodies are crowded together and Cam is a heavy weight in his lap.

When he tries to ease his hands into the back of Cam's pants, Cam pulls away from his mouth with a gasp.

"Don't," he whispers.

"Don't what?" Wren tries for playful but he sounds more confused. "Don't touch you? Don't you want it?"

"I want you to kiss me," Cam's eyes are serious and earnest.

"I will." Wren pushes the hem of Cam's shirt up farther until his hands meet warm skin. Wren urges him closer and closer until they are rocking against each other, imperfectly building pleasure into something aching.

And all through it, the delicious ascent and the brilliant crest, his lips never leave Cam's.

CHAPTER NINETEEN

"I really like Nora's friends," Maggie says one Friday night. They've become weekend regulars at The Cat. Every Friday they meet and gather at the same booth. It's comforting to have a routine, and Cam comes to know who else hangs out here to take advantage of the warm atmosphere. Everything about this bar feels soothing, like the walls, paneled deep brown at the bottom and painted a deep peach at the top, featuring art from local artists for sale. The booths are a bit small for Cam; the seats are lower than most, which makes it a bit awkward at his height, but he knows Maggie and Nora very much appreciate it. Cam usually sits at the end of the booth with his legs stretching out to the side.

Shae, who is almost always their waitress, comes to know them by name. The first two times she waits on them, Cam quietly watches for the tells that lie in the smallest details. She never writes down their order, although the first few times they come in she pretends to. She pulls her hair back in an artfully messy knot—at the end of her shift, he's seen her by the service station taking it down and massaging her scalp. Shae probably doesn't wear her hair up when she's not required to at work. Her apron acquires more and more stains and splashes as the night carries on, but it's always pristine the next time they see her. The other waitresses favor low-cut black tops and darker eye makeup; Shae always looks natural and approachable.

The third time they come in, Cam speaks to her for the first time about something other than what he's ordered.

"Why do you pretend to write down our orders?" he asks. Shae smiles. Her teeth are slightly crooked.

"It's a rule," she explains. "Management rules."

"That's why you wear your hair up, right?"

She gives him a look; he must seem odd to her. "Yes, we have to wear it up."

"I just like to watch people," he says, and then realizes that this probably doesn't make him seem any less strange. "Not in a creepy way—"

"I get it," she interrupts his rushed explanation with a laugh. "I try to do that too—read my tables and customers. I probably don't do it the same way you do, though." She casts a quick look around, scanning her tables to see if she's needed.

"Go," he says when he sees another table trying to get her attention.

"We'll chat more later," she promises, pocketing her useless pad in her apron.

* * *

"Does it bother you, that I kind of shoehorned everyone into this group?" Maggie asks one day. Nora is here with them, but for the moment they're alone in their booth, sharing a plate of cheap appetizers.

"No. Not really. I enjoy it all."

"You know it's not just me matchmaking, right? I really like Nora."

"We hang out with them enough, yes, I got that sense. Plus a little bird told me you've been shopping with her," Cam jokes around a mouthful of potato skins. "The mark of deep love, for you."

"Manners, Cam," Maggie says, only a little severely. He obligingly chews before they continue their conversation. "Which little bird?"

"Christine," Cam says.

"Jealous, a little? I know you've been my shopping partner—"

"A little relieved, actually," he jokes. "My budget can't take that many hits. Who needs that much clothing? Now I can save my money for this wasteland of debauchery."

"Sweetie," Maggie says condescendingly, "two or three drinks on a night out don't count as debauchery."

Cam just barely bites back his retort. Sex in bathrooms and darkened streets are definitely his definition of debauched behavior. The secrecy of those moments feels like intimacy: the press of necessary silence, the rough possession, the frenetic rush of orgasm, his body Wren's to manipulate and take and take from.

Instead, he smiles at her and turns the subject back. "So you've become friends with her beyond transparent plots to hook me up with Wren?"

"I've sort of given up on that," she admits, sipping her Tequila Sunrise and wincing. Every time they go out she tries something new. She'd told him she's on a quest for a signature beverage—and in so doing, is working her way through every mixed drink she can think of. She's depended on Cam to remember the ones she likes.

"Oh good," he says absently. Nora is at the bar rail—she'd gone to order a drink, because Shae has been bogged down at a table of rowdy guys. There's a guy at the bar, too, who has approached Nora. She's smiling in the friendly way she has and twirling a lock of her hair. She's changed her colors to a darker blonde with purple tips and streaks. It's a look Cam likes on her.

There's something about this guy's body language Cam isn't sure of. He's only half-listening to Maggie.

"I still maintain he's perfect for you. You just have to get to know him more. You guys never talk, really."

"Oh don't we?" Something is definitely off. Cam starts to scoot out of the booth, but Nora must suddenly notice it too. With a neutral smile, she says something and starts to turn away. The guy puts a hand on her arm to stop her and says something else, and now Cam is standing because Nora is definitely not welcoming that touch.

But Wren is at her side before Cam can take a step. He says something—his face is a little fierce and his hand is on the small of Nora's back. Nameless guy backs off quickly and turns; he says something Cam knows must be deprecating to the guys at his table, and they all laugh.

When he looks back, Wren has one hand on Nora's arm while the other brushes her hair behind her ear. He's saying something quietly to her, looking into her eyes. He takes a breath and continues to look at her steadily. She breathes too, until her body sags and relaxes a little.

He seems to be compelling comfort, and so sweetly; there is a look of tender concentration Cam's never seen on his face as he strokes the skin of Nora's forearm gently with his thumb. Nora's body is settled into her usual posture when he finally breaks eye contact, and the hug they share is long and familiar.

* * *

WREN GETS BETTER AT SENSING when Nora is going to spring Cam on him, and he wises up to Brokk's involvement as well. He retreats into the comfort of his room, the womblike warmth of his bed and desk and deep blue and gray walls. It's impossible not to sense Cam's feelings when they're together now, no matter what Wren does.

He calls Cam to him only when he can't help it anymore. They don't speak; Wren makes sure of it, compelling Cam into stunned, pleasure-soaked silence. He never allows their eyes to meet unless he has Cam in careful submission. Coming and going erratically, he allows for longer stretches of time between encounters and never indicates when they will be. And they're as fast and impersonal as he can make them—which is not very, not when his idiot need for Cam makes him want to soak in Cam's every molecule.

Cam comes for him, over and over, and more and more often with confusion, sometimes reticence. He wants Wren, it's clear. Wren is careful to always listen to the call of Cam's will. But he's straining for more, reaching for something Wren cannot give him.

* * *

SUMMER WAXES HALCYON AND WARM around them, and with freedom from school, only the gravity of jobs pulling them, they all have more time to spend together. Wren doesn't mind anymore. He's settled himself into a shell he puts on when Cam is with them. This group has come together in a tapestry that he *knows* makes sense, a tapestry he understands would be complete if he didn't work so hard to keep himself away from Cam.

In July, Maggie decides she wants to go to Somewhere O'Clock and try trivia with teams. Wren has a great time with her, especially; he's always wanted to try competitive trivia.

"Do *not* try to be stealthy and manipulate things so I am on his team," he warns Nora when they're getting ready that night. They're both fiddling in front of the mirror in their small bathroom.

"Here," Nora says, turning away from her reflection for a moment and batting his hands from his hair, "you're doing it all wrong." Her fingers are sure against his scalp, and, even though he's not certain he trusts her to do his hair any better than he can, the easy, affectionate touch feels lovely.

"There." He looks at himself. She's done his hair completely differently that he would. It's less messy, shaped differently and swept to one side, with some volume. "It would be even better if you let me put some color in again—"

"Nora, we don't have time for that. And the last time you did it faded and turned pink."

"What's wrong with pink?" Nora says defensively and plucks at her top, which he just now notices is a lovely shade of fuchsia.

"Nothing. I love pink," he says dryly. "I just didn't want it in my hair at that point in time."

"Well." She picks her eyeliner back up and pretends to touch up her eyes, even though her makeup is finished. "The green looked great."

There's an edge to her voice he wishes he could pacify. She's been a little grumpy and high-strung lately, and has been joking about being single for so long. It's incredibly hard for her to find guys to date, because as soon as she thinks she's interested, she reads their auras; after what happened with Matt—trusting him enough to ignore things she'd seen and then realizing how much he'd manipulated and pressured her—her fear has lingered. Nora's a deeply monogamous girl, but rarely finds men whose initial interest isn't just sexual.

"You look beautiful, honey," Wren tugs at her shirt. "Come on, we'll be late."

"TEAMS?" NORA ASKS AS SOON as they are settled.

"I call Maggie," Wren says immediately. He's surprised when Cam smiles widely.

"Excellent." Cam nudges Nora with his shoulder. "I have a good feeling about you, kid."

"Of course you do." Nora tosses her hair back over her shoulder. She's been growing it out; the length gives her waves an at-the-beach, natural beauty. Cam whispers something in her ear, and Wren doesn't try not to stare. Cam is wearing a short-sleeved black shirt with a cowl-neck collar. His skin is dull bronze against it; the winged meeting of his collarbones is visible. Desire cascades through Wren's body.

"I guess that leaves us," Christine says with a laugh. Brokk kisses her cheek.

"We are the only couple," he points out with a completely transparent look at Wren. Wren kicks him under the table, hoping it's discreet enough that Cam won't notice. He' never promised Cam that *he* won't say anything about their arrangement—secrecy only applies to Cam. But he would never have revealed Cam's name had they never met him. If only his friends weren't so fucking nosy. Well, and if only Nora could control her gift.

Cam moves his stool so he's closer to Nora. Wren doesn't miss the look he sends Brokk and Christine; there's a longing in it that feels like needles in Wren's heart. There is no hiding how much Cam wants Wren and loves what they do. But it's also clear how much Cam has come to want more. From Wren, and for his life.

Wren doesn't have this to offer, but he can't stop what he's doing because he wants it too, wants anything he will let himself have from Cam. It's ridiculous and fucked up and out of control.

"We're gonna wipe the floor with you, Allister," Nora taunts Wren, and Cam high-fives her. Wren can't even wrest his smile under control.

THERE IS NOTHING LIKE TRIVIA NIGHTS, because there's no other time Cam gets to see Wren so completely himself. It's nothing like when they're at the bar; a tension underlines those interactions. Plus, they're good at existing at the fringes of a circle of friends.

Here, though, it's so *easy* and becomes so familiar. Wren laughs loudly and makes bawdy jokes whenever a faintly suggestive question comes up. He's more competitive than the rest of them combined, and he and Maggie are a deadly team. It turns out that Maggie is a font of useless facts and a complete secret weapon when it comes to trivia nights.

Cam holds images of Wren close when he goes to sleep at night: Wren's eyes scrunching with laughter as they all banter and trade friendly barbs at the table. Wren mindlessly playing with the plugs in his ears as they talk. The way he fiddles with his drink straw, twirling it clumsily, dropping it so often he steals someone else's. These small things endear him to Cam even further.

Cam is so close to what might be love that by the time he is aware of it, he feels the same way he did after Wren first kissed him—a flash illuminating a room full of familiar objects Cam hadn't realized were there the whole time.

"STOP," WREN PANTS AGAINST CAM'S LIPS. Cam stills the undulating movement of his hips and opens his eyes. It's so dark he can barely see Wren's face; his eyes are the smallest glitter of light in the room. Cam doesn't move, lets himself give in more and relaxes his body against the mattress when Wren presses down harder on his wrists, which are stretched above his head against a pillow. Wren's thighs bracket Cam's and it's so hot they're both sweating. It's wonderful like this, surrounded and overtaken by Wren's body.

"What's wrong?" he manages.

"Stop, *stop*," Wren moans.

"I have," Cam points out, confused. "I can't stop any more when you're holding me down."

"I don't mean that," Wren says.

"What?" Cam squints, as if it will somehow make Wren's image clearer.

"I can't—" Wren's voice breaks, "do this." He untangles their fingers and starts to climb off of him.

"No, no." Cam puts his hands around Wren's biceps and pulls him back down. Wren's arms are wiry, very strong, but Wren is so much smaller Cam can almost wrap his hand all the way around his arm. "Tell me what I'm doing and I'll stop."

Wren shifts and flicks on the bedside light. His face is red; his eyes are skittish and too round. He puts an open palm on Cam's heart, swallows hard before trying to speak and then shakes his head.

"What?" Cam puts his hand over Wren's, and Wren flinches and jerks it away.

"Learn to pull that back or this is over," Wren says between gritted teeth. His eyes are too bright, and Cam wonders for a moment if he's about to cry. He knows now what Wren is saying. It's been harder and harder to hold it in, this huge surge of tender yearning he has for Wren.

"Okay," he promises, not stopping to wonder if he *can*. He'll promise anything to keep Wren here right now, because the hope that he'll figure out how to keep him, how to change this explosive energy into something more lasting, keeps him going and going and going.

Wren closes his eyes and shudders through a few deep breaths. Cam runs his hand up Wren's arm, focusing all of his energy on harnessing what Wren wants—sensuality, desperation and need–and pushing everything else away. His thumb runs just inside the muscle around Wren's armpit and then along the beautiful arches of his collarbone. Cam thinks of his own body, the thrumming need for more, his dick, somehow still hard.

"Wren," he says, "*fuck*. Touch me,"

Wren turns to him, his eyes dangerous and dark. "If you want."

Cam battles back a frown; there's something wrong in Wren's tone, his delivery. Wren sends him something then, hard and fast, and takes Cam down with the hot, wet suction of his mouth.

HE DOESN'T LET CAM GET him off that night. Instead, he brings him to an orgasm in no time at all and feels the edge of pain cresting with Cam's pleasure loud and clear. When Cam reaches for him, Wren shakes his head and climbs onto Cam, holding him down again; with one stare Cam gets the message and lies back passively and obediently while Wren touches and touches him. Wren touches every part of Cam's body carefully—his armpits, behind his ears and knees. He traces each toe and runs his hands up Cam's thighs. Then he spreads Cam's legs roughly and parts his ass cheeks.

"Lube," he commands, and Cam fumbles for it with pleasure-stupid movements.

Wren's hands are shaking, a fact he tries to hide from Cam. His heart pounds so hard it hurts, and something buzzes in his head.

He's got one finger inside Cam, too fast and sudden, when he realizes he's completely shut himself off and isn't sensing Cam's need.

"Oh, god—" he stops his hand immediately. "Are you okay? Is this okay?"

Cam gives him a puzzled look. "You can't tell?"

Wren's rarely asked, and he's not about to explain why he can't tell. But as soon as the words are out of Cam's mouth, he seems to understand. "I'm good. Whatever you want right now—"

"Don't," Wren says roughly, and moves his hand, finger surging in and out. He bends his finger a little at the tip and drags it out until Cam's breath comes short. Once he's found Cam's prostate, it's no work to get another two fingers in and he milks Cam's pleasure slowly. He keeps his touches light but certain with his other hand, fondling Cam's balls and cock and sending him waves of pleasure. He's never done this, managed to bring Cam to dry orgasm over and over.

"Oh god, oh god, *ohmygod*," Cam moans, almost crying. He's gripping the edges of the pillow and his eyes are clenched shut.

"More," Wren says.

"I—" Cam swallows and arches into the next one. "I can't, it's—it's starting to hurt."

"Okay, just one more." Wren uncurls his fingers and takes Cam softly into his mouth. "Should I…" he starts to drag is fingers out, "pull them out?"

"No, just don't move them," Cam asks. Wren keeps them still, three fingers still in the tight vise of Cam's asshole. He works the last orgasm out of Cam so tenderly, with the gentlest kisses and touches and murmured encouragement, until Cam comes with a sob, arching his spine so hard and deep even Wren is surprised.

"You're a lot more flexible than I thought," Wren notes later, once Cam is cleaned up and boneless against the bed. Cam seems to be floating in some space that isn't sleep but isn't quite awareness either.

"I know," he slurs. Wren can feel Cam's energy, untethered, reaching for him. Wren is reading something he's not felt from Cam before, and although he's reeling in a different way, his whole body poised to fly, skittering along a thin plane of fear, he's more afraid to leave Cam alone like this than he is to stay.

He sits next to Cam for a long time. The only part of his body he'll let touch Cam is his hand, heavy against Cam's slowly beating heart. He doesn't time how long it takes for Cam to slip into real sleep, but as soon as he does, he takes Cam's phone from the nightstand, texts Nate an all-clear and dresses. He covers Cam with a blanket and closes the door quietly when he leaves.

CHAPTER TWENTY

"SO WE'RE OUR OWN TEAM BY DEFAULT?" Nate asks, settling at a bar stool next to Ellie.

"Yep," Nora says decisively. "Cam and I are proven winners; nothing's gonna break this magic team apart."

"Please," Maggie breaks in, "who won the last few?"

"I seem to recall that the overall win-to-loss ratio works in our favor," Cam says. Wren rolls his eyes but smiles, eating maraschino cherries from his drink; he likes to savor them slowly. Everyone at the table eventually surrenders their cherries to him if they have them.

"Whatever. We're on a consecutive win streak," Wren points out.

"Okay, then," Nate says. "What you're saying is that Ellie and I are really just decorative?"

"And half of you are so pretty," Cam jokes. Wren laughs suddenly, and then clears his throat and looks away.

"No need to stroke my ego," Nate says, "I know you think I'm hot."

"Shut up," Cam says, and kicks Maggie, who has started giggling too. Wren is biting his lip trying to stop laughing, and Cam shoots him a look.

"All right," Maggie sits straighter. "We're about to start. Everyone stop hitting on each other and get your game faces on."

"Damn," Nate smiles at Ellie. "I don't think I prepared enough for this."

"I didn't bring my study notes either," she jokes back.

NATE IS QUIET WHEN THEY GET BACK to the house, which is a little odd. Cam is only half paying attention to him, though. Wren is fresh in his mind, but also strangely distant. He'd been himself tonight in a way it took him a long time to reveal—joking and competitive and *funny*. But there had been nothing between them, no spark from Wren, no looks that spoke of more. What happened between them the night before seems to have spooked Wren. Cam wants to promise himself that he'll do better at reining his feelings in, but it's impossible when Wren sees past and breaks down every wall. Cam can lie with words, and even with his face if he wants to, but what's deep inside is sewn into him and he can't hide that.

"That was... fun," Nate says casually as he sits on his bed. His movements are careful and precise. He's got something to say.

"You didn't enjoy yourself?" Cam has no idea where Nate is going. "Did Ellie have fun?"

"Yeah, she did," Nate says. He's distracted.

"I'm glad you brought her. Outside of here I don't see you much," Cam observes. Does Nate's bringing her mean she or they have passed some sort of test, or *is* this the test?

"Hmm," Nate says. He plugs his phone in and checks it, Cam knows, to make sure his alarm is set—Sunday is Nate's early workout day, for reasons that completely elude Cam.

"What's up?" Cam says, point-blank. He's tired and distracted enough to want to just get the conversation done.

"What's going on with your man?" Nate asks, looking Cam in the eye.

"What do you mean?" Cam hedges.

"What's with the guy you've been hiding from us? And what's with that guy Wren, too?"

"Uh—what?" Cam says, stupefied.

"There's something strange going on between you two. I can totally feel it."

"Oh, don't be Maggie," Cam dismisses him.

"I'm not," Nate insists. "I know you, man. There's something going on. For a while you were unusually happy or something. But now..." His brow furrows. Cam looks away and swallows down something that is rising in him. "This has been a weird and crazy year for you. I worry that you've gotten yourself into something—"

"I'm a big boy, Nate," Cam snaps, and then tries to soften his tone. "Sorry. Just... trust me?"

"It's not about trust. You have been sitting on some secret, and it's bugging you. And there is something with that Wren guy—like, are you into him? Can you not—?"

Cam takes a breath. He's confused; he has no idea how to lie effectively here, especially when he doesn't *want* to lie. And he's not sure Nate is the font of wisdom on this subject, when he's only *just* decided to try a monogamous relationship. There's no way to do this situation justice, not when it's so nuanced and he's so unsure *and* bound by his promise to follow Wren's ridiculous rules. Well, rules that seem ridiculous now. Wren might be able to delude himself into thinking that this is still a game, but it's *not*.

"I've told you guys, I can't talk about it."

"Cam, dude, that's fucked up."

"What do you know?" Cam says with heat he can't bite back. "Nothing. Just butt out—" He takes a breath. "I'm sorry, never mind."

"It's okay," Nate shrugs. "I want you to talk to me, but I can't make you do it."

"For what it's worth, I want to."

"That's not all that comforting."

Cam shrugs. "I have something I don't want to lose and I have to figure it out."

Nate stares at him for a long time. "I don't understand why you can't—I wouldn't tell anyone—"

"Just... trust me. I know it's a lot to ask. But look. All I can say is that he... has the *ability*," he pauses and lets that sink in, "to know."

"Oh," Nate's eyebrows shoot up.

"Let—" Cam closes his eyes and wonders if these words will qualify as breaking the rules. "Let me think about it?"

"I guess if that's what I can get, I'll take it," Nate says.

Me too. Cam settles back and waits for Nate to shut off the light. In the dark, Nate takes a breath as if he's going to speak; he must change his mind, because nothing follows but a silence so heavy it feels like a blanket.

* * *

IT'S THE MOST GENUINE KINDNESS that does Wren in. He knows Cam is kind, of course, but seeing it when it matters most—

If Wren loves anyone in his life, other than his family, it's Nora. Nora makes him crazy half the time, and often they snipe at each other and slam doors, but regardless, Nora is his constant in this life. She aches for someone to share her life with romantically, intimately, in a way he cannot provide.

Wren has just arrived when he sees Nora and a strange guy at the bar. The guy has awful, bleached-blond hair stuffed under a hipster beanie, and he's crowding Nora's body with his, much too close—she has a *look* on her face that sets off Wren's warning bells. But before Wren can get to Nora's side, Cam is there, smiling at her. His body language is so familiar it could easily read as intimate; it is enough to fend off the strange guy.

"You know," Nora says not unkindly, by the time Wren has joined them, "I don't always need a guy to rescue me." She directs this at Wren as well. Before he can respond, Cam speaks up.

"I didn't do it because I'm a guy, or because I think being a guy makes me some sort of protector. I did it because I care for you and could tell he was making you uncomfortable."

"Which I appreciate," her voice is gentle, "but you helping sends guys like that a message that perpetuates certain behavior. I can do this on my own. And maybe it's naïve of me to think that acting on my own will change brutish behavior from boys who've been conditioned to think I'm weak because I'm a small woman, or just a woman, but change starts somewhere."

Cam looks so pleased that it sends a bright ray of light through Wren's heart. Cam can't know that there is so much more to her story, and how each step like this is her way of fighting to get something back.

"Nora," he says so softly into her ear that Wren has to work to hear it, "I think I'm in love with you."

Nora beams and kisses his cheek. "Thank you for caring enough to want to help."

"Should you ever need it, send up a bat signal. But from now on, I'll let you work it out."

Somehow, in this moment, it's as if Wren has never seen Cam before. Not his face or his body, but his *self*, complete.

Cam excuses himself a few minutes later to go to the restroom, and Wren feels himself pulled toward Cam; the startling realization that there's a reverse pull, that there has *been* a reverse pull, makes his fingers go numb with cold and fear. He's never been pulled before, and this is strong; he's helpless. And so he follows as he must. He leaves the table without an excuse and runs to catch Cam.

Even when he's taken Cam in public, it has always been with an element of secrecy. But the hall of a crowded bar isn't secret. This doesn't stop Wren from turning Cam around to search his lovely eyes in the near dark, even when it feels as though Wren's heart might climb out of his chest, it beats so hard with fear.

BEING PRESSED INTO A WALL AND KISSED by Wren is not something Cam saw coming. It's not shocking, exactly, because Wren is nothing but a hurricane of unpredictability and change in his life. Still, it's surprising. Cam has had a shitty week of terrible classes and fielding phone calls between Peyton and his parents about trouble she's found herself in. Just now his concern for Nora is battling his desire to respect her wishes. And he feels an increasing press of anxiety over wanting to talk to someone about this *thing* between him and Wren. He's been steeling himself for more distance, for some sort of severance.

Instead, what he gets are the sweetest, most insistent and searching kisses Wren has ever given him. When he pulls away, Cam can't help but chase his lips; there's never been a flavor like this between them.

"What?" Cam says softly. The chatter of the crowd and the blaring sports programs almost drowns it. Wren looks as shocked as Cam feels. Cam has a moment to wonder at that before Wren frowns and pulls further away. Not being able to read Wren the way Wren can read him is so frustrating, sometimes. Later, Cam won't know what came first or what influenced it, or why Wren suddenly pressed him back with one hand on his chest and an intense look of concentration.

"You told," he says flatly.

"What?" Cam resists the urge to bat Wren's hand away, as if breaking the physical connection might keep Wren from reading the surge of guilt that rises in him. Cam knows Wren won't listen to his words, or hear the nuances of what actually happened with Nate; Wren's sensing gift is not honed well enough to override his fear.

"You *told*." Wren pushes away and turns. Cam grabs his hand quickly and pulls him back. He's not going down without a fight.

"I didn't. It's not like that."

"Take your hand off of me," Wren spits.

"Listen," Cam begs.

"There were rules. You broke them." Wren wrenches his hand free. Cam winces; he didn't realize how tight his grip was.

"Don't run away," he says with heat, surprising himself. "You're looking for a reason. Don't. Please."

"Fuck you." Wren backs away; in the unnatural lighting of the bar Wren's skin is distorted by shadow. "Don't pretend you know what you're talking about. That you know me. Don't fool yourself."

"Fuck *you*," Cam says, unsurprised by the words despite their foreign taste. "You *know* it's—"

"No," Wren shakes his head and turns, dodging Cam's hand when Cam tries to pull him back again. It's a final insult to feel himself unable to move and follow, and to know in the aftermath, when he's come to himself, that Wren has compelled him and taken away his last chance.

CAM STAYS WHERE HE IS IN A DAZE for so long that Maggie comes looking for him. A framed poster behind his back digs into his muscles. The quality of sound in the bar has changed, and he hadn't realized that trivia has started.

"What's wrong?" she says, placing her hand on his cheek. "Cam, what's wrong?" She shakes his jaw gently to get his attention.

"N–nothing," he manages. He can't feel his hands. Why can't he feel his hands?

"Cam," her voice is infinitely gentle. "Don't lie to me."

"I'm—"

"It's one thing to tell me you can't tell me. But don't you lie to me," she insists. He closes his eyes and tilts his head back against the wall.

"Can we just leave?" he begs.

"Yeah," Maggie smiles. "I'll let them know—"

"No, no, can we not go out there?" he grabs her hand quickly.

"Wren didn't—"

"Just—" Cam interrupts, and her eyes sharpen.

"Okay," she says, understanding dawning bright in her eyes. "I'll text them."

Cam doesn't—can't—wait a second longer, not when the walls feel too close and threaten to press even more. He finds the back exit and stumbles out. The night is so clear it hurts; the air is clean compared to what he's been breathing. The city air is nothing compared to Nebraska air, which is as clear as the bluest waters. But this is cleansing in a different way. This is air he hasn't breathed; this is a new moment, away from the last.

When Maggie comes out, he shakes his head. "You should go back in," he says.

"No, I want to be with you." She's so beautiful to him, even when he knows she's not conventionally pretty. Chicago plays warmly over her skin. She's changed her hair—it's shorter.

"No, go play." He stands his ground. Everything slams home at once. How deeply he's tied himself to a hope, how entwined he's been with Wren, the role he's played in some strange obsession.

Whether it is his or Wren's, he has no idea; he only knows that it is too dark for what his heart needs.

"Cam, don't be an idiot, it's not like anyone is actually going to play right now. With both you and Wren gone, everyone knows something—"

He interrupts her before she can finish that sentence, because even in the cleanest air he couldn't contain this panic. "I have to run."

He hasn't run in weeks. Cam has always centered himself under the sky and into his body with feet hitting the street and breath tearing from his lungs. Has always chased the indescribable afterglow of burnt-out muscles and hot lungs. The memory stings because he hadn't realized it was something he was missing.

"What?"

"Just. I have to run."

"Cam!" she calls after him. But he's already off, overdressed, unprepared and rubbed so raw.

Wren was a high. He lays into the air in front of him too fast. Maybe Cam wanted more, but a high was all he was getting because it's all Wren could give him.

HE'S SOAKED THROUGH HIS SHIRT by the time he gets to his room, panting and red-faced. Nate is waiting for him, which is intensely aggravating.

"Maggie texted me," he states. Cam ignores him, strips off his shirt and gathers things for a shower. "Cam, come on, talk to me."

Cam slams out of the room without looking at him. It's rude and he doesn't care, because riding a wave of anger feels better than what churns underneath it.

He does brief stretches in the shower, as much as he can in a cramped space with his long body, just enough so that he won't hurt unbearably in the morning. He'll definitely hurt, though, and he wants it. Wants the reminder that he's let something—lots of things—go. Wants the impetus to work back to those things and to himself, and then find solid ground on which to figure this out.

In bed, he calculates what he's left behind for this train wreck of a romance that wasn't a romance at all. Or that was, under all of the denial and manipulation and *desire* to be manipulated. Cam lets himself own how much he loved, *loved*, letting someone take him out of his body and his scattered, unexplored self. It's okay to want that, he knows, to seek and pull and desire that, because it is who he is. But not at his own expense. He wants that with Wren for *them*, not just because he wants to be fucked.

Nate snuffles in his sleep. Cam thinks of Ellie, whom he hardly knows. Of Nate changing so much, too—Cam has hardly talked to him about it, he's been so self-centered and caught in this whirlwind with Wren.

Rather than accepting what he's had, he has to convince Wren to come to him for more. Or accept more.

Actually, first Cam needs to think. To separate himself enough to really examine himself and figure out if he can manage to be a good friend and a good brother and good to himself. Figure out how badly he'll need Wren once he's taken the time to look at all that. Can it be healthy to need Wren so wretchedly?

CHAPTER TWENTY-ONE

"TELL ME EVERYTHING ABOUT ELLIE," Cam greets Nate as soon as Nate wakes up.

"Hrm?" Nate mumbles, scrubbing his hands over sleep-crusted eyes and the tiniest bit of scruff on his cheeks.

"I've been a shit friend," Cam says, louder, as if that will help get the message across.

"I'm not awake."

"I can see that," Cam says.

"Hold your horses, man. Are you deflecting?"

"For someone who claims not to be awake, you are using some big words."

"I worry about your education if you think deflecting is a big word." Nate swings his legs over the side of the bed and runs his hand through the mat of his hair.

"Touché." Cam gives up and lies back down.

"Let me shower. And wake up. Then food. And talking if you insist," Nate says.

"You're the one who sat up last night to talk to me," Cam points out.

"About you," Nate stresses.

"Okay, so we'll do both."

"You can, now?" Nate hones in on the nuance.

"Nothing left to lose, I guess." Cam shrugs and looks away and ignores the pang he feels at the words.

Nate examines him, transmitting a tangle of care and sympathy that has Cam closing his eyes. He'll have to deal with it, he knows. But instinctually he wants to put it off, to push it away. But if he wants to turn this around—himself and this thing with Wren and everything else—he'll have to face it all.

"WHAT CAN I DO?" NORA SITS NEXT TO WREN on his bed, where he's mostly under the covers watching the watercolor light seep through the rain outside his window.

"Nothing," he responds, his voice dull.

"I wish—" Nora starts.

"I know. Sometimes I wish you could, too." Wren almost never wishes his gift on someone. Right now, though, a balm warming his bones and easing this ache would be so welcome.

"You could call Kevin," Nora offers. Wren doesn't dignify that with a response. He's been raised to respect his gifts, and although Wren has his own moral compass, he doubts his family will appreciate it—and there's no way he's going to tell his brother how he's been using them.

He feels rubbed raw; even the oasis of his bed and the safety of his sanctuary betray a host of things breaking him down. His sheets scratch too-tender skin and the imagined smell of Cam lingers—or maybe he wants it to linger. Even Nora's fingers petting his head softly are like knives, because it's not her fingers he wants.

"I did everything right," he says in a tight, cracking voice.

"What do you mean?" she asks.

"So this wouldn't happen."

"By this, are you thinking of—" she ventures.

"Yes," he closes his eyes and turns his face into the pillow. He can no longer push away examining what happened with Robert, and how that particular misery left him a complete mess.

"Wren..."

"Just don't," he interrupts. "Please just go." He tries to be gentle, even though he recognizes that there is no polite way to kick someone out of your room when they want to help you. He's not sure that he can he helped, or that he even wants to be right now.

The door clicks so quietly behind her that the sound is almost lost in the calming mutter of rain against the buildings. There's a fleeting memory, an intangible flash of Saturday morning warmth under the sheets with Robert: the rain against the windows, hard pelting, and the sense of something indelibly precious captured in the heat of their hushed laughter.

Wren rolls over and opens the music app on his phone. That Wren is an unrecognizable creature to him now. So young and hopeful and open. So stupidly trusting, easily handing crystallized treasures to Robert only to watch as he dropped them on the floor, glittering shards scattering all around. Wren thought he'd bleed from those wounds forever, had spent days in his bed wondering how he could ever patch himself together again.

But I did, Wren tells himself now. He had gotten up out of that bed and pulled himself together. All he needs now is to pick himself up as he did then, and he'll be fine.

"SO WHAT DO YOU WANT NOW?" Nate asks.

"Swallow before you talk," Cam says. Nate smirks and Cam just knows he's biting back a quip about swallowing. It's not the time for that, though, they both know.

"From him. This thing?"

"I..." Cam takes a breath.

"I mean, do you want to try to keep doing the thing you were doing. The just, um," Nate looks around the restaurant and whispers, "fucking thing?"

"I don't think we can. I don't think he will, because I can't stop him from sensing what I'm feeling, and I can't hold it in, and that scares the shit out of him."

"So, you want more?"

"Well… in a perfect world, yeah. He's so scared. But I think…" Cam fiddles with his fork, using the tines to draw through the pile of ketchup on his plate and making feathered lines across the plate. "I think he wants more. I think that's why he's scared. And I don't want to give up if that's it."

"Are you scared too?" Nate pushes his plate away and folds his arms on the table. "Or is it just fucking with your head too much?"

"Um…" Cam squints and thinks. "Both?"

They smile at the waitress when she comes to collect their plates.

"What do you think?" he hedges.

Nate shakes his head. "Oh, no. You don't want my opinion. I don't know anything but the bits you've told me, and what I've seen, and it doesn't look that good from here. But you know him and whatever you've been feeling."

"I wish I did," Cam muses. He puts his head in his hand and sighs. "You know, I think he thought this whole time that whatever pulled us together was only his doing— that he was doing it all by himself. And I think last night he realized for the first time that it's always been there between us, naturally. That it's been working both ways."

"What about you?"

"I don't know when I realized it. I don't know if I did, exactly. But whatever it is, it doesn't scare me."

"Cam," Nate says, his face calm and serious. "You are literally the bravest person I know."

Cam shrugs, uncomfortable with the praise. "I don't know what you're talking about."

"You… all these things about yourself and your life—you figured them all out, or found them, and instead of being scared or upset, you… it's like they made you happier. Which is awesome. I don't know of many people who suddenly realize they are gay and just keep rolling and don't falter in some way. And now this… being willing to risk yourself for a chance—"

"I guess," Cam starts shredding his crumpled napkin. "I never thought of it like that. I just… it's like, one day someone turned on the lights, and I could see, and it felt good. Easier."

"So, brave one," Nate lowers his tone, adds a little comedy, "will you be going on a quest?"

Cam laughs and shakes his head. "Like I said, there's that *thing*. Maybe he's not ready for it. Maybe he'll push me away. But… I don't think I can ignore it. I don't want to give up."

"Well then," Nate nods, "may the force be with you. Just be careful. Take care of yourself."

Cam laughs louder.

MAGGIE ANSWERS THE DOOR AFTER long minutes of knocking. She's sleepy-eyed, her hair is almost wild and her leggings and long, soft T-shirt show that she was either about to fall asleep or asleep already. Her shirt is a bright and nearly see-through pink. She confessed to Cam long ago that she wears her ruched maternity shirts to bed because they are so comfortable; she discovered them accidentally when she bought a mismarked one, but once she wore it, she was a goner. It's these little things that endear her to him, even if he can see a little more of her in that shirt than he probably should.

"Well, come in," she gestures with quick hand movements. "I'm not offering free shows to the others."

"Just me?" he laughs awkwardly, keeping his eyes carefully on her face.

"Nothing here is a mystery to you," she points out.

"Still, it seems weird," he says. Maggie just rolls her eyes and smiles. Her hand is hot in his when she pulls him toward the bed; she was definitely asleep. Her body temperature always rose dramatically while she slept.

She snuggles back under her covers with a yawn. "Want in?" she holds the corner of her blanket up in invitation. He shakes his head and sits carefully.

"I need his address," he says plainly.

"No."

"Maggie." He's not above pleading, and she can tell.

"This isn't a good idea. And I don't want to take sides. Or misstep."

"I'm not asking you to take a side. Are there sides?"

She looks away.

"Okay, wrong question. Just—" he clears his throat against the raw scrape of helplessness. "I know what I want now, and I know how I want to try to get it. But he won't answer my calls and I don't know where he lives because he was so secretive about it."

"Cam, I feel like this would be a violation of trust. I only know because of Nora, and I don't want to give out their address if they want it kept private."

He swallows back a groan of frustration and the instinct to take it out on her.

"Cam, are you sure this is even what you want?"

"I already told you it is." He says, voice flat, and turns his eyes to her. "I need you to trust me."

There is a long silence. It's obvious she's weighing her words. "I'll try," she says after a bit. "That doesn't mean I'll give you their address, though."

Cam stands with a sigh. "I guess I'll have to settle for that."

"I'm sorry—"

"No," he interrupts, already at her door, "I get it. I'll figure something out."

* * *

WREN DOESN'T WANT CONTACT WITH HIM. And Cam has an idea why—well, he hopes he knows why. Falling in love doesn't scare Cam at all; realizing over the course of this year that he wants to fall in love, that he has something so rich inside himself, is a surprise, but a most welcome one.

Wren, though... Cam can look back at the times they were together, the times they've come closest to actual intimacy, and all the ways in which Wren has shut them down, pushed Cam in another direction. Wren always brought Cam pleasure, but with his gift, and not himself. For some reason, falling in love scares the shit out of Wren. Perhaps it isn't even love—that's Cam's hope speaking—but just something deeper, something that runs further than just play.

Cam is not who he was when he first got off that plane from Nebraska. Nor the one who emerged again at the end of that first summer, puzzling himself out. He's not even who he was last week; he's not willing to stand apart from the world the way he used to. This connection with Wren is something he needs, and he's going to fight for it.

So maybe fighting for it means he does something sort of creepy. Needs must and all that, right?

He sits down and tries to sketch out what he knows about Nora and Wren's schedules, frequenting places Nora goes often, but where Wren rarely does, looking for times when he might catch her on her way home. Once he's made his list, he takes a moment to evaluate his choices; somehow, even knowing how out of line this is, he stays the course.

It only takes a week to luck out. He followed Nora twice that week to places that turned out to be busts, but on the third try he manages to tail her to her apartment. It's not in the student housing neighborhood, but north of campus among much nicer homes. Theirs is a lovely deep green with cream scallop trim and a two-story bay window. Obviously, at least one of them has a lot more money than he.

Once she's inside, he tries peek into sneak in. There are two doors outside the house, and the one she goes into leads to a hallway and what appears to be an upstairs and a downstairs apartment. Checking the mailbox, he sees that theirs is upstairs.

Back in his room, after the longest and most tedious and trying day he's ever had, he's thankful to find Nate gone. In his desk drawer is the schedule he'd made. He tries to pin down a time when Wren will be home without Nora, and manages to narrow it down. There's a better chance of this conversation happening—of something happening—without someone else nearby.

Through the window, a glooming light throws his furniture into strange relief, lighting the faux wood top of his desk, but throwing the further recess of the room into darkness. Cam closes his eyes and feels his body absorb the last warmth from the day's end. He's caught there, between something incandescent and tethering and a darkness that he could live through but that would never feel right.

He thumbs over his contacts thoughtfully. He has the number Peyton gave him a few days ago. She might still be where she was, since his parents refused to give her more money. Taking a chance, he dials the number.

"Hey you," she answers nearly immediately, quietly. The lingering annoyance he's carried since their last conversation, the frustration from believing he had to mediate and from being hung up on, melts away.

"You too." Cam closes his eyes and lays his head back against his pillow.

"Tell me about it," she says.

"I think I'm falling in love," he admits.

"That's... Cam, that's amazing," Peyton says in a thickened voice.

"Don't cry, Pey."

"I can't help it. I've been waiting. Ever since you escaped home and changed so much. You woke up. I'm so sorry, you know?" she tacks onto the end of her sentence. Cam frowns, watching the last of the sunlight wane in ripples across the ceiling. He's not sure he'd ever describe his choice to go to Chicago as an escape; on this side of it, he sees it more clearly as flight.

"For what? Me changing?"

"For being a part of what put you to sleep."

"Peyton," he starts, but doesn't know how to finish. It's not her fault. Not entirely. Retreating was his coping mechanism. He just never figured out how to come back out—probably because he'd never examined his own reactions to the turmoil in their home until Wren had come and jolted him into his body and mind and self with a single kiss.

"So, love," she says.

"It's not... I don't know. It's complicated," he says.

"Isn't it always?"

"Don't throw clichés at me right now," he says, laughing.

"What's the complication? What are the complications, I mean?"

Cam thinks this over. The room is mostly dark now, which feels good, feels close and safe and anonymous.

"I don't think I can tell you some stuff yet. But I can tell you that he's scared. I don't know the details—"

"Cam—"

"I know it's probably something obvious, like having his heart broken. But I want him to tell me and I want him to trust me with it. The problem is finding him, getting him to talk to me."

"I gather that's not simple. You don't know where he lives?"

"I think I figured it out. Um..." he bites his lip, "I followed his roommate home. Is that awful?"

"Well," she's laughing, "it might qualify as desperate."

"I feel desperate," he says earnestly, and she stops laughing.

"So what next?"

"Knock on his door when I think he's home alone? I don't know, it's going too far, isn't it?"

"Honey, I don't know that you're asking the right person. You know me. I'm the queen of risk and following your gut. If it's love, the question might not be *what will I do* but *what won't I do*."

Cam is quiet for a long moment. The jangle of keys and a door slamming in the hall, indistinct conversations, muffled through walls and doors, sound loud in the presence of his silence.

"I love him," he states plainly.

"Yes," she replies immediately, and they both know what that means.

CHAPTER TWENTY-TWO

CAM ISN'T SURE WHAT TO WEAR that will sway Wren, mostly because Wren has taken him regardless of his attire. He has a slight idea of what Wren might like, but everything has to be perfect this time, just right. Maggie has told him he looks good in jewel tones; he picks out a shirt she said is ultramarine. He'd laughed so hard, imagining her closely investigating the names of colors; she'd rolled her eyes and forced him to buy the shirt, a simple boatneck T-shirt.

He ties a linen gray scarf around his neck in a slipknot and pulls on the darkest-wash jeans he has. He's still pretty unpracticed at figuring out how his hair looks best, but he flat-irons the ends and creates a far part, a compromise between neat and messy.

In the mirror, he sees something smaller than his tall frame. He sees a boy, scared and nervous, not a man willing to take risks. Squaring his shoulders with a deep breath, he closes his eyes, counts to three and lets the reality of what he is going to do settle in his bones. Wren is worth fighting for, he's worth risking for, and doing anything less would be the real wrong.

He has to collect himself again outside Wren's door, between thought and action. But when he does finally knock, it's with confidence.

It's loud, his knock. Or perhaps it sounds loud, echoing over the mad thump of his nervous heart. Beyond the door is silence, but Cam knows as soon as Wren approaches the door because his body calls Cam's immediately.

"Wren," he says as loudly as is needed for his voice to travel through the door. He puts his open palm on the door. "Please."

WREN IS SURPRISED THAT HE DIDN'T KNOW who it was until he'd almost opened the door. He's been in a haze, closed in and confused. But it's not his gift pulling Cam's energy through. That energy just is. It exists beyond his will. Wren puts his forehead against the door, reeling and bewildered and aching. His palm connects with the door, and crackling energy like lightning exits through his skin from his marrow. He's so close to Cam through this thin piece of wood.

"Just let me talk." Cam's voice filters through the door. "Just this once, and if you tell me to go afterwards I will. But I can't let go like this."

Everything inside him is compelled by its own imperative, a call wound so deep it's a song he can't ignore.

He opens the door.

Cam doesn't step in, not immediately. It's early afternoon, but the hallway window is on the far end, so Cam is cast in shadow. He looks like everything Wren wants to touch, so different from when Wren first saw him. He's defined himself. It's not just style—which is a part of it. He seems so *true*.

"You want to say something?" Wren manages through numb lips. He curls his hands into fists at his sides.

"I—" Cam says, and stops. He steps in lightly, shutting the door behind him with an almost inaudible click. Fascinated, Wren observes the acceleration of Cam's breathing and the staining of his collarbone, which flushes in a way his cheeks rarely do. It's not quite the hectic red he gets when Wren has taken him apart with pleasure, but definitely an indication of something strong surging in him.

Wren understands that all too well.

He closes his eyes because Cam's are so bright on his, but he can't dam the undercurrent he feels washing through him; it slips through him like quicksilver, and the more he tries, the stronger it flows.

"Cam, I—" he swallows because his mouth is so dry. When he opens his eyes, Cam is closer.

"I know I said talking," Cam whispers, and it sounds like an afterthought because his hand is already wrapping around Wren's neck and pulling him closer. Wren gasps into the kiss, he has to push forward and up onto his toes to meet Cam. Cam kisses him as if Wren is air, as if he is sustaining himself on the sweet, wet press of Wren's lips. His palm is wide and commanding against the back of Wren's head.

"Oh god," Wren says faintly when Cam pulls away, then shivers into Cam's mouth as it works down Wren's neck. He comes to the awareness that he's clutching Cam's shirt at his shoulders so hard his fingers ache. He unfurls them with difficulty and forces himself back a bit, with a palm against Cam's chest.

"Don't, don't," Cam says, chasing Wren's mouth.

"No, not that." Wren wraps his arms over Cam's shoulders and bites his chin lightly. "Take me to bed, *god*, now." Wren's tongue traces Cam's ear and the cord of his neck and he smells Cam's hair, clean and sharp and *Cam*. Cam shakes with laughter.

"Where?" Cam's fingers dig hard into Wren's waist. Wren points vaguely down the hall to their left.

"Second room," he presses himself closer, then lets out a shocked huff of air when Cam picks him up easily, hands under his thighs. Wren wraps them around Cam's waist and that fire inside flashes so hot and bright he's tempted to take Cam down right here. "*Fuck*," he groans, "don't hurt yourself."

Cam laughs and staggers toward the hall. "You're so small."

"Jesus," Wren pants, his lips barely on Cam's, biting and licking softly and trying his best to coax Cam into another kiss. "I can't believe you—"

"Stop talking," Cam commands. He lays Wren on the bed, then lies on top of him. Wren does get his kiss then, many of them, frantic and biting; their bodies writhing in a desperate race.

Cam manhandles Wren quickly out of his clothes, manipulating the unfettered weight of Wren's body as he tugs and pulls, and it's perfect, it's all so good, heat curls deliciously in Wren's belly and brings his cock up so achingly hard and wanting.

"Stay," Cam says. He puts his hand on Wren's chest and strips efficiently, tossing his scarf carelessly on the floor. His hair flies wildly where taking his shirt off has ruffled it.

"Hurry." Wren's fingers are clumsy at Cam's belt, and they both laugh because Cam has to struggle out of his tight jeans. It's sweltering between their bodies, too hot and too fast, and a free fall when Cam takes Wren back into his arms. He bites down on Wren's neck and uses one hand to pull Wren's knee up and out, fitting Wren's cock snugly between the crease of Wren's groin and his own dick.

"What do you want?" Cam asks, his mouth gently brushing Wren's nipple. He speaks so faintly Wren almost misses it.

"I—" Wren whimpers weakly. Cam's fingers are in his hair now, tugging it, pulling Wren's head back to expose his neck. Cam pins him down; it's a most desired weight when everything is skittering out of his control. Cam keeps him centered with only the heat of his skin and the heft of his muscle and bone.

"No, *nonono*, don't ask that," Wren says, shaking his head as if to clear it. This isn't right, it's not how he does this. This thing, it's bigger than he can shape with his hands, it's the breaking of a promise he made himself. He gasps and pulls away from Cam's lips, which are feasting on his own, and tries to center himself. He pushes himself into Cam's energy and tugs.

"*No*." Cam says. He doesn't pull away, doesn't stop the drive of his hips against Wren's. "Can't you feel it?"

Wren closes his eyes and turns his face. He can, because there's such a strong *no* pulsing from Cam, an impenetrable wall rejecting his ability.

"Like this, without it." Cam stills and Wren cries out softly, his teeth digging against Cam's lower lip.

"I can't." Wren feels something collapsing inside and shakes his head hard.

"You can," Cam chants with his mouth against Wren's cheek. "You can, you can, just be here with me."

Wren pulls further inside, withdraws what he was compelling Cam to feel and closes it inside himself, and then pulls himself in too, putting up walls.

"No." Cam traces Wren's cheek with a soft finger. "Please don't." He nudges Wren's nose with his own, and when Wren opens his eyes Cam's are on his, steady and wide open and ready. They're always dark, a lovely deep chocolate brown, but right now his pupils are so wide they almost swallow all the color. "Let me in, please let me in."

Wren exhales. Exhales and wants and listens to the clamor of his skin, so desperate for Cam's touch. *It's only fucking,* he tells himself. *It's only fucking.* He opens his legs further, and keeps chanting even when his body betrays that it's not, even when his heart feels as if it will burst because Cam's hands are all over him, his lips too, his whispered praise and affirmation making a tender wreck of Wren's heart.

Cam slithers up Wren's body from the deep red mark on his hipbone where Cam's mouth has been busy, inhaling as he goes as if he's taking in every part of Wren. He tucks his face into Wren's damp neck and pulls his hips away a bit.

"Tell me what you want," Cam asks again.

"I—I don't..." Wren stops when his voice breaks.

"What do you need? What haven't you gotten that you want?"

"A million dollars?" Wren jokes weakly, trying to divert him.

"Who doesn't?" Cam pulls back. His face is bright with amusement, but his eyes are dark and focused. "You always give. You take sometimes, but not like that. I want that. I want to give too."

Wren forces his whole body to still. Forces his mind to quiet, to pause before he lets Cam gather him into this storm. He asks himself if this is what he wants, to be pushed into fierce winds.

"Fuck me," Wren whispers with trembling lips, before his mind has come to a conscious decision. Before he means to speak. Before he can reason himself out of it. "I want you inside."

Cam's eyes close and he groans. "*Wren*," he whispers, lips wet against Wren's. He licks them slowly, then frantically, his mouth opening and accepting Wren's tongue and harsh breath and swallowing the soft moans his kiss elicits.

"Make it so I can't think," Wren begs. "Fuck me until I don't know my own name."

Cam pulls away, one hand cupping Wren's balls and then drifting lower. "That's a tall order for a virgin of this sort."

Wren covers his eyes as Cam's finger explores. He wants this, he feels empty, but he can't look at Cam while he lets him do this. Cam notices, stills his hand and softly kisses the inside of Wren's thigh.

"Do you have lube and condoms?"

"Yeah." Wren sits up halfway, grateful for the distraction, and pulls them out. When he moves to lie back down, Cam stops him with a firm hand on his shoulder.

"No, let's try this. Roll over, maybe?" Cam says.

"Hands and knees?" Wren asks as he does, uncertainty creeping in.

"No." Cam guides him until he's on his side, facing away. The day is so bright outside Wren's window it almost hurts his eyes. Cam takes a breath; Wren is calmed enough that he can open himself a little now, feel the edges of Cam's feelings. It's a beautiful chaos there, lust and sweetness that hurt when Wren touches Cam with his gift. It's a stilling of nerves with an inhalation and then a cool wash of confidence Cam must know Wren needs. He needs to be close but not too exposed. He's afraid that being really open might fracture everything.

Cam pulls one of Wren's legs up so his knee is bent, and then strokes between Wren's legs with his fingers, balls to sacrum, barely touching him. For years Wren has ignored pleasure his body has wanted, intimacy he's longed for, and now, on the cusp of resignation, that's all he can feel, as if all the desire in his body has coalesced in one spot.

"Touch me, touch me," Wren whispers, turning his face into the pillow. "You don't have to be gentle."

Cam groans against Wren's neck and shuffles around a bit before pushing Wren farther into the bed, hitching his leg up and out even farther. One hand grips one buttock hard, spreading Wren as wide as the position will allow, until the cool slide of one finger connects. Wren closes his eyes and gasps, biting the pillow under his face, moaning when Cam's finger pushes in. He concentrates on that, on the sparking of nerves all around his asshole, on the indescribable rush of his body opening and begging for more.

"Fuck," Cam breathes from too far away. "I can't believe—you just…" Wren presses back against Cam's finger, unable to speak but hoping his meaning is clear. "Okay," Cam says. He clears his throat. "Okay," he says more confidently as the second finger slides in.

It's so easy, so simple even after years without. Wren's whole body feels as if it's melting; the edges of Cam's pleasure and desire to please Wren are so bright he can't not feel them even when he tries. As the feelings spike and the build of *yesyesyes* cascades from his mouth, Wren doesn't want to try.

It's a bit of a fumble by the time he's ready, with Cam positioning himself and Wren for an unfamiliar act.

"How?" Cam kisses the knob of Wren's shoulder. His whole body is shaking. "I don't want to hurt you—"

"It's okay, you won't. Just go slow, I'll tell you if it's too much." Wren tilts his hips and presents himself a little more. It takes a few tries, but Cam does manage, pressing until something comes loose and he slides so easily into Wren that the sensation wrests a broken groan from Wren and a shocked gasp from Cam.

"*Oh my god*," Cam moans, and bends forward to kiss the spot between Wren's shoulder blades. It's that kiss that's too much, though. It's as intimate as looking into Cam's eyes would be.

"Fuck me," Wren urges, more loudly than he meant to. "Come on."

"Wren…" Cam moves slowly inside him, covering Wren with his body. Too close. Too slow, too much.

"Fuck me, *fuck me*," Wren tries to demand.

"No," Cam whispers against his back, and then slides into him, against him, with care and deliberation, and Wren feels a pressure build against his eyes, the threat of tears. Cam knots their fingers together and kisses Wren's ear until Wren turns his face down and into the pillow.

Wren tries to keep it in, keep the wracking shudder of pleasure spiraling from the epicenter of Cam inside him, but he can't. The slow slide of their bodies and the relentless movement of Cam's body feel so *good*. A shocked little moan slips out when Cam presses down with his hips.

"Yeah?" Cam says breathlessly, adjusting himself. He untangles one of his hands to splay it over Wren's belly; the backs of his knuckles just brush Wren's cock.

Wren cries out, spreads his legs and tilts his hips and lets Cam ride him senseless. A building press of pleasure is grabbing him. Cam fucks him and listens, fucks him and listens to every direction Wren gives when he can, voice pleasure-stunned. Every movement carries Wren further into helplessness, drives and drives slowly until he's cracking open, crying out and moaning with tears gathering and filling his eyes. Wren's fingers tighten against Cam's until they hurt; he clamps down around Cam and just barely hears the way Cam grunts, his movements becoming less coordinated.

"Oh my god," Wren says, his voice splintering with tears. His body feels like this beautiful live thing, this glowing presence, perfectly held with Cam all around him, Cam inside him, Cam taking and taking him. "*Oh*, I can't, I don't think—" He's not even sure what he's saying, just that what builds inside him is too big.

"You can," Cam says against his scapula. "I won't hurt you. I have you."

Wren bucks and shivers and comes, Cam's words a match that ignites his orgasm until it flashes resplendent, so long Wren loses himself to it completely.

He's still gasping when he comes back to himself. Cam is plastered against his back, heavy and breathing hard and trembling. One hand is cupped around the curve of Wren's forearm, running up and down it with uncoordinated, jerky movements. Wren supposes that Cam must have come too but can't discern much more beyond the complete and boneless give of his body. It settles in him, like a deep, safe silence he's never experienced before.

CHAPTER TWENTY-THREE

CAM WAKES TO GRAY DARKNESS and the sound of rain lashing against windows in a room he's never been in. There's a small lamp with a Tiffany-style shade in the far corner. The butter yellow glow from its tiny bulb barely breaches the night pressing against the rest of the room. Above him is a half-canopy of soft white, running on a bar across the ceiling halfway above the bed, swooping to the wall and cascading down. The grays and blues of the walls give him the feeling of being inside a cocoon, sheltering and close and comfortable.

It's cold; he's barely under the sheet, and the body that had tumbled into dreamlessness with him, heavy with something like physical trust, a body knowing it won't be hurt, is gone.

Cam sits, tugging the sheet a bit higher and letting his eyes adjust slowly to the lack of light. He finds Wren curled up on a window seat, looking out the window. One hand mindlessly traces the small rectangular wooden frame of a pane. Cam clears his throat and Wren doesn't look up. The expectancy in the air curls suddenly into Cam's belly, the pause preceding the drop, just before Wren speaks.

"I was too young," Wren starts softly. He rests his head against the glass, eyes closed. "Much too young to fall in love."

Cam waits for more. Should he let Wren take his time before asking questions? A slivered shadow of a smile crosses Wren's face. It's not a happy one, but rueful and quickly repressed. Wren looks at his knees, which are drawn up by his face. He is dressed again; his jeans are torn at the knees, frayed strings a clear white against the dark denim even in the low light. He's wearing the loose-knit sweater he'd worn the first time Cam saw him. It's comfortable-looking and too big, and slips precariously to the edge of his shoulder. Did Wren choose it on purpose?

"But I did." Wren shrugs, picking and picking at loose threads. "It's not like we know when we're stepping into something awful when we do it. We see it later when the dust settles."

Cam wonders if that's what this will be, what Wren will be, if what's been kicked up by this storm will settle and things will be clear in a completely different light.

"His name was Robert, and I was seventeen. We went to school together."

"Where?" Cam dares to ask, hoping it won't stop Wren from speaking all together.

"Le Grange," Wren says absently. "It's nice. My family is just a regular family, you know." He looks at Cam briefly. It's hard to picture that, because Wren is so startling, such a powerful force, Cam's never been able to really figure out how he inhabits the world when he's not busy taking Cam apart.

"My brother Kevin is gifted, my mom too, but not Dad or Sean," Wren says.

"Is Sean—?" Cam can't help but interrupt.

"Brother," Wren waves this off impatiently, obviously wanting to carry on with the story. "It's not important, other than to say that no one but my family knew. It wasn't quite the city, where people are more cosmopolitan. It's not dangerous, necessarily, to be gifted, but it's easy to be misunderstood."

Cam nods.

"I don't know why I did it—why I trusted Robert with it. It was just this stupid high school romance; it was a stupid fucking high school cliché. But it began to feel like lying when I kept it from him for so long, when things got so serious. The more I loved him, the worse it felt to keep it from him."

Wren looks up at Cam with something burning in his eyes. "We'd been together for a while, over a year. We had *plans*, we were going to go to college together. But—"

"But?" Cam's voice is just barely louder than the rain against the window.

"But I couldn't hide being gifted forever. And it was stupid, to think he'd be okay with it. It was so *stupid*—I was—not to see how much it hurt him." Wren shakes his head and looks back out the window. "I didn't know I could sense, then. It's not a strong gift; I've worked on it a bit since I came here, and it's grown too, which happens."

"Anyway," Wren says as he lifts a shoulder, "things were a little off after that, for a while. I thought he needed time, because I knew it must have hurt to be lied to, no matter how good my reasons were. Or had been. I could have told him much sooner, because holding off was my fear speaking louder than my belief in him."

"You were a kid," Cam says. Wren snorts and ignores this.

"He was with me, but not, after that, you know?" Cam nods. "After a while he said he understood. And it was fine. It seemed fine, everything was as it had been for a long time. But once we came here... I mean, you know this. There's a lot more freedom once you get to college. My parents are progressive, but it's not like I could kick my brother out of our room while my parents watched TV to fuck my boyfriend." There's such bitterness in Wren's voice. "It had been *months* and Rob knew about it the whole time, so it didn't raise any flags when he asked to see what I could do. It didn't seem unusual when that became more about… what we did together. To me, that meant something. I thought, 'Oh god, he trusts me so much,' and it was like giving him a present, like something just for the two of us."

Cam's heartbeat steadily speeds up as Wren speaks—it's becoming clear to him what happened.

"I lied to myself for a while, because I was blindly in love. I used to be such a romantic." Wren says. "So stupid," he says softly. "Because that's all it became. Because he pulled away in the in-between times, and every time he came back to me in bed, I thought that was equalizing everything. Like all the silence and Rob being grumpy with me and going out with other people but not inviting me… him asking me to compel him when we fucked—" Wren's voice cracks, and it's a long moment before he continues. "I thought that was *love* Cam. *Making love*." Wren says it with venom, with a voice laced with self-loathing.

"I let myself be used. My gift—it wasn't a gift to him. He made it ugly. I guess he never got over me lying. And I was so wrapped up in him that I let him make me desperate. I let him manipulate me into fucking him any way he wanted and thinking I was *giving*. And in the meantime, I was alone. I was in this new place and I had no one until I met Nora. It was so lonely when he wasn't there."

He stops talking. Cam leans forward, catching the smallest glimmer of a tear track on Wren's cheek.

"So you made rules," Cam says softly.

"Well, not at first," Wren says wryly. "Because I was nothing when he left. He erased me."

"You're here," Cam tries to point out.

"Oh," Wren's whisper is laced with something fierce, furious, "don't kid yourself. I'm not who I was. You don't really know me."

Cam looks at Wren and remembers him in unguarded moments. He bites back a smile; Wren must believe he's hidden himself. Maybe he's changed, but he's definitely not the enigma he believes himself to be.

"But, well, you're not wrong. It took time, but yeah. I made the rules. I made myself a promise, because I'm never, *never* letting someone hurt me like that again. Erase me and leave me alone." His words crack, revealing resonant pain in the deepest timbre of his voice.

Cam lets the silence play out for a long time. He watches as Wren slowly tries to pull himself together, crossing his arms over his tented knees and calming his breathing. After a while he sits, locates his underwear and pulls it on; Wren stiffens when Cam kneels next to him.

"Wren," Cam starts softly, barely daring to speak. "Doesn't this hurt too, though?"

Wren pulls away a bit and curls his lip. "What do you know about it?"

Risk and reward. "I think I love you," Cam confesses quietly, heart tripping in his chest. His hand barely touches Wren's elbow.

"Stop." Wren covers his eyes. "Stop, please."

"I think you love me too," Cam dares. "I think if you walk away, it's going to hurt even more."

"Cam, please, I can't do this—"

"You can," Cam insists. He kneels forward and puts his cheek on Wren's knee. "I know you're scared. Fuck, I'm scared right now. But don't break our hearts without trying."

"You'll break me," Wren says, voice cracking.

"No, no," Cam whispers, kissing the tattered denim across Wren's knee, feeling the texture of strings and the hint of Wren's skin under them. He kisses the back of Wren's hand and pushes up to bury his face in the thick chaos of Wren's hair. "I won't. *I won't.*"

"You can't promise that, Cam," Wren says thickly.

"Sure I can," Cam nudges Wren's face up and looks him in the eyes. "People do it all the time."

"People lie. They break those promises," Wren's lips tremble where he's pressed his mouth tight and his eyes flit away. "They use each other."

"I'm not using you," Cam points out softly. Wren snorts.

"Are you kidding? What do you think we've been doing?"

"Wren," Cam says evenly, "*I've* been trying not to. Every time we get close to something real, you push me back. I don't need it. I wouldn't care if you never did it again." Wren's skin is cold under his fingers. "I want *you*."

"Cam," Wren manages, face crumbling. Wordlessly, Cam opens his arms to him; Wren's tears are hot against his neck. He's so small and fragile right now and Cam wants so badly to shelter him.

"I don't know how to do this," Wren says through shuddering breaths. "I don't know if *I* can promise not to hurt you."

"It's okay. We'll figure it out. I don't think you will," Cam says, petting Wren's head with one hand and keeping the other banded around Wren's shoulders. "I'm willing to take the risk. You're *so* worth the risk."

"Cam," Wren says against his neck, and pulls away. He combs shaking fingers through Cam's hair. His face is wet and flushed and his eyes are red-rimmed. "I—I can't jump into this. I have to think."

"Wren," Cam says as helplessness swamps him, "don't send me away."

"It's not… it won't be forever." Wren kisses him so softly. "No matter what, I won't leave you in the dark."

"But… this—" Cam splays his hand against Wren's chest, over his heart.

"I *cannot* rush into this. I won't make promises if I don't think I can keep them."

Wren stands, pulling Cam up with him. His lips are damp when they kiss Cam's shoulder.

"You should dress."

Wren smiles, his quivering lips just barely managing it, and then leaves the room. All around Cam is too-thick air and a silence that breaks him. He closes his eyes and focuses but can't feel Wren anywhere.

WREN CURLS ON THE COUCH under the softest throw he and Nora own, eyes stubbornly closed, while Cam dresses. He doesn't move or acknowledge Cam when he comes in and hovers awkwardly by the couch. He most definitely doesn't lean into the soft kiss Cam leaves on his cheek.

And when the door closes quietly behind him, he most assuredly doesn't fall apart.

He does, however, open his eyes. Unfocused and post-tear sticky, they roam the cluttered shelves surrounding the television: framed family pictures, candid shots of him and Nora, of his dog, left in Sean's care when he came to Carlina. Sean's off to school this year; he supposes Cinnamon will have to make do with his parents. It's not as if they don't dote on him anyway.

The loud slam of their door shakes him from his scattered thoughts.

"Oh my god, Wren, what happened?" Nora says immediately. She drops her purse on the floor in the entryway and climbs onto the couch with him. He tilts into her warmth even though he promised himself he wouldn't.

"I'm fine," he sniffles. His eyes burn, and he's so cried out he can't tell if it's because they're trying to produce more tears or if they're just tired.

"You—" Nora waves a hand.

"He came," Wren interrupts.

"Oh," she says, careful and quiet. "And you ended it?"

"No." He plays with the blankets. "I don't think so."

"You don't think so?"

"How does he know me so well?" Wren turns his face into her shoulder.

"Maybe you're not as much of a mystery as you think," Nora says.

"That's not what I mean," he replies. "I mean, that too, I must have been off my game, but that's not the point."

"So what is?"

"You know," Wren says, settling back into the couch and letting himself relax muscles that have been impossibly tight, "when I first saw him—there was something immediate. I've never felt anything like it before. I assumed it was because he was searching."

"Cam didn't even know gifted people existed," Nora points out.

"Well, I didn't know that then," Wren says. "And then when I did, I didn't really think about it too much. What was happening was so intense. I think if I had let myself really explore it, I would have been too scared to move on."

"Haven't you been scared anyway?" Nora asks

"Not like I would have been, had I seen it," he says.

"Seen what?"

"The connection. Every time I felt like I was pulling him, everything—it was there. It was always there, and it had nothing to do with me creating it."

"You think it's just a natural thing?" She turns to look at him.

"Well," he swallows; all of this is new. "It's not like we understand everything even though we're gifted. It's not like new things aren't found all the time."

"True," Nora says, then leans back against him.

Wren looks up at the ceiling, then down at his hands. He searches inside where he can always feel his gifts—one stronger than the other. "I think I could live without it," he says at last

"Do you plan to?"

"I don't know. I don't know if I'd ever feel *right* without it. I could go on. But I can sense, inside, where it fits."

"Oh?"

"I told him I wouldn't let him hurt me. And he said—" Wren bites his lip to try to keep himself together. "He said that walking away is the only thing guaranteed to hurt me. He says he'll keep his promises."

"Do you want to know what I really think?" she asks carefully. He turns to look her in the eyes; they're a blue that makes him think of clear Easter skies, the lightest blue of early spring. He shrugs and she answers softly. "I think he will."

* * *

"YOU JUST HAVE TO WAIT," Maggie says, taking his phone out of his hand and turning it face down on the table. "And eat."

Cam shakes his head and looks away. The sun is too bright and he has to find the will to go to class.

"No really," she says, putting a fork in his hand. "You're not going to change his mind by starving. Eat something or I'll call your mom." He rolls his eyes at her. "Fine, point taken. I'll call Peyton. I have her number now."

"What? What the hell?"

"It's taking a village to keep you together, Cam."

He just puts his head down.

IN THE END, HE EATS, mostly because Nate comes home and chimes in, and the chorus of people harassing him is not worth it.

Outside, the wind is sharper; maple leaves cascade in golds and reds as he walks to class. His feet kick them up as he shuffles along.

Cam has never experienced heartbreak. He's not sure that's what this is; he hopes it's just the strain of waiting for an answer, the not knowing if he will be heartbroken. But something inside doesn't feel right, and he doesn't have a clue how he'll fix it by himself.

CAM KNOWS THERE ARE A FEW THINGS he should do. First, he should stretch, because he ran hard and opted to skip cooling down and stretching in favor of a shower. There's something more soothing about showering than running. All the things he's drawn from running —sharpening and exposing his senses, opening up and feeling connected to the world around him—feel like sandpaper. He runs now out of obligation.

The shower is like a mute button. Time stands still and all the sensory input feels right: the murmur of falling water and the white wall in front of him; the steam and heat that leave him in a stupor—it's all he craves right now while he's living in the in between of putting his heart in Wren's hands and waiting to see if it will stay there.

So. Stretching. A thing he should do. Also: drying off. He'd dropped his towel on the floor and crawled into bed the moment he got to his room. His hair is getting his pillow wet. But he's so warm and tranquil and, for a moment, perfect.

Until Wren pierces through him. Cam can tell he's here, senses him close and bright and *fuck*, Cam is naked and his hair is half in his eyes and everything is damp.

He tries to hop into some pants as fast as he can, but he's only gotten on boxers and has one leg in when Wren opens the door and slips in. For all the quiet of his entrance, his energy—their energy—is anything but. It's a cacophony that resonates so deeply Cam vibrates with it.

"Uh," he manages brilliantly.

"You... aren't dressed. I should—um, I can—" Wren seems flustered and turns to open the door.

"No!" Cam fumbles into his pants. "No, don't go." He reaches for a shirt that's hanging on the foot of his bed.

"It's inside out," Wren points out with a small smile, and holds up a hand when Cam moves to take it off. "No, leave it."

A silence stretches, in which they examine each other. Wren looks devastating, beautiful but strained; exhaustion is written around his eyes and slumped shoulders. He's wearing a very un-Wren cardigan, very slim black with red accents around the arms and shoulders. He looks tiny in it.

"So..."

"I want to talk," Wren states.

"Okay." Cam steps back and offers Wren his desk chair, which is pretty much the only thing he has to offer other than his bed. Wren's look is careful; his movements are deliberate when he steps close and puts his hand on Cam's cheek. It's cool and cupped perfectly to the shape of his face. Cam closes his eyes and turns into the touch. Relief is a torrent through him.

"Look at me, please," Wren whispers. He doesn't make him though, and that small thing, the freedom to keep his eyes closed if he wants to, is sweet surety to Cam. When he does open them, Wren's are a steady, rich green. "Yes."

"Oh god." Cam bites his lip and he's lost his breath.

"*Yes.*" Wren's other hand traces Cam's ear and cheekbone; Cam sits back on the bed and pulls Wren with him until he's curled precariously on his lap. "If you'll still have me."

"Shut up," Cam manages weakly. "Of course." He kisses the tip of Wren's nose and his cheek and his Wren-redolent hair.

"*Oh.*" Wren presses his face against Cam's skin and wraps his arms awkwardly around him. Cam tugs, rearranging them so that Wren is still on his lap but leaned against the wall more comfortably. He feels Wren's tears and the moisture of his shuddering breaths against his neck. Cam just smoothes his hands over and over the muscles of Wren's back until he is calmer, marveling at the compact weight of his body and how it fits Cam's just right.

Finally, Wren pulls away; when he looks up at Cam, his face is like something Cam's never seen before, hesitant and young. It's almost unbearable, the feeling of being trusted, finally. Wren's breath fans over Cam's cheekbone before he dips in for a gentle kiss. It's a kiss not meant to heat, but to comfort, long and so soft it's barely a whisper. Wren is beautiful, so close and openly vulnerable, all lovely male lines and boneless, a trusting weight in Cam's arms.

"I have no idea how to do this," Wren confesses again.

"Neither do I. We'll figure it out," Cam says. He feels a confidence glowing solidly inside, one with an origin he can't discern but doesn't really want to.

"I'm probably getting heavy," Wren says after slow and newly shy kisses, spilling off of Cam's lap and onto his damp pillow. Cam wants to protest, but he can't really feel his left leg. Wren laughs when he feels the dampness on the pillow and pulls it out from under him to flip it over. He curls one hand around Cam's waist to pull him down so they can lie next to each other. He looks sleepy. Cam can feel how hard it is for him to be so open, as if he's poised for the moment Cam will hurt him. Cam slips two fingers against Wren's collarbone and takes in the slight shiver that runs through him.

"What now?" Cam asks.

Wren cuts Cam off with a kiss, pulling him in with grasping hands and the smallest exhalation.

"Wait," Cam says. He pulls back and smiles, then runs his thumbs down the line of Wren's neck to settle him. Wren shakes his head and kisses Cam again, sending a wave of fervor from his mouth through Cam's body. "Don't do that," Cam says more softly. "I told you I want *you*."

"So..." Wren hesitates, drawing his hands back, and Cam flounders for a second. Wren sits up and moves to the edge of the bed, knees together; his pale fingers fiddle with one of his plugs, a bright lapis with darker blue streaks. Cam wants to kiss him there, tender and sweet, where Wren's nervous fingers meet his ear; he realizes with a flutter that he *can*. That all the little gestures and touches and words he's been holding back, he can say and do now. He props himself up near Wren, facing him, and puts one hand on his knee.

"Cam," Wren pleads, "I don't know how to be with anyone without it. It just happens most of the time. How will I unlearn it?"

"I have no idea," Cam admits. The littlest moments, the details they've never let themselves linger over—those are what he wants the most. "I just think that—I... will you lay back down, with me? We'll figure this out. We can learn."

He stretches out carefully on his side next to Wren, adjusting so that Wren can pull the blankets up over them. He sips Wren slowly, each kiss a little different, the flavor of exploration, of newness—of uncertainty, even—coloring each a different shade from the last.

EVERY TIME WREN FEELS HIMSELF SLIDING into his old habit, Cam pulls back; sometimes with a tiny smile, his eyes dun, sleepy and happy, sometimes with a whispered *hey you* or a finger tracing the curve of Wren's eyebrow or the bow of his lip. It's like being banked in the loveliest fog; Wren can sense the shape of his desire through it, though everything is tamped down and muffled in mists. It shimmers through him, as if wanting Cam is millions of sparks and refracted lights held carefully in the gray. But more, almost frighteningly powerful, is the sensation of home.

Cam pulls away after a moment, settling his head on the pillow so that Wren can only see half of his face. Wren can't remember the last time he let himself settle with someone like this, their knees pressed together, delicate touches lighting like dragonflies on water—his cheek, the plush give of Cam's earlobe. The bump of Cam's shoulder, discernible under his cotton shirt.

"Tell me something about you," Wren says, finally. There has always been a hunger in him that Cam has been able to rouse without trying, a hunger he's indulged and fed time and time again with his body and Cam's. But tucked further away has been a denied hunger to know Cam as a person, more than a body. "There's so much I don't know."

"Tell me about it, Mister 'I have two brothers and a dog,'" Cam says lightly.

Wren laughs too. "Good point."

"So you tell me a thing," Cam whispers.

"A thing?"

"I'd say everything," Cam explains. Happiness is blinding, building and coming out of him in waves Wren can't help but sense. "But we have time. Let's discover it all slowly. I want to savor every bit of it."

"So. One thing." Wren feels wonder, wondrous realization, with each of Cam's words. Because he wants everything. "And then everything."

"*Everything*," Cam whispers, his eyes holding Wren's with a power that makes him believe, and hope, and trust.

THE END

Acknowledgments

So many thanks to the hardworking team at Interlude Press. Annie, for every morning you held my hand and told me to believe in myself and all the work to make this book better. Candy, for fierce support and hard work and belief. Lex, for answering each of my silly questions with patience and for memorable GIFs that often made my day. Becky, for having a vision for this amazing cover I would not have imagined, and Victoria for bringing it to gorgeous life with the cover art. Zoe Bird and Nicki Harper for holding me accountable to each detail and helping me craft this novel into something wonderful.

To the beautiful women in my life who have encouraged me to write: Mo and Emily, I'd never have taken first steps without you. So many thanks to Riah, April, Carrie, Kate, Kathryn, Mel, Jess and Jenni—each hug, each moment and each story I've written in the last four years I've done with your encouragement and support. Thanks to everyone who answered my questions about Chicago, and to each friend, fan, writer and beta along the way, thanks for the beautiful crazy community we made together.

To my husband and kids, who have put up with a tremendous amount of "Mommy is busy now," thank you, thank you, thank you.

About the Author

JUDE BEGAN HER WRITING CAREER at the age of eight when she immortalized her summer vacation with ten entries in a row that read "pool+tv."

As a sucker for happy endings and well-written emotional arcs and characters, Jude is an unapologetic bookaholic. She finds bookstores and libraries unbearably sexy and, to her husband's dismay, is attempting to create her own in their living room. She is a writer of many things that hope to find their way out of the sanctuary of her hard drive and many that have found a home in a fanfiction community.

Jude has been determinedly aging backwards from thirty each year. As such she's really twenty-seven and not actually thirty-three, although her addiction to tea and tendency to crochet anything in sight make her sound like an old biddy. Her two cats, husband and two young boys are determined to fill her life with chaos and love. Visit Judesierra.com for more.

One Story Can Change Everything.

interludepress.com

*Twitter: @interludepress *** Facebook: Interlude Press*
*Google+: +interludepress *** Pinterest: interludepress*
Instagram: InterludePress

www.ingramcontent.com/pod-product-compliance
Lightning Source LLC
LaVergne TN
LVHW091035080826
845145LV00002B/503

* 9 7 8 1 9 4 1 5 3 0 2 7 6 *